# The Parrots

*By the same author*

Can We Still Be Friends

# The Parrots

## ALEXANDRA SHULMAN

WITHDRAWN
FROM
STOCK

FIG TREE
*an imprint of*
PENGUIN BOOKS

FIG TREE

UK | USA | Canada | Ireland | Australia
India | New Zealand | South Africa

Fig Tree is part of the Penguin Random House group of companies
whose addresses can be found at global.penguinrandomhouse.com.

First published 2015
001

Set in 12/14.75 pt Dante MT Std
Typeset by Jouve (UK), Milton Keynes
Printed in Great Britain by Clays Ltd, St Ives plc

A CIP catalogue record for this book is available from the British Library

HARDBACK ISBN: 978–0–241–14635–4
TRADE PAPERBACK ISBN: 978–0–241–14640–8

www.greenpenguin.co.uk

MIX
Paper from
responsible sources
FSC
www.fsc.org   FSC® C018179

Penguin Random House is committed to a
sustainable future for our business, our readers
and our planet. This book is made from Forest
Stewardship Council® certified paper.

For David

# Foreword

## July

It must be a westerly. Katherine Tennison enjoyed the thought, with its pleasing combination of factual knowledge and natural order. Tide timetables, wind directions, lunar movements – she liked their names and numbers. As she ran the wind was mirrored on the surface of the ornamental lake, rippling from left to right, the confined water depositing ice-cream wrappers, sodden bags and a thick scum of toxic-looking algae along the eastern edge.

The lake part of her route had the great advantage of flatness, but the competition for space was fierce: small children escaping the distracted eyes of au pairs; an army of dog-walkers; elderly couples propped up against each other; and other jogging women, many of them remarkably similar to Katherine, with blonde hair tied up in a ponytail, well-preserved muscle tone in their limbs and on their faces no hint of the exertion needed to keep at bay the unwelcome and extraordinarily determined process of ageing.

It was at the small gate on to the boundary road, the 6km point where on certain days she would allow herself to stop, that she first heard the rumble. At first she thought it was the pounding Beyoncé through her headphones but then, almost immediately, she saw, moving towards her in the pale sky above, the bright-red machine. Helicopters were always scudding over the park and were often to be seen landing near the ambassadorial mansions that bordered one side of it, but an air ambulance was different.

To her left, the playground began to empty of adults and children, the red shape pulling them like a magnet as it neared the ground. It was just like that moment in *ET*, Katherine thought, watching as parents bundled up the smallest of their brood in one arm, leaving the elder children to run towards it. In seconds, a circle was formed of buggies, bicycles and crop-headed Saturday-morning fathers with weekend stubble doing their childcare bit, grateful that something unusual had infiltrated the normal routine of swing-pushing and nose-wiping.

Leaving the ambulance and its audience behind, Katherine pushed on. The run helped to empty her mind. To ask for clarity or direction would be too much, but she could keep moving, leave behind the messy chaos that was overtaking every part of her life. Her phone was in a sticky clamp on her upper arm. She could feel it vibrate, but if she stopped right now she wasn't sure she'd recognize who she was. Instead, she thought about the ambulance behind her and how, once, when Josh was small and they were in that same playground, a child roughly his age had fallen from the tall wooden climbing structure and, unlike the others, who constantly tumbled off and jumped up, had lain, a twisted, unmoving shape. She had seen his mother rush to her child and was part of the initial communal concern that shifted collectively into terror as everyone waited for what seemed like hours for the ambulance to land, just as it had that morning.

The phone buzzed again as she spotted the tree that marked the end of her run, and she pushed herself to a last burst of speed, which was meant to keep the calories burning off for hours. She passed a man in brief silky shorts, his legs mottled hams, before finally allowing herself to stop, then waited a moment before bending slowly from her waist to massage her calves in turn. For a minute or so she was able to feel content in the zone – flooded with achievement, a swamp of endorphins and music.

She didn't want to look at her phone, knowing that even a glance would puncture the moment. Missed calls and texts would intrude into this space into which, briefly, she had escaped. Smudging her T-shirt against her sweaty ribs, she pulled her ponytail tighter in its band. At the same time, there was the *ping* of another text coming through, and this time she looked. Three missed calls from Josh lined up on the screen: 9.10, 9.11, 9.15.

The change from warm post-exercise flush to creep of chilly fear was instant. She remembered the air ambulance, its red shape now terrifyingly personal, and Josh with that goofy, accepting grin he still had, and that small child years back twisted on the ground. As she jabbed at the phone she told herself it was ridiculous. Why should there be any connection? But she could feel her heart rate speeding up even further with terror.

'You have one message,' she heard, tormented by the gap between the automated voice and the real one. There was a moment when she thought of replacing the phone in the clamp on her arm and ending the call, as if not listening to it would stop it happening. Whatever *it* was. 'Mum, we're in the park.' Josh was clearly terrified. 'It's gone properly wrong.'

# Chapter One

*The Previous September*

It was the year there was no summer. The optimism of spring with the promise of sunshine, rose- and lavender-scented gardens, bare limbs and smoking barbecues was confounded by relentless grey and torrential downpours, the gardens devastated by the rain, the roses battered, their leaves riddled with mould.

Yes, there were the occasional hours of almost painfully sharp sun when the sodden lawns and borders and dripping trees would suddenly sparkle like fairy lights. And sometimes the arrival of the two, three, sometimes four parrots on the branches of the morello cherry tree would coincide with this brilliance in a flash of emerald, turquoise and gold, startling anyone spotting them for the first time. But more often in the dank grey it was their colour alone that would transform the neat lawn, box hedging and tragic beds of 30 Norland Terrace into something other than a nicely sized patch in one of the more expensive London streets. Despite their incongruous presence, the parrots were entirely confident in their ownership of wherever they happened to land and some days would remain perched for hours, unchallenged by the drab pigeons and starlings more often found there.

Katherine Tennison glanced at a pair of the parrots as she prepared her breakfast. Now, in late September, the morning was warm, a frustrating reminder of what had been missing the whole summer. She was still not immune to the transforming effect of the birds on the garden, although they had been appearing since early spring, when the bare branches made their visits all the more obvious. There were no rules as to when they would arrive. Sometimes, like today, they would be perched there casually in the morning, sometimes it would be early evening; guests for cocktails.

The silence in the house seemed louder than its usual soundtrack of washing machines and vacuum cleaners, the housekeeper Mariella's commentary on its deficiencies, ringing mobiles and chatter from a distant television which Josh, if it were up to him, would leave on for days when he was still at home. She watched the sticky trail of honey from the wooden drizzler make a pattern on her yoghurt. The ceramic honey hive reminded her of the weekend they'd found it on a cluttered table on a Cotswold high street. It had been the spring before Josh was conceived. Rick's arm was across her shoulders, clamping her to him, demonstrating his ownership of her. And how flattered she'd been to be claimed in that way. To be his. Momentarily, she was nostalgic for that couple, for the narrow vision of their youth, the absence of knowledge of what was to come, the years dominated by her desire to have a second child.

Her vision (and she acknowledged that it was hers, not Rick's) of a family had never been just them and Josh. Both she and Rick were one of three: she had two brothers and he two sisters. But despite her determination and diligence, despite the money, despite the injections, supplements, timetabled sex, shrinks, examinations and endless waiting rooms with dusty pot plants and property magazines, they had been unable to conceive another child.

'Morning, darling!' Rick bellowed from the hallway, dropping the squash racquets from his regular morning session on to the floor. He pressed his lips to her forehead, simultaneously flinging the mail down on the kitchen island. 'I hope I didn't wake you earlier. Rubbish game. Ed destroyed me. *Destroyed* me.' He swiped an imaginary ball towards the glass doors leading on to the garden. 'It was obvious right from the first serve. Must have been that second bottle last night that did for me.' He squinted through the glare on the glass. 'Parrots in residence, I see.'

As he walked towards the doors Katherine could smell the game on him, rich and tangy. Often, she had less of a physical sense of him when he was right next to her than when he moved away and she looked at him: solid; ginger hair faded to a pale sand but still gratifyingly *there* in thick waves, when most of his contemporaries were either bald or grey.

'I'll make some coffee. Toast? Eggs?'

'Just the caffeine hit, I think.' Rick stretched, arching his back and bending his knees, his loose cotton jogging pants hiding sturdy thighs. He pulled down the locks at the top of the high doors to the garden. As he walked out, the parrots, first one and, seconds after, the other, flew from the branch in a crackling rush into the clear blue of the sky.

The large kitchen was at the back of the house, transplanted from the front when the Tennisons arrived five years before. The tall stucco-fronted building in a terrace of similarly gleaming properties had been in perfectly reasonable condition, but they wouldn't have bought it if Katherine hadn't been able to see that work could be done to improve it. It might be Rick's family money, but it was her skill at renovation and her vision when it came to interior decoration that had made their property buys so successful.

'I might get on with some deadheading later!' shouted Rick as he squatted by a border, resisting the impulse to tear a dead flower from its stem by hand. 'I must buy some new clippers this weekend.' Despite his poor performance that morning, playing squash had filled him with a sense of well-being. 'Did you see? There's a letter for you. It's on the top of the usual pile of crap. All that do-good stuff dropped through the door. I reckon we could save a rainforest simply by losing all their flyers.'

Katherine didn't immediately recognize the handwriting on the heavy cream envelope, though the stamp was foreign.

'Dear Katherine,' she read. Of course. It was Ann.

*It has been such a long time since we've seen each other, but I write to ask you a favour. My children Matteo and Antonella are coming to London for a stay and I would love them to visit my dear friend Katherine. I've been away for so long that I feel quite out of touch with the place and it would be helpful to think that you might introduce them to some friends. Of course, they are now adult and independent. But it would*

*be great if they could see you. And that might mean that you will finally*
*visit Milano?*
   *For ever*
   *Ann*


Annie Berthoud. It must be more than ten years since they had last met, for dinner in that mirrored Italian restaurant on the Pimlico Road. Katherine had felt ridiculous suggesting Italian to an Italian couple, but the place was always filled with noisy Romans in blue blazers and loafers and it seemed to tick the box. Annie and Massimo. He had the longest, thinnest fingers she had ever seen on a man. They moved almost independently of his hand, like the tentacles of an octopus. When they found him after the car crash, there were reports that he had been decapitated. She imagined those fingers, still moving on reflex after the head had gone.

'It's from Annie Berthoud. I still think of her as that, but of course she's Fullardi now. She's sending her two kids to London and wants us to have them over.' Rick turned the pink pages of the *FT* 's Saturday package.

'Aha.' After twenty-two years together, much of the time, only a vague audible acknowledgement was needed to qualify as interest from Rick.

Annie Berthoud had arrived in London for A levels. Teenage myopia had allowed only a few details of her family circumstances to register with Katherine: they were Belgian; her father's job had brought them to a large mansion-block flat which always smelt of stew; and Annie had been given a car by her parents the day she turned seventeen. Annie's sporty appearance – arms with freckles clustered thickly around her elbows, small breasts, thick, short auburn hair and long legs – was an effective disguise for the fact that she had sex with a different boy every Saturday night. Until Annie, the designated pool of boys had been pretty sure that it was *they* who chopped and changed and that girls were after a *relationship*. Annie didn't need any such thing, and this, and her attitude towards sex – that it required pretty much the same level of commitment as a game of tennis – caused immens... she'd been a close friend and, when the ... sels, Katherine missed her chatty confidenc... engagement to Massimo Fullardi, the eldest so... Italian fashion dynasty, when she read about it in the p...

'She doesn't say when they're arriving,' Katherine co... realizing that she was talking to herself now that Rick had mov... on to the *Daily Mail* and was also checking his BlackBerry. 'I wonder if they're about the same age as Josh. No. They must be older. She married Massimo at least four years before we were married.' She looked again at the writing on the envelope, this time with a professional eye. Ever since she had taken up calligraphy she found it impossible not to judge handwriting in any form. But that reminded her that upstairs, in her study, there was a garden plan to be finished off for the Jellicoes.

'You remember I'm in Paris a couple of days next week?' Rick said, stroking the striped ginger cat that was sprawled on the floor. 'Got to seal the deal, haven't we, Carrot?'

The Tennison Gallery, which Rick had taken over from his father, specialized in the abstract shapes and evocative landscapes of mid-twentieth-century British art. Michael Tennison had been a well-liked figure in the art world but, had it not been for his wife, he would have become a competent gentleman banker, like so many of his contemporaries. Instead, Lady Christabel Clarendon's money and social skills, combined with his knowledge, intuition and gambler's enthusiasm had created a gallery that merged the mutually attractive worlds of old money and sixties cool. As a child, Rick and his two sisters would be presented at exhibition openings, drab in school uniform against the peacocking velvets and colourful silks of the time. His father held court, a glass in one hand, a paisley scarf draped around his neck.

'How long are you gone? I know it's in the diary . . .' There were so many diaries now: in his office, on her computer, in a brass-clipped leather book, on his BlackBerry. Katherine folded the letter back into the envelope.

this LVMH guy, and
...apore but he may get
...n hanging on for. We've

...his shoulders, experiencing
...at moment, derived from the
...ther he was fucking someone
...she had decided that there were
...uld keep it in their trousers and
...any sense, you married the former.
...seduced by the allure of the latter,
...idence to the contrary, they would be
cap...friend's roaming eyes and of converting
Jamie, o...to the alternative pleasures of familial
monogamy.

With Rick, it was a different story. From those first days in his small flat with the brown sheets and view over the treetops of a London square, she was sure that a carousel of girls was not what interested him. He had seen Katherine standing at the bar of a party, helping herself to a glass of wine. Her composure had been evident from yards away: her long, pale face registered little as she poured the drink, turned to look at the crowded room and raised a hand to tuck a strand of blonde hair back into the pile on her head. Rick had since told her that she had seemed to exist in her own ecosystem, and he'd approached her with a, for him, unusual determination to invade that calm space, at the same time imagining what it would be like to have her legs wrapped around his waist as he moved her against him.

Within weeks she had moved into his flat, changed the brown sheets for white, hung curtains in the bare windows and offered him an alternative existence from the cocaine-crammed nights he'd spent with a posse of male friends. In less than a year they were engaged. Katherine, still only twenty-four and drifting in and out of short-term office jobs, was more than content to make the idea of them as a couple the centre of her existence. Rick brought a world with him, one which, with its proximity to art and wealth and sense of sweeping family, she was eager to embrace. He loved her easy enthusiasm for it all and, not only that, he recognized in her a clearness of purpose that offered salvation from his own lack of it. And nobody could say that Katherine bore any resemblance to CeeCee, the mother who was such a powerful presence in his life.

'We could bring Ann's kids out here sometime,' said Katherine as the London suburbs were replaced by open green countryside. Since the letter's arrival the previous day, she'd been surprised how much time she'd spent thinking about her old friend's request.

'I'm sure my mother would be thrilled,' answered Rick, who was driving. His inability to give up his position in the outside lane was a dominant feature of the way he drove and was now creating tension, since the blue Audi behind him appeared equally determined to force Rick to move over. 'You know how she likes to be involved in everything she can get her mitts on. Personally, I'd keep them a good distance from her. She has long arms and, before they know it, she'll snap them up and she'll never be off the phone.' Katherine could see the muscle at the side of his mouth flex with the competition from the Audi. 'This guy's a total loser. He can just suck it up. We're coming off at the next exit anyway,' Rick muttered, in pointless explanation.

Sunday lunch with CeeCee was a frequent engagement that induced very little pleasure in either Rick or Katherine, but on a day like this, when the September sun was dappling the chalk hills to the north, it was possible to imagine that it might be enjoyable, even if years of experience had proved this unlikely. Rick drove at speed across the three lanes to the junction exit, while Katherine wondered whether lunch with CeeCee was a good enough reason to be killed in a car crash.

Charlwood was the Lutyens-style house CeeCee had made her home when she was widowed. 'It will suit me to have a project,' she had briskly replied to the many concerned friends who had pointed out that size alone made it an unsuitable purchase for a single woman, let alone one of sixty-five. Not to mention the condition of the place.

Now, fifteen years later, the large house combined authentic architectural details with an extravagant degree of comfort, and the gardens had been restored to their Jekyll-inspired haze of colour: smudges of blues and greying greens, aubergines and muted silvers even in winter, when, in the mornings, the lawn was a frosted sheet.

They found her standing on the wide terrace at the back of the house and Katherine leant in to offer a kiss to the small portion of her face not covered by her large blush-tinted glasses. They covered not only her eyes but the fine skin below. She had always been known for the beauty of her full-lipped mouth, which was still painted a girlish pale pink and made all the more prominent by the glasses.

Roland, one of CeeCee's two black Labradors, leapt up, snagging his claws in Katherine's cardigan. CeeCee both noticed and ignored the victim's grimace, glancing instead at her watch while Katherine readjusted her expression to a bright smile, determined not to let in the feeling of distrust that informed most of her meetings with her mother-in-law.

'It's so glorious today, isn't it? Probably the best weekend we've had all year.' Immediately disappointed in herself for embarking on such a predictable topic, Katherine was also exasperated with her husband for wandering on to the lawn and throwing balls for Roland, thereby avoiding having to talk with his mother.

'Let's have a stroll before lunch.' CeeCee's tiny white-trouser-clad legs set a smart pace as they walked towards Rick, in the direction of the red-bricked loggia. 'What news of Josh? When does he go up? Or is that the wrong term? I forget. Does it only apply to Oxbridge?' CeeCee rarely wasted an opportunity to show her disapproval of her grandson's attendance at a provincial university. 'I do wonder how he will take it. You know . . . I still think the States might have been a better route for him.'

Katherine moved the conversation on. 'What did you think about those figures at Sotheby's last week? Not entirely predictable?

The Gorky went for a huge figure, but a couple of the Irish were disappointing.'

'When you get to my age,' replied CeeCee, 'you realize, in most matters, timing is all.' Katherine's mother-in-law, having reached her son at the far end of the lawn, was positioning herself at an angle that would make further conversation with Katherine difficult.

'I was just saying to Katherine that I hope that Josh will be happy where he is. I know you agree that the States would have suited him so well. Couldn't he have come with you today?' She watched Rick throw the ball to another corner of the lawn. He had his father's build, but he was stouter than Michael had been at his age.

'We don't know where he is. He didn't text us last night, otherwise we might have packed him into the car with us,' Rick replied, keeping his eye on Roland, now chasing the ball. 'You know the States wasn't something he was particularly keen on, though of course he wasn't particularly keen to do anything much. Let's see how it goes. I'm starving. When are we eating?'

'You're just like darling Michael about your food. He always had to have it on the dot.' CeeCee looked back towards the house. Katherine had wandered back. 'Lunch will be ready in a few minutes. Do look at the amaranthus en route. They've done particularly well this year.'

Inside, a round table had been laid with a white cloth in a low-ceilinged square room, the silver cutlery and glass half-moons for salad placed at an angle next to crystal glasses. Pale, tobacco-coloured scrims at the windows added a flattering filter to the light.

'How clever,' observed Katherine. 'Roses. Still. These must be the very last.' She stood, even though it was only the three of them, waiting to be directed to a seat by CeeCee.

'Why don't you sit there?' Her mother-in-law waved at one of the high-backed oak chairs. 'And, please, help yourself.' An Arts and Crafts dresser sat in a niche between bookshelves, and on it pale green, soft lettuce interspersed with the veined reds of radicchio lay in a broad, shallow wooden bowl next to a soufflé inflated to a crusty dome from its white china casing.

'Have you met Mr Oblomovik yet?' CeeCee asked Rick. Her habit of adding a formal prefix to the name of certain acquaintances, far from endowing them with status, clearly indicated her disdain for them. 'Mrs Oblomovik has gutted Drayton Hall – almost completely, I gather,' she continued, as Rick helped himself to some food. 'Simply a shell left. It's over there.' She gestured towards the window. 'Literally, the other side of the M40. Very close to the motorway.'

'We've met Olga,' Rick replied, his concentration focused on piling his plate with soufflé. 'She seemed a nice enough woman, though I can't say I spent much time with her. He wasn't there that night. It was at the Jellicoes, wasn't it, darling?'

'Yes, that's right. She and I had a chat after dinner and she said she'd be interested in meeting Flo. I'd be surprised if she'd gutted it. She seemed pretty clued up on conservation and that kind of thing. I guess Drayton would be a minefield. Anyway, she said she'd like to meet her.' Katherine knew that CeeCee had little time for Flo, her closest friend and an expert on domestic and architectural history.

Rick reached out to the decanter on the table.

'Katherine had a letter from her friend Ann, who married Massimo Fullardi. She's sending her two children over to London. I think you knew the father, didn't you?'

'Yes. Gianni Fullardi. He bought really quite regularly from Michael. An excellent eye, I remember. He was one of the few Italians to invest in the British relatively early. Are they still in charge of the company?'

'Nope. I don't think so. They got bought by some conglomerate – I can't remember which right now. You sometimes see the family members dragged out for publicity. I'd feel like a performing monkey, but the money they sold the company for would lighten the burden. Anyway, it'll be interesting to see what the kids are like. Their father was a good guy. That was a terrible story, that crash. Poor kids.'

# Chapter Two

Flo O'Connell knew that, when people met her with Katherine, they were confused. It was the same as when a handsome man marries a very plain woman and the couple is analysed and discussed as if this might shed a light on other people's and their own relationships. They'd met over a pair of naked bodies at a particularly dire second-year university party. It was in the upstairs bedroom and they had both been searching for their coats. The shape of their friendship had remained exactly as it had started out, comfortingly throwing up no surprises to either. Flo's cleverness, loyalty, humour and complete availability were paired with Katherine's competence, sociability and easy attractiveness. Katherine would invariably be dressed neatly, prettily, like a present waiting to be unwrapped, and the slight gap in her teeth gave her blonde good looks the flaw necessary to make her memorable, while Flo would hover nearby, broader, taller, with a frizzy mop of dark curls, a creamy Celtic pallor and a body that never quite seemed to be contained by her clothes.

Looking down on the street, where tubs of bay trees stood sentry outside the houses opposite, Flo experienced the discomfort she always felt in Katherine's workroom. It was a place of purpose, every corner and surface allocated. Visitors were extraneous. And although she appreciated the ordered paraphernalia of equipment, the large table, the architect's chest under the window, the rolls of paper tied with ribbon, it was, to her, a transit lounge. You wanted to get the hell out.

She waited as Katherine screwed the top back on to a bottle of ink, giving it an extra twist to be sure, then placed it on a tray with other bottles, all identical in height and shape and differing only in the colour of their labels. Steel-nibbed pens, brushes of badger hair, sticks of black ink in their wrappers and white china mixing trays were laid out as precisely as a surgeon's tools. Flo couldn't remember ever seeing a brush lying outside its designated spot, or a forgotten glass filled with murky-coloured water. Katherine had none of the constructive chaos of an artist.

'Nearly ready.' Katherine gave a final wipe to the nib of a pen, glancing at the large white sheet of paper fixed to a board. 'My deadline for this garden plan is the weekend, but it's taking longer than I thought. When doesn't it, though? It's all the Latin names that slow me down. I keep having to check the spellings. But it's a pretty fabulous scheme – look at all these rooms. This one in the centre is all dark purple and white planting, like a floral chessboard.' She pointed to a square outlined in dark-green ink, a fountain marked on it. 'Is it cold outside?'

'Yes. It's no longer pretending not to be autumn.' Flo had reverted to the treasured black biker boots she lived in as soon as the weather permitted. Katherine didn't think they flattered her legs in the slightest, but Flo imagined they made her calves, now encased in the reassuring camouflage of black opaque tights, look thinner. The two of them never discussed clothes. Although Flo admired the way Katherine dressed, she couldn't for the life of her have described what she wore, and neither did she aspire to being well dressed herself. And if Katherine was sometimes confounded by Flo's lack of style, she knew there was no point in becoming involved. It was fine. Flo wasn't about clothes.

The trees in the park as they walked from Norland Terrace to Mayfair had begun to turn. The sprawling picnics and impromptu after-work football matches had been ended by the shortening of the days, and the conversing mounds of Middle Eastern women watching their striped T-shirted little sons playing from behind designer sunglasses or the restricted view of the burqa had left the city weeks ago.

In forty minutes the pair had reached the moneyed core of the capital. Here, the window-box displays were changed weekly. The monumental designer stores displayed all the pomp of a pharaoh's tomb, and paparazzi huddled in clusters outside hotels and restaurants while chauffeurs sat in waiting Bentleys watching DVDs.

Katherine nudged Flo to look at a woman outside a hairdresser's, with waist-length hair streaked with silver foil and a plastic bag on her head, shouting into a mobile and flicking ash on the pavement. 'Not a look to aspire to. Memo to self next time I'm getting my colour done.'

'Oh, I don't know – makes a change. Sort of *Star Wars* meets *Game of Thrones*.' Flo readjusted her large bag, which was slipping from her shoulder. 'It's weird round here, isn't it? It's like the land that time forgot. Shiny. Carpeted. If you listen to your footsteps on the pavement they might even sound different.' Flo tapped the ground with a laugh.

There was a single painting in the window of the Tennison Gallery, rich swirls of colour in a thick, carved frame, the space beyond it dim. On either side of it were galleries, neither quite as impressive in size or façade. Across the road, mannequins, dressed in autumn fashion, gazed unseeing. Katherine led the way inside and to an area set apart at the back, where a young man was staring at a computer, distractedly scratching his head. He jabbed a key and stood.

'Girl-on-girl action, was it, Fred?' Flo smiled.

'Hi. Ignore.' Katherine greeted her husband's colleague. 'We're meeting Olga Oblomovik here.' Standing beside Fred, it was impossible to miss the smell of tobacco coming off him. Rick, who was also a smoker (*still* a smoker, Katherine would emphasize) had rebelled against making the gallery a smoke-free zone for as long as possible, but now he and Fred were often to be found around the corner on the pavement sharing a fag, huddled like the teenage tailoring apprentices in the doorways of neighbouring Savile Row.

'Sure.' He waved at them. 'I'm expecting her any minute.'

Catalogues were piled on a counter – the cover image of each an example of the work of a different artist. Katherine stroked the smooth surface of the one on top as she asked, 'By the way . . .

how's it going with –? What's she called? Sorry. Rick tells me she's totally gorgeous. He's confused. Can't understand what she's doing with you . . .' Katherine was fond of Fred. He had worked for Rick for several years now, and Rick and she often discussed Fred's more often than not unsatisfactory love life. It was a useful topic, which could often be revived due to Fred's revolving-door policy when it came to girls. 'Don't know what you mean,' he would say when this point was drawn to his attention. 'It's never me that fucks off. I'm the one with the broken heart.'

Unlike family, money, houses and holidays, Fred's relationships had the great advantage of being discussed without any emotional consequence.

'Don't ask. She's called Daisy. I don't understand women. I'm smart enough to realize that much, but I really don't. I mean . . . Okay, listen to this. I'm doing all the right things. You know, stuff like flowers when she doesn't expect them. I've called when I said I'd call – big mistake, I'm now thinking. I've got this weekend booked in some fucking pricey hotel with a spa that she's been banging on about. Now . . . now! . . . she's gone radio silence on me.' He rubbed his eyes. 'You tell me . . . ?'

'I'll come, if you need a stand-in,' Flo volunteered. 'But I guess we haven't heard the whole story.' Fred watched the smile crease her face, creating a double chin that one day would probably be permanent. He'd just been in the lunch queue at Itsu and, looking at the girls there, he'd wondered whether, if you ran the metrics, the thinner ones all asked for chopsticks rather than forks. He always went for a fork himself. Made it easier to shovel the noodles in.

The only natural light in the main gallery came from the window at the front but, at the back, a large skylight exposed the pale-grey afternoon sky and lit a flight of stairs leading to a lower floor. A car drew up outside and Flo looked towards the window. A black-suited man emerged, opened the passenger door and positioned himself in the centre of the pavement, requisitioning the space before his passenger stepped out.

Fred moved towards the door as the buzzer sounded, first pressing the lock release.

'You are expecting me, I think.' Olga held out her hand, which was as eagerly accepted by Fred as a spaniel seizing on a biscuit.

'Of course. Good to see you.' Fred had done his research on this new client but, even so, he wasn't prepared for the effect she had in real life – her skin made you want to reach out and stroke it. He was having trouble stopping himself thinking about what he'd heard about Russian girls and blow jobs. Where had that all come from? That they had a technique that totally did your head in.

Olga pointed to a large seascape the colour of water and the same as her short velvet skirt. 'Alexander and I are fond of his work. Rick told me to have a quick look, as I was near here. But I'm looking for a piece that will work in a particular placement at Drayton. I'm not sure now.' Her eyes were wide in a face framed by a soft curtain of light-brown hair. 'Maybe it is a little less interesting than I expected.'

Katherine approached from the back room, her flat black shoes tapping on the polished wood floor.

'Hi, Olga.' She leant in to the brush of a kiss bestowed by the substantially taller woman. 'It's a lovely selection, isn't it? A lot of them from the best years.'

During her marriage she had learnt enough to be able to voice judgements on art with reasonable conviction. Although, when they met, Katherine had been aware that Rick's well-known family had been part of his appeal, in no time at all she had decided that it didn't matter what it was about somebody that was attractive so long as the relationship worked. The success of the Tennison Gallery was simply as valid a reason for her to want to be with Rick as his sense of humour and the fact that *Heidi* was one of his favourite childhood books.

Throughout Josh's childhood she had dipped in and out of Rick's professional life, but now, looking ahead to the empty nest that was as unavoidable as the proverbial death and taxes, she was searching for something else. It was as vague as that – *something else* – but she was clear that she didn't want to feel that her future was behind her.

Olga looked across the gallery to where Flo was standing, apart from the group.

'And this is Flo, of course.'

Olga walked over, her face breaking into a smile which made her beauty less daunting. 'I'm so pleased to meet you. Katherine has told me that you are an expert in period houses. Alexander and I are determined to restore some of the original details. I know that everybody thinks we're rich Russians who have torn everything out but we have done some research and, of course, so much that was there was taken out many years ago.' Olga spoke with the clipped pronunciation of the non-native tutored in a foreign language. Her deep voice and the formal delivery of her words formed a striking contrast to the soft smudge of her mouth.

'I'd love to have a look. It sounds interesting. I'm not a great expert on the eighteenth century, but I do know quite a bit. I always think old houses speak. I like to hear the tales.' For years Flo had been working on a book that would examine how the concept of the individual had influenced domestic life and architecture over the last four hundred years. Flo knew she had done more than enough research now; it was all over her flat, literally climbing the walls in boxes of folders. But she was paralysed by a conviction that what she would write would never be good enough. This lack of confidence, inconveniently combined with a conflictingly strong degree of belief in herself and her talents meant that she was constantly battling with her own high standards. Katherine was always urging her just to get on with things, but she simply couldn't. Instead, she freelanced as a researcher, more often than not to those with less intelligence than herself.

Olga turned to Fred. 'We are going to have tea, but I may bring Alexander back. It's hard, don't you find' – she turned for the first time to Katherine – 'to get men to focus on the things you need? Alexander, he always says to me, "You do what you want. I don't need to see it. I trust you." But that is not the point, is it? You would like them to be involved in the choice.'

'Actually, I've always thought it best that Rick has absolutely no interest in what I do in terms of the house and other things. I mean, if we had to agree on a colour every time I wanted to paint a room, or he wanted to choose furniture with me, I don't think we'd still be married. That's my territory. Let's go have that tea, shall we?'

'We'll drive.' Olga gestured to the pavement. The substantial form of her driver was already filling the door. 'Goodbye!' She waved at Fred, adjusting the collar of her short fur jacket. 'I'll be in touch in the next day or so.'

Her coat was mink, probably, Katherine guessed, unable to remember where mink stood in the canon of 'bad' furs. They all wore fur, the Russian girls. They managed to get away with it, pleading sub-arctic temperatures in Moscow, even though they were in a restaurant in Mayfair.

Olga sat in the front seat of the car, allowing Flo and Katherine to enjoy the capacious leg room at the back. A crystal tumbler of water nestled in a leather cradle and a television screen was soundlessly showing daytime crap.

'Do you know the Fullardis?' Katherine asked, leaning forward, close to the shaven neck of the driver. 'There's no reason why you should, but I just wondered.'

'I've met Ann a few times. She never married again, did she? After the crash. Though there have been lovers, of course. And so many rumours.' Olga was dabbing lip balm on her mouth from a slim tube. 'The last one, I heard it was a guy from the circus. A high-wire walker. She met him when they were in Florence. It was one of those troupes. High-end circus stuff. He ran away to be with her, like in a kids' story. The man who ran away from the circus. But it didn't last. I think he went back to try and rejoin the circus in Vienna, or wherever. But by that time they had found another high-wire man.'

'In a way, that sounds like the Ann I was at school with,' Katherine said. 'She was this strange mixture – very sporty and straight in some ways, but very into boys. The rest of us were always anguishing about whether somebody fancied us, but she just screwed around. It was a long time ago, obviously.' Katherine was aware that Olga was much younger than her and Flo, but what was she? Thirty? Maybe a little more, even though she could easily pass for twenty-five.

'When do the kids arrive?' asked Flo. 'It must be soon.'

'Those kids, they've had their problems,' Olga said. 'It's been difficult, everyone says, at home. Are they twins?'

'No, they're not, but they're very close in age. They must be in their early twenties now. Once she'd married Massimo, I remember she popped them out one after the other,' Katherine replied.

The car pulled up at a side entrance. Olga waited for the driver to come round to her door and slipped out before the other two women. The streets were filling up with early office-leavers, the late-afternoon sky shafted with the pink of a chilly sunset.

Really, Rick could have done without this dinner. It had been a hell of a week what with one thing and another, although Paris had been worth it, no question. He peered at himself in the mirror above the basin to check whether he should shave. There'd been no meetings today, so he'd left it alone, but now, as he stroked his lower cheek, he couldn't ignore the speckled whiskers. Too many white ones. Maybe it would wake him up a bit.

The room smelt of Katherine's bath oil. She was well ahead of him tonight; already bathed, dressed. He pictured her downstairs, checking over the living room – candles, cushions, flowers, the displays on the various mantelpieces arranged to convey the desired message. They were a couple at the centre of things. They had people to see, places to go. There were invitations to private views, fundraising galas, birthdays; nowadays, some of them were like books, fat with dietary requirements, lists of local hotels, notifications of train stations, car-parking facilities, even available heli pads. They'd dropped out of the wedding loop, though. When they had first married, every weekend there seemed to be another wedding. Now it was fiftieths.

Rick understood that, for Katherine, most of the pleasure of their entertaining lay in this moment. Making sure that everything in their house looked perfect was what made her happy, and he liked it, too. She'd always had a talent for it, right from the start, when he was, truth be told, a bit of a case and she was smoothing him out. When the guests finally did arrive, it was almost as if they were an afterthought.

He shouted downstairs. 'Darling! What do you think? Should it be the blue shirt tonight and a jacket? Or do you think I can wear a sweater?'

'What? I can't hear you!' Katherine yelled up. 'I'm in the kitchen with Mariella.'

He left the bedroom and leant over the staircase, unwilling to walk into the kitchen in his underpants. 'I was asking what I should wear. A jacket? What would you like?'

Katherine left the kitchen to go and stand at the bottom of the stairs. From there, she could see her husband, his chest bare, rubbing a towel around his neck. 'For heaven's sake. They're just kids. Wear what you want.'

'That's not much help.' Rick retreated to the bedroom, crossly pulling a clean shirt from a hanger. If she was going to be like that, he might as well wait till they arrived to go down.

In the kitchen, Katherine was going through the details with Mariella. If she, Mariella, seared the fillet of beef ('Really hot, Mariella, so the tin is *smoking*') when Antonella and Matteo arrived, it should only take twenty minutes in the hot oven. Maybe not even that. It would be best to eat early so that, if conversation was sticky, they wouldn't have to make it a long evening. Oh Christ. What if they were veggie?

The French oak refectory table in the kitchen was laid for four, although it was capable of seating many more. The kitchen was where they hung out and, when they had people over, Mariella could position herself far enough away for her presence not to intrude. Anyway, over the years, they'd developed a routine where she would disappear discreetly throughout the meal, returning with well-rehearsed timing to serve up and clear plates. Katherine glanced across at her aide, standing out in a fluffy pink sweater against the steel of the kitchen, and felt a rush of gratitude and affection towards her. Twelve years together. It was almost like a marriage.

Returning to the living room, Katherine looked at her reflection in the mirror. With her blonde hair in a half up-do, a necklace of sea-coloured laboradite, her black top with a scoop neck, she wondered if she looked her age. What *did* her age look like now? When the doorbell rang she moved first to the bottom of the stairs to shout to her husband: 'Rick. It's them. Can you *please* come down?' Then she went to the door. The light from the porch shone on two figures standing side by side, drops of rain sparkling on their shoulders, the street dark behind them.

'Come in.' She held out her hand. 'Antonella?' The girl held out a cool, limp hand.

The pair were negatives of each other. Antonella's deep-brown hair was a similar length to Matteo's dark blond, both had the straight nose of a Florentine page, but his complexion was olive while hers was strikingly pale. Against the soft, creamy walls of the hall they cut a stark presence. Antonella's slim black jacket was buttoned, revealing ridges of bone rather than flesh where the lapels met, and her brother was, similarly, in a black suit with a white shirt buttoned to the neck.

The pair looked towards the stairs as Rick ran down them. His arrival was immensely reassuring to Katherine at this moment, wiping clear her previous irritation. She was taken aback by their looks. Annie had been pleasant but unremarkable looking and, as she remembered, Massimo had been fairly standard-kit Euro. Apart from those strange fingers, he was sturdy, clean-shaven, with a short, dark back and sides, good teeth and expensive loafers. Their children were unlike either of them, with their etiolated physiques and combined androgyny. Even at first glance they were curiously compelling.

Once inside, Matteo accepted the glass of champagne Rick offered. 'It's kind of you to have us. Ann told us that you' – he looked at Katherine – 'and she were schoolfriends but that you hadn't seen each other for a long time.' The way he called his mother Ann jarred with Katherine. She preferred 'Mum!', yelled throughout the house, even if it was almost always a demand for her to do something.

'Yes. It's been forever. I don't know why. We were really close when we were at school together for the few years she was in London and then, when she left . . . I guess life gets in the way. We had dinner with both her and your father – years back now – and of course I spoke to her after he died. Please. Sit.'

Matteo claimed the end of a sofa across from the fireplace, crossing his legs in a way that drew attention to their length, while Antonella remained standing. Katherine remembered Josh coming home from school one afternoon and saying, 'Mr Jacobs told me today not to cross my legs. He said men don't sit like that.' She had told him it was nonsense and to sit how he wanted.

She addressed Antonella, who was lighting a cigarette with the click of a heavy gold lighter.

'I'm right, aren't I, that you are the elder? I remember you were born quite close together.'

'No.' Antonella spoke with more of an accent than her brother. 'My brother's older. There is a year between us. A little more.' She gestured to the room's carefully cluttered artworks, long, pale curtains and side-table tableaux.

'Your house is very nice. Very English. All this furniture, and the comfort. At home, you know, everything is much more – hmm, how do you say? – *formale?*'

'Well, of course, the Milanese are leaders in modern furniture design,' said Rick enthusiastically. 'Personally, I love a lot of that stuff. But I bow to Katherine when it comes to furnishing, and she certainly makes the place pretty comfortable. I don't think you're that into the Milanese thing . . . darling, are you?'

'No, that's wrong,' replied his wife, with a lift of her brow that indicated she had heard this before. Katherine had now sat beside Matteo, and turned to him to ask, 'Where are you living in London?'

'We have a flat in Maida Vale. It belongs to somebody our mother knows, and has been empty, I think, for some time. It's fine. It's kind of a quiet neighbourhood, but we're used to that with Milan.' As he tucked his hair behind his ears, Katherine noticed he had the same extraordinary fingers as his father.

'I want to have a kitten.' Antonella spoke up. 'I think you need cats to have a home, but Teo, he is not so sure. He doesn't trust me to take care . . . do you?' For the first time, Antonella smiled as she looked across at her brother. 'He is better at being the caring one.' The smile disappeared quickly, as if it had arrived by mistake.

'At home we have hundreds of cats. Some of them just arrive and the maids feed them. Antonella can't, or maybe won't, feed herself even. The poor cat, if it had to rely on her for its supper!' her brother said with a laugh.

Rick drained the champagne bottle into his glass. 'Talking of supper,' he said, 'when are we planning on eating? I'm starving.'

'Rick's like a baby when it comes to feeding time.' Katherine stood up from the sofa, adjusting her skirt and pushing up the sleeves of her top. 'Josh is just the same, I'm afraid. You'll meet him soon, I hope. He's at uni, his first year. Did you study?' Katherine was finding it hard to assume the usual trajectory – school, gap year, university, first job; the traditional stepping stones that let everybody know where they were – for these two.

'Oh yes. We have studied. Haven't we, Antonella? And here? Oh. We are doing an art course.' Matteo shrugged. 'We just started. I don't know how interesting it will be. But Ann, she wanted us to have a plan. "I don't want you just hanging around in London," she said. He mimicked the more British inflection of his mother's international accent. 'So . . . we live her plan, for now.'

Having dimmed the kitchen lights and lit the candles, Mariella walked around the table with the platters of food. It came as no surprise to see the small portion Antonella took from each, carefully lifting and depositing it precisely on to her plate, separating each item, islands of different colour with a clear white china sea between.

Rick had produced one of his best Italian reds from the cellar. He had opened it earlier, and gave it a sniff now before pouring.

'We love Barolo,' Antonella spoke after taking a sip. 'We have the vineyards and produce some every year. It was one of our father's favourite things. He would take us to watch the harvest when we were younger. We would taste the wine with him.'

'Now, it's still done on the estate, but we don't have anything to do with it,' Matteo added. 'We haven't been there for a number of summers. We've been in exile.'

'Really?' Katherine replied, conversationally.

'Yes. Really,' endorsed Antonella, stubbing her most recent cigarette out in the neat pile of rainbow chard left on her plate. 'It's our mother . . . she's kind of insane.'

Matteo pushed back his hair from his forehead. 'It's not such a big deal. It's not the same there now. You know you don't really want to be there anyway, Tonne. We've moved on.'

'Well, it's great that you're here and, as we said, we must get you together with Josh. He's younger than you, but he knows the city pretty well and can show you some of his dives,' said Rick. His tolerance for what he called 'atmosphere' was minimal, and one was clearly building. He didn't put up with it from his own son and he certainly wasn't going to from these two. 'Before you leave we'll check when he's next around and get something sorted.'

'Not exactly straightforward, are they?' Katherine spoke to her own reflection in the corner of the bathroom mirror. She pulled at the skin just to the left of her eye in a vague attempt to remove a fine line she wished she couldn't see.

Rick fell back on to the bed, lying with one arm folded behind his head, the other adjusting his balls. 'You can say that again. I'm exhausted. Done in. That was all I needed after the day I had. Two cracked kids to talk to.'

'Sorry. Thanks for doing it. I'm really surprised. There's something unsettling about them that I can't put my finger on. Ann wasn't ever like that. She was solid in every way, whereas they're . . . febrile. At least, Antonella is. She made me feel on edge. Teo was a *bit* more relaxed. Anyway, I'm sure it'll be easier next time we see them. Maybe they were nervous.'

'Nervous? Who are you kidding?' Rick sat and turned the pillows over as Katherine came into the room. 'Come to bed. I need compensation. It's payback time.' Rick reached towards his wife. He was tired, but very little overrode his desire for a quickie. It would help him get to sleep, which he was finding harder and harder to do now he was approaching fifty. Katherine's slim body hadn't changed much since the first time he'd seen her naked. She had kept the small, firm breasts she was always insecure about, even though she knew it was legs that did it for him. Those legs of hers, with their slim thighs leading to the patch of brown hair on her pale skin.

Katherine allowed him to move her on to him, feeling his hands on her hips and watching his face when he entered her. The light on the bedside table illuminated his freckled shoulders. She counted the freckles as she waited for him to come, first on one shoulder, then the other.

# Chapter Three

There was no reason why Flo was late. But she was. She was always late. Running late, people *said*, when that was *literally* what she was doing now, and she was undoubtedly going to arrive in a muck sweat. It was beyond her how people could be on time. This morning was a case in point. She'd made it out of bed in time to wash and blow-dry her hair; usually, she always left the house with it damp. But this morning she was meeting Olga and she'd wanted to buy into the whole Olga deal, and her hair looking like she'd at least made a bit of an effort was one way of doing that. She'd selected one of the deep-berry shades of lipstick she'd worn ever since a friend of her dad's had said she had a mouth that could carry colour like a tune. It was true, she acknowledged, that she could have been quicker making the choice, and then of course her phone went just as she was about to leave, and she could see on the screen it was her mum, who she hadn't spoken to in at least a week . . .

If it hadn't been Mum she wouldn't have answered, but then she couldn't stop her talking, seeing as the council had decided, in their infinite wisdom, that the new development in the village would mean that the local shop would have to close. Dermot had said, 'Ah Mum,' in that impatient way he had. 'You're not going to miss it at all, what with all the choice nowadays. Anyways, there's always the supermarket just past the top of the lane.' But Flo could tell she was upset. Dermot had never done touchy-feely, even when they were kids. Emotional intuition in its most basic form had bypassed him. It wasn't the shop Mum was upset about, not really, but change. Dermot didn't get that. When you're close on eighty and living in a small village in Ireland with your kids skedaddled to

29

a different country, change is threatening, it's got to be. Flo could see that.

She peered to find the numbers on the houses that curved in a crescent around the park. Set back from the pavement by a barricade of cheerlessly maintained gardens, there was none of the usual detritus of urban occupation: no wheelie bins, plastic bags, beer cans. The road and gutters were completely clear of those single children's shoes she always wondered about (how did they lose just one?) and sodden car-wash flyers.

The front door of number 48 was opened by a young woman in the black dress and white apron of domestic staff, her face free of make-up and her hair pulled back so tight that the appearance of any generosity in her gaze was impossible.

'Mrs Oblomovik will be with you in a minute,' she offered, pronouncing the name in quite a different way to either Katherine or Rick, and showing Flo into the hall.

*Oblo*movik, Oblo*movik* – which was correct? Flo wondered on hearing the maid's pronunciation. Maybe they just give up on the Brits and let us say it any which way. On the wall above a huge mahogany table hung the graded canvas of a Rothko, at the ends stood a pair of red, lacquered Chinese lanterns.

Olga appeared in the hall through a door Flo hadn't noticed. Her hair was tied back today, which drew attention to her wide cheekbones and made her look older than she had that afternoon in the gallery. For the first time, she wondered about Olga's history.

'I thought we'd make a start immediately.' Olga buttoned her tan leather coat, tugging the belt tight around her waist and pulling the collar up high to frame the lower part of her jaw. 'Oh, this phone. It rings and it rings.' She pulled it out of her coat pocket without looking.

'Yes?' Her exasperation quickly changed as she recognized the caller's voice. She laughed. 'No. It's not. I'm on the way to Drayton. I think I mentioned to you yesterday. Yes, it was . . .' Another laugh, and her expression took on a softness Flo hadn't previously seen in it. 'I'll call you later on, I promise.' Olga kept the phone in her hand when the call ended.

At the door she turned back. 'Paulina!' she called. The maid reappeared instantly. 'Will you tell Mr Oblomovik that I expect to be back here this afternoon. He'll be leaving himself soon.'

As the door closed behind them she said, 'I am looking forward to having this house in the country so Alexander will have somewhere, I hope, where he isn't always working. Even when we're on the boat he spends all day on business. Apart from first thing. He likes to talk with me over breakfast.' Flo saw a man standing guard as they walked towards the black Range Rover parked outside. Was a shaven head part of the job description when it came to bodyguards?

As they were driven out of London Olga explained that Drayton Hall had not been her first choice. She had originally set her heart on a Palladian house in Wiltshire, one of the first in England she had been told, but in the end Alexander had said it was too far out of town.

'I was upset because, really' – she shrugged – 'it is not so difficult to take the helicopter. He'll probably use it anyway, most of the time, but he had in his mind that he didn't want to *have* to use it, and I guess, in the winter, it can be difficult, with the weather and everything. So I had to pass on that and now it's been bought by an Uzbeki couple we know. They have no taste at all. I hate to think what they will do to it.'

'But I've heard that Drayton is very beautiful, and your husband is right – it's so near London.' In the reflection of the darkened window, Flo's face was blurry, her dark curls wild, despite the blow-dry.

Olga leant over and put her hand on her arm. 'I am very much looking forward to showing it to you.' Flo felt ridiculously flattered by the younger woman. 'Now. Tell me about yourself,' Olga asked as they travelled through the west of London, with its big family homes ringed by towering culs de sac of council estates. 'Do you have family? A boyfriend? Children? Husband? A girlfriend?' She laughed.

'Definitely not a girlfriend,' Flo replied. 'Never a husband, and no boyfriend at the time of speaking. I have a mother in Ireland. That's where I was brought up. And I have a brother, Dermot, but, like me, he's moved over here.'

'You don't want them?' Olga pursued. 'Boyfriends?'

'Oh, I've had boyfriends, but I've been on my own for the past year or so. It gets harder once you're my age, and I guess you get pickier. Not that I had a very high bar.' Flo's gutsy, self-deprecating laugh echoed in the car. 'You should ask Katherine. She can be very vocal on the subject.'

'We must find you someone.' Olga extended her hand to examine her nails, pushing at the cuticles; each half-moon was as clear as a child's. 'Alexander has lots of colleagues.'

Flo was grateful for Olga making the effort to pretend this was a possibility, even though men like Alexander Oblomovik would be more likely to find a three-legged donkey attractive than a middle-aged woman with frizzy dark hair and an interest in domestic history. The younger woman exuded a certainty which Flo found intriguing and which prevented her comment from being patronizing.

Outside the city the morning fog still hung in the hollows of the distant hills, drifting in patches across the tame landscape. After less than an hour the car slowed at wooden gates, which slowly slid to one side at the touch of a control. The drive was surrounded by tall shrubs so that the final right turn unexpectedly revealed Drayton Hall itself. The gravelled area in front of the large house held a central fountain and as the driver opened the car doors a pair of peacocks emerged from the right, strutting proprietorially in front of the stone portico.

Flo pointed at the birds, the male's feathers fanned in full display. Olga replied without looking, 'Alexander gave me them recently. A house present, he said. He had been going to buy me parrots – I think it was macaws he had in mind – but then he considered that they would be more trouble. They look divine, don't they?'

Flo followed Olga through the front door and into the substantial, square hall. A young woman appeared, wearing the same uniform as the girl in the London house, and took first Olga's coat then turned to Flo.

'Nina. We will have some coffee in the garden room,' Olga announced. 'As you will see, the house is not habitable at the moment. We have a small kitchen now and, because I come here all the time, I have made a useable space to work in, but we have so much to do.' She led the way directly into a splendidly sized room, long windows running its length and a pair of double doors at the end leading to a smaller room, where a log fire had been lit and a pair of deep armchairs sat on either side of a vast leather ottoman, covered in magazines and fabric swatches. A large desk was placed opposite the windows, empty apart from a telephone, a laptop and a pair of lamps, recognizable to Flo by their bases of bronze cubes as the work of a seventies Italian designer.

'We hope to be in by the spring. Alexander is not a man who enjoys things taking time.' Olga's expression was tense for a moment as she looked around. 'Why don't I show you some of the house before the coffee arrives? Then, maybe, you can advise me on a few points.' She picked up the handset of a landline telephone and pressed a button. 'Alexander wouldn't come here until we had the telephone line put in. He is addicted and, in the country, you know, it's not always easy with the mobiles. Nina' – she spoke crisply – 'I have left my mobile in my coat. Please bring it in for me when you bring the coffee.'

She led the way back into the empty room they had passed through. 'For example, this fireplace. I think it is hideous, but we are not allowed to do anything with it. It's a treasure, so we are told, and has a preservation order. What do you think?' But before Flo had time to consider a reply they were climbing the wide curve of the staircase to an upper floor. The rumble of a drill could be heard from another part of the house, and the inane chatter from a radio drifted in and out as they toured the huge number of bedrooms, each of which was to have an en suite bathroom.

'How many of these bathrooms were here when you bought the house?' asked Flo.

'I think they had approximately one for every three bedrooms, but Alexander and I . . . that's not our style. Alexander likes to bathe often. Two or three times a day. And, of course, I like to have my own space, so we have one each. You don't want to share a bathroom with a man, do you?' Olga replied. Flo wondered when it was that Olga had become used to a life in which she never shared her bathroom with a man.

Olga moved through the house quickly, efficiently pointing out the qualities of each room – the aspect, the cornicing, the unusual wooden parquet on several of the ground-floor rooms which she was considering retaining, the height of the ceilings in proportion to the windows, the depth of the sills. She explained that the north and south wings had been added to the original house and that it was here that you could see the Adams influence on the ceilings. It was not thought that they themselves had been involved but the ceilings were still of interest and she was keen to keep the plasterwork in its original form, restoring it only where necessary.

Occasionally, she asked Flo a question, but the occasion was, Flo felt, more an opportunity for Olga to demonstrate her own knowledge and education than any desire for information. As they completed the circuit, she linked her arm in Flo's, guiding her back to the room they had originally been in.

'So, now you might like to come back here, alone, to study it in more detail. And then we could work on a plan.' Olga poured thick, dark coffee from a jug into small cups in a matching delicate, floral design.

'Certainly.' Flo reached to accept the coffee. 'It's a marvellous house. A classic. And from what I can tell, you've cleverly managed the conservation issues so far.'

Katherine had mentioned CeeCee's comment about Olga 'gutting Drayton'. It was typically ungenerous of CeeCee. And completely wrong. She went on, 'I'm always intrigued by the flow of a house. Nowadays, it's very different . . . the way we move around homes. If I may, I'd like to look at how the positioning of the staircases has changed.'

'I think it will be entertaining to have someone to talk to about these things. And I trust you. It's like we have known each other for some time. Do you feel that? I love to be in London. It's a wonderful city, and Alexander and I have met so many interesting people, but a lot of them feel very foreign. Or, probably, it is they who make it so obvious that I am very foreign to them. We are "the Russians", aren't we? All big cars and big money and football. Cultural philistines. And of course now with the Ukraine situation . . . there are new issues. Sometimes I find the stereotype amusing. But not always.' Olga sat back in one of the armchairs, stirring her coffee for some time, as if it were a Tibetan singing bowl. 'How long have you known Katherine?'

'Oh, we go way back. From university. I knew her before she met Rick. We became friends immediately. We found each other at some god-forsaken party which neither of us was enjoying.'

'I only really know of her as Rick's wife. I met him, of course, through his business. He seems a good man.' Olga caressed a few strands of hair back from her face. 'I know a lot of the gallerists and dealers in London now. I think they are always pleased to hear from me.' She laughed.

'Mm. No doubt you've got that right,' Flo agreed. 'They can probably smell you coming.'

'You seem very different. Though I have only met her a couple of times, she is more . . . closed. Is that what I mean?' Olga returned to the subject of Katherine.

Flo was surprised by the younger woman's intimacy; she hadn't expected it. 'Yes. It's true. Katherine is very different to me. That's probably why our friendship works. She's extremely organized and self-contained, whereas I'm all over the place. Sometimes people find her a bit cold, but she's not at all. She cares deeply about things. Anyway, isn't it often the differences to yourself that make other people interesting? It's probably the same with a marriage. You don't want to spend all your time with a reflection of yourself. Not that I would know,' she acknowledged, leaning forward to replace the cup on the tray.

'No.' Olga looked towards the door with a vague smile, as if a slightly amusing idea had struck her. 'Rick's mother, Lady Christabel, has invited us to the party she is having next weekend. A bonfire party? We thought we might go. It would be good to meet some of the people who live around here.'

It was predictable of CeeCee to invite the Oblomoviks, thought Flo, despite her suspicion of the newcomers. She would enjoy their presence as a talking point – entertaining fodder for the other guests' curiosity. 'Oh yes. It's one of CeeCee's – that's what everyone calls her – annual events. Guy Fawkes Night. It's a family tradition, but she invites a big group of people, some from around here, but quite a few come from London.'

Attendance at CeeCee's bonfire parties had been mandatory for Rick and Katherine ever since she had introduced them on moving to Charlwood. What was the point, she announced, of having this large place in the country if she couldn't entertain her grandchildren?

A magnificent pyre would be erected by her gardeners and the guests helped to make the guy. Until Josh was ten he had been terrified at the sight of the object he and his cousins had built, knowing that it would soon be burning on the fire, but he had tried not to show it.

'It's quite a spectacle, and it's a trophy occasion for CeeCee. Katherine's got Josh coming back from uni – even though he's eighteen he's still expected to turn up – and she's invited the Fullardis.'

'We shall go for a short time. I don't imagine Alexander will have the patience to stay for long. But I will find it interesting, I am sure.' Olga stood up and walked towards a window that looked on to a stone terrace edged by a balustrade. Rain was starting to pool on the slabs. 'I hope you will be there.' She turned back to face Flo with a smile that transformed her face. 'Then I would have a friend.'

★

There was just enough desultory afternoon light for Katherine to avoid switching on the Anglepoise beside her. The work was absorbing, and she treasured having to concentrate so intensely. It was almost meditative: the calculated pull of the pen for each stroke, the precision of the ink, the space between words, measured with an accuracy equal to that of the letters themselves. The parchment currently stretched on the tilted board was at her favourite point – empty, apart from the initial light pencil markings. Since nothing had been committed, there was nothing for her to scrutinize and find lacking. The Reynolds family tree was not so much complicated as highly populated. There were a few unwieldy deviations in the form of second marriages in recent decades, but, generally, the branches conformed to surprisingly similar patterns of matrimony and offspring as the generations passed. She enjoyed these more substantial undertakings: family trees, illustrated poems, bespoke pamphlets; she could get her teeth into them. So much more rewarding than writing names on invitations. She was lucky she didn't have to do that stuff – or only occasionally, as a favour for a friend, or the gallery.

Katherine looked at the information on the table beside her detailing each coupling, and noticed that there were no single children in the Reynolds lineage, although it looked as though there had been several young deaths. Catholics, of course. They were a fecund lot – on average, four kids per marriage. Even now, that thought reactivated her insecurity about only having managed to produce Josh. Just the one. She hated that phrase. It designated them both victims, making her son sound as if he were missing something and as if she had failed on some level. Which was, of course, only what, deep down, she herself felt.

It was quiet at the top of the house, and Katherine worked well there. Once she got going she didn't need to look for diversions. Rick had bought a Nespresso machine for her study, which, in truth, she didn't really like, preferring the stove-top ritual downstairs in the kitchen, but it had at least given her an excuse to buy some exquisite stoneware mugs. She was always grateful for an opportunity to justify a new purchase. The house was already filled, and they hadn't been in it long enough to start having to replace things, so she was reliant on breakages and spillages and even the kindness of moths (when their targets weren't her favourite cashmeres) to allow her some completely guilt-free shopping.

By the time she heard Josh shouting from below, the sallow darkness of evening had replaced the grey of the November afternoon.

'I'm up here!' she shouted as she stood and stretched, hinging her tailbone back and then forward to massage her calves, as she did after running. 'Come up. I'm longing to see you.' She heard the lovely, familiar crashing noise before she saw him, filling the low-ceilinged room like Alice after she'd drunk the potion. He draped a big arm briefly around her shoulder.

'Hi. Is there any food?'

'Is that the first thing you say to your mother? You haven't seen me for weeks. Let me look at you. I need to examine you. Is there any change?' Josh stepped back, his dark-blue hoodie grubby and creased, jeans hanging from his hips. His red hair stood up in the same thick brush as it had since he was a small boy, gaining him the unimaginative nickname Basil at nursery. He rubbed his eyes and reached his arms towards the ceiling – tipping on to his toes in an attempt to touch it – in an attempt to diffuse any emotion at the reunion.

'I had to stand on the train. It was packed, totally packed. My legs are agony.' Josh began to pace the room, picking items up and putting them back down. 'What's this?' He stopped at the board.

'It's a golden-wedding gift that Julia Reynolds is giving her husband. A family tree.' She watched him walk over to where her inks were kept and a shallow slate mixing bowl contained a small amount of dense black. 'Don't stick your fingers in that,' she added.

'What do you think I am? Five years old? Why would I want to put my fingers in a bowl of ink?' Josh pulled a phone out of his pocket, looking at the screen as he tapped quickly, using both hands.

'What are you doing this evening? Do you think you'll go out?'

'Don't know. Probably.' Josh kept his eyes on the phone. 'I might go and see Rob. He's around. There's a party over in Clapton, but I don't know if I can be arsed to get there. What time are we going to CeeCee's thing? I hope it's not ridiculously early.'

'Well, our definitions of early aren't quite the same, but I said we'd get there mid-afternoon. In time for you to do the guy stuff.'

'Shit. I'm not still going to have to do that, am I?'

'Maybe not. Luckily, there are lots of younger ones around who'll want to do it, but you know she'd like you to be there. Even if it's on the edge of the action.'

'I don't really understand why we have to do this. Why we have to go at all. I mean, it's not like any of us like fireworks anyway. I've always hated them, but I've always been made to go,' Josh whined.

'Look. There's no point having this conversation now. I guess, sometimes, we all have to do family things. Anyway, I want you to meet these children of an old schoolfriend of mine, Antonella and Matteo, who have moved to London. They're Italian and a bit older than you, but I'm sure you could show them around. I've invited them tomorrow, too. I thought they might enjoy it. Or' – Katherine readjusted that statement – 'be interested. Whatever you think about the whole event, CeeCee does put on a show.'

Josh stuffed his phone back into his pocket. 'I'm starving. I'll see you downstairs.'

Katherine sat back at the board, reassessing her afternoon's work. The first generation of Reynolds were now in place at the top of the page, their children spanned out neatly beneath them, the carefully scripted letters and dates revealing nothing of what each family's life might have been. Had any of them, she wondered, rereading the names, been an overbearing mother-in-law?

# Chapter Four

By the time Rick pulled up alongside CeeCee's Bentley, the parking area to the side of Charlwood House was already filled with cars. His mother had always been infamous for her cavalier attitude to the Highway Code, terrifying her children, who were jammed into the back of the dark-green Jaguar with cream leather seats that made them feel sick. Now she'd given up driving and instead employed a man who not only acted as chauffeur but doubled as butler and general factotum.

Robert, the current occupant of this position, greeted them at the door.

'Afternoon, Robert.' Rick put an accomplice's hand on his shoulder. 'Are we the last to arrive?'

'One of them, Mr Tennison,' Robert replied. Rick had told him, as he had all his mother's previous aides, to address him as Rick, but Robert, having acknowledged the suggestion with a compliant nod, continued to avoid first-name terms. 'Her Ladyship is in the afternoon room, where they are assembling the guy.'

'How's the bonfire? Josh and I might go and have a quick look.'

'It's in the normal place. We had a lucky break this year. There's been a lot of ash come down around Spalling. I believe Her Ladyship is planning to take the younger children shortly, to join in.'

'We'll drop in and say our hellos and then go for a walk – don't you think, Josh?'

Josh shrugged. In the end, he had made it to the party in Clapton, returning to Kensington only in the early morning. Rick was exasperated by his son's hangover, which had literally hung over their drive to a degree which he regarded as unacceptable, but although he would have preferred otherwise, he understood Josh's reluctance to be here at all. CeeCee's ability to force her family's attendance whenever she wished was a constant source of frustration. He had never been able to figure out how she contrived to play both on her children's sense of duty and their emotional reliance on her. But, infuriating as it was to be summoned, there was a part of him that acknowledged the event as an endorsement of the successful family she had always and still intended to have. Hangover or not, he felt his son should appreciate being a member of it.

The afternoon was bright and chilly, a cobalt sky showing off the deep ochres and russets of the trees. After the sodden summer, autumn had bathed the countryside in lush colour for weeks longer than usual. To the left of Charlwood House the tulip tree was a burnished gold and the dark reds of the copper beech clashed cheerfully with the brick of the building. Rick could sense Katherine muster herself as she walked in front of him, chatting to Flo, who was wearing a striped woollen hat, an incongruous touch of jollity that topped off her usual head-to-toe black. Flo – Katherine's one-woman household cavalry. How many times had she been produced over the years to give his wife moral support at gatherings of the Tennison clan?

The afternoon room lay at the end of a long hall punctuated by leaded windows. In the centre, a large guy lay on a trestle table, the body of stuffed sacking ready to be manhandled into an old coat. The room was so crowded with adults and children that, for a moment, Rick couldn't recognize the members of his immediate family, then he spotted CeeCee seated in an upright armchair, a small boy pinned beside her. That must be Amelia's, he thought, looking for the hearty presence of one of Charlwood's nearest neighbours. CeeCee refused to allow herself a predictable snobbery when confronted with the plastic dome of their indoor swimming pool and their fondness for Marks & Spencer canapés. 'Amelia, such a *kind* person,' she would say, 'and *darling* Jerry – though I do wonder why he didn't stick to Jeremy.'

Children stood around the table, dabbing finishing touches: painting a grimacing face, sticking on straw and twigs to create a thatch of hair. Rick could see that the guy was nearly ready for its ceremonial procession to the funeral pyre. There would be no escape for him and Josh just now.

Followed by a raggle-taggle of children and attendant adults, Rick, Robert, Josh and Jerry carried the unwieldy bulk across the lawn, past the brick loggia, over the gate and into the field known as Michael's Meadow, with its tribute wooden bench at the far end. Rick had always been irritated by his mother's assumption that his father would have liked to walk around that field, admiring the gentle English view. Experiential evidence pointed to his never choosing to walk anywhere if he could avoid it but, as with so many details, CeeCee's certainty had turned wishful thinking into a kind of fact.

'Why don't you help Amelia's little boy?' Katherine asked Josh, as she watched the child scrabble in the wicker log baskets where dried pine cones, twigs and small branches had been gathered for the children to throw on the bonfire.

'Sure.' Josh started to move over. 'When are those two people coming?'

'Which two people?'

'You know – the Italians. What other two people would I mean, duh?'

'I said to them to come for drinks. I didn't think they'd enjoy building a bonfire.'

'Well, neither do I, and I'm here.'

'Yes.' Katherine reached up to flick a piece of leaf from his hair. 'But you're family. You're stuck with it. Go on. Look at him on his tiptoes. He's about to fall into the basket.'

Rick watched his wife and son from the other side of the bonfire, his gaze following Josh as he loped towards the child, hearing the laughter of the small boy when Josh bent to speak to him and help him with a satisfyingly large piece of firewood, then walked alongside him to place it on the pyre. It was a pity Josh didn't have brothers or sisters. He was good with small kids. It would have been much better for him not to have the full beam of Katherine's adoration focused so sharply on him. She'd never allowed him to make his own mistakes and was always able to find excuses for any shortcomings.

After Josh's birth they had both been delighted by the appearance of this ruddy, robust baby boy, but a couple of years later Katherine had become so driven by her desire for a second child that Rick had started to feel deprived physically and emotionally. Originally, she had been there all the time for him; her body, her focus, her whole life plan one hundred per cent engaged on him. But then her need for this other baby, the baby that never arrived, had changed that, and she had never quite returned to him in the same way. So when it came down to where they now were, which was the chicken and which the egg? Which had come first? And did it matter?

By the time the large clock in the hall had struck six the drawing room was filled. The group had been carefully chosen to show off the range of CeeCee's acquaintance: neighbours such as Jerry and Amelia, the Harringtons from over at Chalk Farm, and Tobias Jameson, whose successful novels had bought him one of the prettiest manor houses in the area. A convoy from London had just arrived, spewing a land artist, his new girlfriend and their entourage into the mix, along with the newly ennobled Lord Patel and his wife, Priya, and the family of a priapically incontinent television presenter and his long-suffering wife.

'Fucking freezing out here.' Josh was standing with Flo outside the front of the house, cupping his hand around the flame as she lit her cigarette. Flo was an occasional smoker, or she supposed that's what you'd call it. But at least she bought her own. She didn't do that 'May I? I don't usually' rubbish that most occasional smokers did as soon as someone else lit up.

'So how's university?' asked Flo. Her godson was wearing an oilskin jacket he had grabbed from the corridor, where jackets, scarves, boots and hats congregated in a murky mass. She had hoped to become his friend but, right from the beginning, she and Josh had failed to find any connection. Even when he was a small child he had shown a hurtful lack of interest in the presents she gave him – the complete Tintin series, a kit where you built a house of bricks with real concrete you mixed yourself (what kind of kid wouldn't like that?), a remote-control boat he could use in the park. She sent him garishly coloured postcards every time she travelled, marking the location of her hotel or the beach with an X, but he'd never mentioned them.

She knew that minding about this was *her* failure, no doubt an illustration of arrested development. But she did mind and, even now, faced with this giant of an eighteen-year-old, she found conversation with him daunting.

'It's fine,' Josh answered, blowing out smoke, which was indistinguishable from their breath in the cold air.

'Have you made friends? I remember I didn't talk to anyone at all for the first few weeks. I didn't do any of that Freshers stuff. I stayed in my room. It was awful. I'd made this big effort to get away to a new life, and then just when I'd got there I was too frightened to . . . well, practically to speak. But then it changed suddenly and I was well away.'

Josh smiled in polite appreciation. 'No. I'm fine. I've met some cool people. It's fun.'

'Katherine misses you.'

'Yeah. But I haven't gone far, have I? I mean I didn't go to the States, which everyone was talking about. And look. Here I am. Present and correct.'

They both turned towards the curve of the drive, hearing the roar of a powerful engine in the darkness before the motorbike appeared and crunched to a halt in front of them. Two figures were straddled across the huge machine, unbuckling helmets.

'This must be them,' Josh muttered, while Flo moved to greet the new arrivals. Teo stayed astride to shake hands as Antonella slithered from the bike, adjusting her body with a shrug under a shaggy white fur.

'Hi. I'm Flo, and this is Josh, Katherine's son.'

'Hello, Josh.' Antonella leant in to kiss him, assuming their identity was known to both, or not caring if it weren't. She smelt of something sharp and dark, not like the sweet, pinky stuff of most girls he knew. 'So this is a fireworks party?' She opened her arms to the silent countryside.

Josh laughed. 'Kind of. Is that the new Monster?' he asked Matteo, eyeing the bike with fascination. 'Sweet.'

'I brought it with me from Italy. I love it.' Teo stroked the handlebars. 'I'll take you for a ride sometime if you like. Antonella, you go with them. I'll follow.'

They moved into the house. 'I'll wait for my brother here,' said Antonella, standing in front of the hall's deep stone fireplace and rubbing her hands in the heat before putting them to her face. 'The bike. It was cold, but super-fun. Teo and I, we love to be speed.'

'You mean fast,' Josh suggested. 'Cool bike.'

'Like he says, he adores it. For me, I don't particularly care . . . bike, car, boat . . . just the speed. *Whoooosh!*'

Flo came up to them. 'Let's go in. You probably want a drink before the bonfire?' she asked Antonella. 'Ah, here's your brother now.' They were led by Flo into the drawing room, where Katherine stood beside a deep window seat supporting Amir Patel. Flo was eager to hand over her cargo, leaving them as Amir stood to greet the newcomers, his dark-green corduroy trousers and the collar of a checked shirt neatly poking out of a navy crew neck more English than the English. The Fullardis towered over him, like praying mantises.

'You should come and meet my mother-in-law,' said Katherine after a few moments, and ushered the pair through the crowded room, past waiters carrying trays loaded with champagne coupes and hot toddies in Bavarian red glass nestled in silver-handled cribs.

'Ah yes. I knew your grandfather.' CeeCee remained seated as she greeted them. 'Gianni. Oh, he had exceptional taste . . . in everything. Never predictable, but always spot on: houses, art, women. Michael and I spent a memorable weekend with him and your grandmother on Capri. That was many years back now. Of course, they were a little older than us. We were very flattered to be invited, as I recall.' Her smile – the same girlishly flirtatious smile – was still employed to effect. 'Your father was still a small child then. He was allowed on the yacht for a treat in his little blue shorts and smart white shirt, and then an enormous grasshopper landed on the plate of biscuits he was eating and he screamed and screamed. And his nanny scooped him up and removed him. Such a beautiful yacht.' She stroked the long gold chain she was wearing, her fingers caressing the links as if they were prayer beads.

Her head moved a fraction to the left, catching a movement. 'I see the Oblomoviks have arrived. If you'll excuse me.' She stood, slowly. Teo and Antonella turned to the double doors, where Olga now stood beside her husband, his dark, flat head bent over a smartphone. Antonella removed her fur to reveal the white branches of her arms in a black tank top.

'That's a wonderful jacket you have,' Katherine remarked, stroking the shaggy pelt.

'It's just an old one of my mother's that was made when the family worked with the fur houses. She had them all taken out of the storage when we left.' Antonella draped it over her shoulder. 'I don't suppose she will miss it.'

'She has so many furs, our mother. She likes to have so much of everything,' Teo added. His hair was pulled back in a ponytail from a severe middle parting that emphasized the rich colour of his lips and the sharp line of his jaw. Like Flo, they obviously had a thing about wearing black, thought Katherine, but while Flo's black was deployed as an anonymous, shape-disguising device, theirs was the opposite: it drew the eye towards them, a challenge to the traditional heathery camouflage the other guests wore for a party in the countryside.

It was only recently that CeeCee had given in to the golf cart. She was entirely steady on her feet most of the time, but she had to acknowledge that walking down the lawn, across the slightly uneven terrain of the brick-floored knot garden, and climbing the slope of Michael's Meadow in the dark, was hazardous. This evening, the cart took on a stately element as it led the way along the route, which was lined with flickering flares, yet another demonstration of CeeCee's ability to turn threat into opportunity.

Alongside her sat Olga and Alexander Oblomovik. 'Did you landscape this yourself?' Olga asked, although the minimal light could only allow her to guess at the content and layout of the gardens.

'Yes. It was an act of faith. All gardening is, don't you find? Particularly trees. Of course, there was a structure already in place with most of the parkland, but it was a question of how to link the gardens to what was there and how to make an effective progression. Do you have extensive plans for Drayton?'

'We do.' Alexander spoke for the first time. 'We are bringing mature trees in, which will help.'

'Not too mature, though, Alexander.' Olga spoke fondly, correcting him without any hint of criticism. 'You remember that you discovered there is the perfect moment for the planting? It has to be a balance, doesn't it, so that the roots will be safe.' She patted her husband's thigh. 'Alexander is impatient. This kind of thing is difficult for him. Once he has a vision, he wants it done immediately. His mind works so quickly.'

CeeCee pointed out the glow on the other side of the thicket to Tommy, her youngest grandchild, who was sitting on the bench behind. If the timing was correct – and the timing would be – the fire would have been lit and taken hold but, when the procession arrived, the flames would not yet be dancing their lethal tarantella around the doomed guy.

Katherine was pleased to see that her niece, Amy, had latched on to Antonella. Teo, his hands in his coat pockets, walked more slowly at her side, helping her over the stile at the entrance to Michael's Meadow with a surprising display of good manners.

'Why did you come to London, Matteo, both of you?' asked Katherine, holding his hand briefly as she jumped from the wooden step and feeling the unfamiliar boniness of it through her gloves. Rick's palms were padded, as if he were wearing a baseball glove on each hand.

'It's Teo.' He pronounced the 'T' softly, making it into a completely

47

different consonant. 'We wanted to breathe some different air. I could put it that way. There were reasons, some things happened, but it's not worth explaining. Antonella and my mother needed time apart. Anyway, Milan is very intense, we know everybody and both of us were bored. The same restaurants, the same ski weekends, the same bars. It was a drag. We thought of New York – perhaps we will go there next. We thought of Shanghai . . .' He laughed. 'But our mother always told us that London was where she had the most fun, so that was a good reason to come here.'

'And both of you? You wanted to come together? That's really unusual. Most brothers and sisters at your age want to get away from each other.'

Teo stopped to look across the field. Some people had already reached the fire and were beginning to gather in groups of small, dark shadow players. 'We're very close. Why would we want to be apart?' he said. 'We like to look after each other. We've learnt that. Antonella needs me.' He touched her arm before quickening his pace to catch up with his sister, an icy dandelion in her white fur.

Katherine let him walk away from her and stood alone, listening to the crackle of the flames as they crept upwards and watching the sparks dart and fly. She wished for a moment to be the Katherine Wilson she once was, before becoming Rick's wife, Josh's mother. But was that possible? Did you eventually become another person, or were you, like an onion, made of layers? And if she peeled away the outer layers, would she find that same Katherine Wilson who, as a child, had enjoyed the pretty Roman candles flaring on the ground but had always been waiting for the thrilling, noisy starbursts in the sky? Was that person still there?

By the time she reached the bonfire the flames were licking around the guy. To the left of the pyre, caterers had set up two huge contraptions for CeeCee's celebrated fondues. Bubbling pans of cheese, a piquant barbecue-style sauce and nutty bagna càuda were lined up and, beside them, heated griddles waited to sear cubes of steak and bread. The smaller children waved sparklers, writing their names in the darkness, sketching hoops of sputtering light, or grabbed sausages and miniature baked potatoes from another table.

Katherine looked for Josh. Where was he? Not that it mattered, but she would have liked to see him, just briefly. When had her job changed from being the mother of a child demanding undivided attention – 'What does my dive score?' 'Peel my egg, pleeese.' 'Are you *there*?' – to being required, in ways less vocal but equally insistent, to keep a distance?

'How you doing?' Flo approached, holding a glass of mulled wine. 'CeeCee is in her element tonight, isn't she? Everyone in place, even Olga and Alexander standing to attention. You know, I was surprised that Olga was so keen to come, but she seemed genuinely excited by the idea. She's a queer girl. I can't figure out what it is she wants from me. But, hey . . . it's going to be an interesting trip.' She took a glug of the wine and pulled her hat further down around her ears. 'I don't know about Alexander, though. What's that relationship about? Maybe I'm just being my old, cynical self, but I can't help feeling there's a story there. I guess it could just be the usual . . . rich guy, beautiful chick, no surprises. But she sounds devoted to him, and she's certainly attentive, from what I've seen.'

'I think she's okay. She's certainly staggeringly beautiful. I find myself looking at her all the time,' Katherine replied. 'Anyway, they've added something new to tonight. Them and the Italians, who, I'm pleased to see, are chatting away. Have you seen Josh, by the way?'

'He's over there, with the Fullardis and Amy. Look.' Flo directed Katherine's gaze to the group smoking around a brazier. 'Isn't Teo a total ride?'

'Huh?'

'Fuckable. That's the Irish in me.'

'I guess . . . I hadn't thought about him that way. The cordon sanitaire of age, perhaps. Is he?' For a moment Katherine appeared genuinely concerned, as if she had suddenly forgotten how to spell her surname. 'I suppose he might be. You could give it a whirl,' she teased her friend. 'He's certainly got something. Do you think he's straight?'

Flo put an arm around Katherine. 'I'm sure we'll find out soon enough.'

CeeCee had placed herself at the front of the crowd. Amir Patel was shouting into her ear on one side of her; Alexander Oblomovik was standing silent on the other. Katherine looked past her mother-in-law, vaguely trying, now, to locate Rick. CeeCee liked the family to engage in a public display of connection at evenings like this – sharing jokes, the generations mingling together – which friends, neighbours and acquaintances could observe and, ideally, envy.

But she couldn't see Rick in the lilac glow, until after the first rocket had whistled into the air, opening the display at the far end of the field, where the ground offensive was launched in hissing colour. By the time another rocket soared above he was beside her, and they watched together, the odd cry of a small child audible above the rush of the comets and cascades of stars that lit the sky.

When the air had eventually cleared of the smoke after the last spectacular bombardment, Katherine saw Josh approaching the bonfire with a group, throwing his cigarette down before he thought he was in her clear view. They stood together a short distance from her, lit by the embers and the flames, which were now dying down. Suddenly, Antonella removed her fur jacket, whirling it above her head like a lasso, and straining to watch as she swung it around and around, faster and faster, until it was a pale blur and she hurled it into the fire.

Even from a distance, Katherine could tell that Josh was unsure how to react. He waited until he saw Teo stroke his sister's dark head before he laughed, the loud, honking sound he produced when he had an audience. It took a few seconds before the flames flared up around the fur and, as they did, Antonella flung her bare arms around Josh's neck, jumping up and down and shaking her head, chattering all the while. Teo came up and opened his coat to wrap her inside with him as the burning fur turned the flames into a thick, black smoke.

Katherine looked for somebody to share Antonella's perverse

exhibitionism with, but the rest of the party was heading back towards the house. The fur must have been worth several thousand pounds, but it wasn't that which bothered her. It was Antonella's bleak expression in the seconds before the flames took hold that had made the gesture something more than just an oddly adolescent showing-off. It wasn't the fur she was burning, but something else. The woods to the side were a dense black now, and the red embers of the bonfire were imitated by the circle of metal braziers, similarly at the end of their lives. Katherine set off towards the house alone, walking quickly to catch up with the others, and pleased that, as she reached the stile and the fog moved in, she could make out Rick walking just behind the golf cart.

# Chapter Five

Rick checked the watch Katherine had given him for his fortieth. He'd never been an expensive-watch type and had managed with cheap ones for years. Once, he'd grabbed a watch with loads of dials in transit to Singapore, but Katherine had thought it was totally naff. 'You have to be kidding. It's like some Y division footballer's kit,' she'd said with a vehemence out of any reasonable proportion to what he'd done. That year, she presented him with the one he was wearing now, along with a card saying 'Time to grow up, my sweetheart'. It was a Patek Philippe with a dark-brown strap and only a single set of Roman numerals circling the elegant face. Given their shared bank account, he had wondered, briefly, what else he might have liked for that money.

The London art scene had changed in recent years, and now he had to contend with the huge multi-gallery dealers like Gagosian and Pace coming to town and turning up the volume. Michael Tennison had been a great one for decrying the jack-of-all-trades-master-of-none crowd, and specialism had stood him in good stead, and this was an approach that Rick had continued. They had a loyal following who appreciated their expertise in their particular field. He knew that he hadn't inherited his father's flair for spotting new talent but, at the final count, he was the more acute businessman.

Ever since his parents' day, the gallery had given good parties, and he wasn't going to change that. It was part of their DNA, as everyone kept telling him, as if the double helix had only just been discovered. Brand DNA. If he'd had a pound for every time somebody had brought up that old chestnut.

Rick picked up the sample invitation that had just been delivered to the gallery and ran a finger down the side of the thick card.

'It looks rather attractive, doesn't it? I'm pleased with how it's turned out. I know you think I should have gone with the Hitchens, but I reckon I made the right call with this one.' There was a nude in charcoal on a creamy background, the outline of her body voluptuous and abstracted and, on the reverse, 'Tennison Gallery Christmas Exhibition' and the details beautifully written by Katherine. Fred nodded agreement without thinking much about it. He thought the nude was a clichéd choice, but it was Rick's show, not his. It was always Rick's call.

Walking on to the street, Rick turned right, pulling his heavy wool coat closer to him as he strode along the parade of restaurants, galleries and shops. They'd had a good autumn, all in all. The first half of the year had been dodgy, no denying it. There'd been a lot of chatter and, when he woke in the middle of the night, he'd begun to feel the fear. He remembered his father puffing on a cigar one evening and telling him that the gallery was 'five per cent talent, twenty per cent luck and seventy-five per cent good old chutzpah. Never let them see the whites of your eyes,' he'd said. It wasn't just him: everyone was finding it slow going, but that didn't help. The auction-house figures weren't as straightforward as they appeared. Heaven knows what deals they were making to get the results sometimes. Thank God it looked like there'd been a sea change in September, but nobody was sure how long it would be until the tide turned again.

He could feel the shape of his BlackBerry in his coat pocket and pulled it out to check for messages as he arrived at the hotel, walking past the doorman, who nodded at him in a manner which avoided specifying whether it was out of acquaintance or politeness.

The foyer was busy as he strode through towards the lifts. A group of Americans crowded the reception, surrounded by their suitcases; a young girl sat on one of the stiff-backed armchairs, her phone lodged in the crick of her neck as she used both hands to apply her eye make-up. The doors of the right-hand lift opened on a couple standing side by side who momentarily stared at him as they exchanged places. He pressed '4' on the brass plate and glanced at himself in the mirror set into the wood panelling.

The thickly carpeted corridor shared the anonymity of all hotel corridors; behind each door lay a different story, hidden from view, changing daily. This was what Rick liked about hotels. You opened the door to a room and you could be anyone, you could be anywhere. It was liberating. He knew room 42 was at the end of the corridor, past the fire hydrant, just before the path swung round. He felt a familiar rush of anticipation before he pressed the bell, aware that, as always, he had a choice. He could just walk away.

Truth be told, Bonfire Night had been a close call. Rick could see his mother placed, as usual, at a short remove from the fire and in the centre of a crowd. He would put money on the fact that she was bending Alexander Oblomovik's ear about the provenance of Michael's Meadow. As the years passed, the picture she drew of her late husband had become increasingly adoring, his many desirable qualities now enshrined in a greatest hits of recollection.

To the left of him, through the drifting smoke, Katherine stood a little stiffly, chatting to Flo. Now seemed a good moment – before the fireworks were launched, when he would be expected to be at the centre of things. Olga was listening to Amir Patel near the fondue, but she was looking straight at him. He turned his head left towards the dark copse, before moving towards it, resisting the urge to look back and check if she was following. It took only seconds to move out of the view of the gathering and into the copse, where the ground was a damp mass. There was a scuttling sound ahead. A fox? Or maybe a disturbed badger. Enclosed by the trees, he was now able to look back at where he had come from, hoping that Olga would be able to find the opening he had just walked through. He wanted her right now, with an urgency that overruled everything else. At times – most of the time – Katherine, Josh, the gallery and all the other components of what he regarded as his world effectively blotted out his desire but, occasionally, like now, the reverse was true. True enough to make it worth the risk, only yards from his wife, his mother and Olga's husband.

A slushy tread announced her passage through the branches. He reached out to hold her, smelling the smoke in her hair, feeling the coldness of her nose on his cheek and the warmth of her lips as they kissed. He reached under her thick, downy coat to discover the body there, unzipping her jeans and pulling her against him, moving them clumsily back into the support of a tree.

'Sweetheart,' he whispered.

'Ssh!' She clamped a hand against his mouth as he lifted her up and she unzipped him. 'Ssh.'

It was over in a minute, leaving him breathless. As she found her feet, readjusted her clothes, smoothed that fall of hair and tucked it into the collar of her coat, he wondered vaguely whether she minded that she hadn't come.

'I must get back to Alexander.' Olga spoke quickly. Now it was over, he could sense her tension. 'This was a little crazy. Too close.'

'You go first. I'll follow. He had my mother banging on at him, so you'll be fine. She wouldn't have let him wander off.' Rick watched her walk towards the flickering light outside the thicket, his body still hot, the sound of his uneven breath louder than her footsteps. Allowing her to get well ahead of him, he used the time to recalibrate, setting the dial back to family. When he emerged, Olga was standing with her husband, the light of the fire illuminating the small space between them. As he neared the crowd he looked over to the right, where the figures of Josh and Teo were standing alongside Amy, and at a slight distance from them, looking directly at him, there was Antonella. Even in this light, he could clearly see that she was smiling at him, raising a hand, but not waving. He thought of walking over to her. What had she seen, if anything? It was so dark that it was unlikely that she had spotted both of them leaving the wood and, if she had, what of it? Never apologize, never explain. That had served him well in the past. And, anyway, he wanted to watch the fireworks with Katherine, and that was what he was going to do.

★

Olga opened the door of the hotel room, standing back for him to enter. For a second, he appraised her beauty professionally, as he might a piece of art that he had no personal interest in. But as they kissed and he pressed her body against his, running his fingers down her spine to feel the bones and soft skin, any distance vanished.

It had started in Venice in the early summer. A *coup de foudre*. They had been seated next to each other at a dinner after a long day bouncing about in water taxis during an uncommonly hot spell for June. He had seen her name on the card next to him and recognized it, of course. Although many of the Russians who had been big players around the European scene had recently gone underground – their assets either frozen or displays of ostentatious foreign spending frowned upon in the motherland – Alexander Oblomovik was still a high-profile operator. Rick didn't know a great deal about the intricacies of his status vis-à-vis Putin but the word was that his fortune was still in play. Everyone said his wife was a real beauty and in the art world she had a reputation for a surprising shrewdness and knowledge. But they hadn't ever met.

Rick was flattered but surprised that he'd been given such a big hitter as his dinner partner and watched her walk down the table that spanned the length of the huge room of the canal-side palazzo. She was bending to peer at the place cards tucked into the arrangements of white roses opposite each seat, the candlelight picking up on the sheen of her faintly tanned skin. She looked cool, despite the heat that had reduced most of the guests to damp imprints of their normally crisp selves.

'I think you've got me,' he said, pulling out the chair beside him for her to sit.

The party was business, the guests more interested in ensuring that they had committed their precious time to the right occasion than in the eating of the meal, and it took a long time for the food to be served.

But Rick enjoyed every minute of it. Olga's eyes hardly ever left his, and whatever they discussed – the design of the Scandinavian

Pavilion (curiously brutal), the choice of the Russian artist for the Biennale (a brave decision), the new place Olga and her husband had bought not far from Charlwood – was a minuet of flirtation.

By the time the first plates were put in front of them, he knew what was going to happen. He knew that he would leave the dinner with this woman and sit, their bodies touching, on the bench of the boat that would drop them in the small, dark canal at the side of his hotel. He knew they would walk wordlessly to his room to fuck all night, on the bed, in the bath, on the balcony in the dark with the vaporetti splashing by, across from the white dome of Santa Maria della Salute.

There had been many hotel rooms since. They liked to recite the list of cities: Paris, Florence, Barcelona, Zurich. And London. He didn't know how she managed to be there, but she never discussed it. Once, he had asked, more out of politeness than interest, not wanting to make the assumption that it was easy for her to meet him. They had been lying, his leg flung heavily over hers, and she had immediately left the bed, snapping that it had nothing to do with him. It should be enough that she was there. Whenever they parted he sensed that she simply wanted to disappear without going through the process of leaving and, indeed, some part of her had always gone before she physically left. It kept him on edge; he was never quite sure that there would be a next time. He hadn't ever really understood how there had been that first time, but that was part of the thrill and the joy. It wasn't clear, quantifiable or explicable. It was just that here they were now in the vacuum packing of another hotel – super-king bed, champagne in a bucket, double-glazed windows – and all he wanted was to be inside her. She was pure pleasure.

Olga moved to the dressing table and poured champagne for them both, walking back to him and stroking the cold glass against his cheek. She took a sip and removed her slip in an elegant slither, standing naked before him, the black silk in a pool at her feet. Rick lay back on the bed, one arm pulling her to him, the other loosening his tie and removing his watch.

57

After they had made love Olga lay on her stomach, smiling like a child hoping for a gift.

'You know, you always take off your watch. Why is that? I like it. It shows a . . . carelessness, is that right? You don't care about the time?'

'Do I? No idea,' Rick replied.

'I was thinking, just now. About this.' Olga sat up quickly, resting on her haunches to look around the room. 'It's simple, isn't it? It feels so good. Like you are the sun on my skin. Not everything is so simple.' For an instant her easy flirtatiousness disappeared and she had gone somewhere else, but then she bounced from the bed and looked out through the window. The curtains were still open and the sulphurous glow from the street was the only light in the room. She closed them using the control panel at the door, mystifying in its array of options. Rick grimaced as, suddenly, a recessed spotlight beamed straight down over the bed. 'Too much reality,' he muttered.

Olga played with the control. 'Now, that's better.' Rick spoke softly. 'Come back here.'

'Tonight . . . what are you doing?' Olga asked as she stretched herself out alongside him.

'We've got dinner with friends we haven't seen for ages. Katherine did a plan of their garden.'

'She is a gardener, your wife? I had no idea.'

'No. She's a calligrapher. In this case, she's used the text partially as an illustrative device in the scheme.'

'Ah. She is an artist,' Olga teased, jumping up again and tossing her hair backwards and forwards like a feather across his chest.

'No. Not that either.' Rick was uncomfortable discussing Katherine. Since the start of their relationship Olga had shown herself to be completely at ease with any mention of his married life, although she was less predictable when it came to her own. In his previous liaisons he had learnt not exactly to deny Katherine's existence in any way but to downplay it – using 'I' rather than 'we', avoiding any description of the things they did together unless absolutely

58

necessary, ring-fencing conversations to make them as neutral as possible – discussing books, films, sometimes mutual friends or colleagues. But, with Olga, such dissemination was unnecessary. And there hadn't been so many other women, really.

He'd begun to be unfaithful during those difficult years when Katherine was so desperate for a second child, when their love-making had been reduced to scheduling and acrimonious recriminations. It was hardly surprising that he'd been tempted by sex as he once remembered it, just for fun. After the first, brief fling it was as if a barrier had been lifted, and his infidelities had become part of his life – harmless liaisons that had nothing whatsoever to do with Katherine and Josh. If anything, they probably made him nicer to be with. Katherine had no idea. He knew she had him placed firmly in the good-guy slot, playing for the home team. And he was. Ninety-nine per cent of the time.

'What did you think of my mother's party?' Rick asked, curious to know her answer.

'It was beautifully arranged – the fireworks, the food. Yes. The choreography. She moves everyone around, doesn't she?'

'You could say that.' Rick stared up at the ceiling. 'What about Alexander? Did he enjoy it?' He was able to separate the urgent, exciting minutes Olga and he had spent in the wood that night from a genuine interest in what her husband had thought about the evening.

'He said that he had been one time but that it wouldn't become a habit. You know, Alexander is not a good guest. He likes to be in control of everything. When he is not in charge, he becomes bored. But he was impressed by your mother. She charmed him.'

'Yes. She's a pro.' He reached out idly to stroke the skin of her arm. 'Katherine's planning a trip to Milan in a couple of weeks to stay with Ann Fullardi. How are you placed then? It would be nice to spend some time together if you can manage it.'

'You know I can't make plans, but I will try to fix something.' She leant over to him and gave him a quick kiss on his forehead before getting out of the bed. 'I must get to the airport. We are leaving for

Geneva tonight. We have a late dinner there. And there's a sale tomorrow. I have my eye on some pieces for Drayton.' She laughed. 'It's fun. It's like I have a new doll's house.'

Rick watched her pick her slip up from the floor and shake out the skirt lying over an armchair. She was completely at ease naked, never showing any uncertainty about her body. So different to Katherine, who, even after all these years, was never entirely comfortable unclothed. He knew she beat herself up about her stomach, with its small folds, and the faint veins that were inking her legs, and her movements when she was naked were careful, as if she didn't want to run the risk of unexpected exposure. He reached over to the bedside table for his watch, buckling the strap and checking the time.

# Chapter Six

They had always liked to hide out in the old olive press, some distance from the main house. When Antonella was a young child Massimo would carry her on his shoulders through the newly planted avenue of jacaranda trees while Teo ran behind, turning the trees into a giant xylophone by striking them with his stick. They would look at the huge wheel on its stone base under the vaulted ceiling, and Massimo would pretend that he alone might be able to move it with just his shoulder, putting on a drama when it naturally remained immobile, and then chasing them around the building with its wooden rafters and plaster walls.

One morning, they had taken Teo's iPod and speakers and were dancing together among the wooden barrels which still remained, though the oil was no longer produced, and Giulia had come running in. Her always cheerful face, the one that greeted them in the mornings and made them eat breakfast, was blotched from crying. The jacaranda trees had now grown tall, their slim trunks arched to create a cathedral of shady green, and it was through this that Giulia bustled them, back to the house.

As they approached, two cars of the local *carabinieri* were racing away, dust spitting out behind them. Giulia guided the two towards a small sitting room, where their mother was standing by the fireplace. Their grandmother, Valeria, stood opposite, beside a large, silver-framed photograph of her wedding and a smaller one of her son's to Ann, both couples posed outside the same church door.

'We have some terrible news.' Valeria spoke first. 'Your father has been in a very bad accident. It is a tragedy for us all. He has not survived.' Teo was surprised to hear her stop so abruptly, and waited for the silence to be filled. Ann was smoking, in short, tense drags, and pulling at the chains of the necklaces hanging down over her long shirt. When she moved closer to the children they could see she was crying, but her voice sounded the same as usual.

'I have to leave now to sort things out. I will be back as soon as I can, but I don't know how long this might be. You must be good to *Nonna*. Teo, take care of Antonella. You are the man here.' She touched a finger to his face, and was about to do the same to her daughter, but she twisted her head away.

'Where is he? Where is he now?' Antonella shouted, already at twelve almost as tall as her mother. 'I want to come, too. I want to see him! I have to see him!'

'What happened?' Teo asked.

'It was his car.' Ann answered her son before turning to Antonella. 'No, darling. That is impossible. You can't come with me now. We'll see, later. I always said I hated that Maserati – he would drive so fast. In the car he was a different person.'

'Ann. This is not for the children.' Valeria stepped towards them.

'I'm not such a child, you know!' Teo shouted. Antonella had begun to sob, a choking, retching sound that only increased when her mother approached. It had always been her father who could calm her. She would become first furious then inconsolable about something, sometimes real and sometimes imaginary. And often she would pinch herself again and again, hard enough to hurt, leaving bruises on the soft flesh on her arms and stomach. Massimo could always talk her down, but when he was away it would be left to Teo and a nanny to ride it out. Her mother's presence would only prolong the crisis.

Teo, though, was always close to his mother, happy to drape himself over her shoulder and hold her hand – until a year ago, that is, when she saw him wince as she approached to kiss him. Now, he kept his distance from her, each one of the four unable to find any solace by being close to another. Antonella was the first to move, running to Teo and clinging to his arm.

'You can't leave us here! You have to take us with you! He can't go! He can't!' she cried.

'This is a terrible thing for us all,' Valeria continued, 'but your father would want you to be strong. It is a shock to lose him like this, I know.'

'I need to get the Fullardi press office to work on a statement immediately. I should do this right now, before I leave, before every-one starts calling. They need to manage this.' Ann looked helplessly at her two children then left the room. The pair stood with their grandmother, looking out to the hills beyond, the olive groves slop-ing into hillsides of oak and chestnut, the spikes of cypress lining the ridges. It was a landscape that had scarcely changed for centuries.

Meeting Ann's children had made Katherine curious about what had happened to her schoolfriend since they last met. Even with her limited acquaintance of Teo and Antonella, it was clear that their feelings about their mother were, to say the very least, complicated. True, the Annie she had known at school was not a particularly caring type – more of a just-get-on-with-it-no-fuss, rather than someone into over-empathizing, so it wouldn't surprise her if, when it came to motherhood, she hadn't been much good at doing cosy – but Katherine couldn't imagine anything more damaging.

And Annie had always been fun to be with. Ready to dive in and grab the moment. But there was something about that scene at Guy Fawkes, the peculiarly childish and exhibitionist display from Antonella as she burnt her mother's fur, that hinted at something deeper. Teo, Katherine found easier, the more appealing of the two. But then maybe he was less able to show what he felt and was happy to allow Antonella to be his dysfunctional proxy.

When Ann had suggested that Katherine visit Milan she had been keen to accept. All the same, now, as she waited for her flight, which had been delayed by morning fog, she couldn't help cataloguing all the reasons not to take the trip. It was almost December and her self-imposed Christmas deadlines were looming. And although the original plan had been for Josh to come along, that had fallen apart when Ann insisted that there was no point in visiting the city at the weekend: 'I tell you, Katherine, *nobody* is here for the weekend, we all leave the city, and I would like to give a dinner for you when you visit.'

Josh, when she told him this, had been oddly reluctant to miss any lectures, even at the end of term, and when she'd dithered about going alone Rick had been persuasive. 'Darling, it's not often you get the chance to get away and do your thing. If you don't stick to the plan now, God knows when you'll go. It'll be good for you. I'm looking forward to hearing all about it, circus boys and all. Ann sounds a real character.'

But once they had landed and she was walking down the jetty stairs to the tarmac at Milan, where a platoon of fat-bellied planes was lined up for departure, and saw ahead of her the vast Emporio Armani logo bearing down imperiously from an industrial building nearby, her reservations lifted.

Ann had phoned her the previous evening, offering to send a car to collect her.

'Don't be ridiculous,' Katherine had replied. 'I'll just jump in a cab.'

'That's crazy. Linate's only twenty minutes outside the centre, but sometimes there's a terrible queue for a taxi. It's the easiest thing in the world to send Angelo. It's good that you're flying to Linate rather than into Malpensa, but both of them are suffering with fog now. In the winter, that's usual. He'll check if there is a delay.'

Katherine walked out into Arrivals and scanned the clusters of drivers brandishing boards with names written on them. It had been a long time since she had travelled anywhere alone, she was always attached to either Josh or Rick or usually both, and it was liberating to emerge quickly, with only one small case. Her father used to quote Kipling's 'Down to Gehenna or up to the Throne / He travels the fastest who travels alone' when he tussled with the family luggage, trying to fit it into the boot in advance of each summer's drive to a rental in the French countryside. For the first time, she could identify with that.

She was enjoying that sense of freedom and considering joining the queue at the café for coffee when she felt a touch on her arm.

'Hello. I'm taking the ride with you.' Katherine was startled to see Teo beside her, and immediately the vista of the foreign space foreshortened and snapped her focus closer. Unlike all the other passengers, he appeared not to have a suitcase, briefcase or bulging shoulder bag, and took the handle of her case to carry it for her. 'There's Angelo. Come.' He guided her to a group of chauffeurs near the foreign exchange desk and handed the case to one of them with a joke, judging by the laughing response.

'I didn't know you were on the flight. Your mother didn't say anything about it. How strange.' Teo's appearance had shattered Katherine's pleasure in arriving alone and she made no attempt to mask her irritation.

He looked more adult, more substantial, on home ground as he marched ahead to the waiting car. In their previous meetings she'd had the sense that he was flying in briefly, ready at any moment to depart elsewhere, but here he seemed grounded. 'I only emailed to tell her last night and, anyway, she wouldn't think it was relevant. I had some things I wanted to do here and it makes no difference to her. We exist quite independently.'

'And Antonella? She's still in London?'

'Yes. She's got a friend staying with her. I think she said she might see Josh, too. There's some concert. Something, anyway, they had connected over.'

'I hope not. He was going to come here with me but he said he had too much work to leave university. I'll be majorly pissed off if he's back in London for a concert. I was looking forward to bringing him.' She could see a young woman spinning her small child around and around while they waited for a man at the Avis counter, and felt a sharp envy of her ability to make somebody so happy so easily. She couldn't remember when she had last been able to do that.

Teo disregarded this last comment, opening a door of the Mercedes for her then establishing himself in the front passenger seat while the driver placed her luggage in the boot. He jabbed at his phone before leaning back to talk into it. Although she couldn't understand what he said, Katherine noticed that his general tone was no different to when he spoke in English. He was still emphatic and economic with words. She looked out of the window as they drove into the city, taking in the featureless houses and rushing cars. The billboards on stilts above the roadside, with their vulgar colours and clumsy typography, shrieked messages about detergents and shampoos, television programmes and dairy products. No understanding of the language was required. There was none of the warm glory she associated with the Italian landscape – the faded terracottas and olive greens, the classic proportions of old farmhouses and gracious villas.

In no time they were in the city, and the scrappy warehouses set back from the road had given way to smaller shops, cobbled roads and a network of wires that criss-crossed the grey sky, a giant cat's cradle that contrasted oddly with the sturdy stone buildings lining the pavements. It was only when the car turned into a series of narrow streets then stopped outside a pair of forbidding dark-green doors, decorative but unwelcoming iron bars across the windows on either side, that Teo stopped talking and turned around to her.

'We have arrived. You know, after London, it looks . . .' He mimed a tight space with his hands. 'But you will see.'

Stepping over a stone ridge, they entered a dark, cobbled area, the only light coming from a courtyard ahead of them framed by a wide archway. Teo turned to the left before they reached it and walked through a small side entrance, leading Katherine up a flight of thick, curving marble stairs polished smooth by generations of use to another pair of huge doors on the first landing. In the silence, even the air seemed trapped in the past. He pressed a bell on the side, which was immediately answered by a man who nodded a welcome to Teo, his sage-green jacket buttoned to a high collar by brass discs. Teo disappeared down the hallway just before a clatter of heels announced Ann's arrival.

The last time they had met, all those years back, Katherine had been struck by Ann's new gleam. Her once auburn hair was an impressive, sleek copper and a white jacket and silk shirt lent a smart structure to her ranginess, yet she had also kept her athletic stride and fresh, freckled face. The woman now approaching was almost unrecognizable, either as her cheerful Belgian schoolfriend with a passion for Heinz tomato soup or that married woman in the Italian restaurant so clearly enjoying the status of her husband's family.

She remembered Ann had told her in the restaurant how ironic it was that the Fullardis were in the fashion business when they were a family who found any kind of change in the smallest of details unacceptable and unnecessary. She had pointed at the bread basket on the table. 'I think they have eaten the same loaves at every meal for the past century.' Massimo had smiled fondly at her before saying that she exaggerated, but it was true: they had a certain way of doing things.

'Katherine. I can't believe you're finally here!' Ann put her hands on her friend's shoulders, delivering a movement of her head rather than a kiss. She stepped back. 'Let me look at you. You haven't changed at all. Still your beautiful hair.'

Katherine was unable to return the compliment, since there was so little about the original Ann that remained. The legs that had sped her so effectively across the tennis court as part of the lower-sixth team were now needle thin in black leather jeans, and her hair was a streaky blonde, backcombed mane. In some private operating theatre, a surgeon had spent several hours reconfiguring her face, pulling tight around the eyes and jaw, so that, although she was smiling in greeting, there was no connection between her features. Her brow was disassociated, a flatland without history.

'It's so good to be here. Now I've arrived, I can't imagine why I haven't come before,' Katherine said as they walked to a large room. Ann fell on to a deep, velvet-cushioned sofa, her skinny frame scarcely making a dent as she waved at Katherine to sit opposite. She could smell a medley of fig and some deeper note from the array of candles in thick dark glass jars scattered on a low table between piles of books more like sculptures than reading matter.

Although she had expected there to be a period of readjustment while the two old friends dug for what it was that they had originally found appealing in each other, she had been unprepared for how alien these first moments would be. Even the physical environment was oddly disorientating. 'I'm trying to get the sense of this place,' she said. 'Is it a house or a flat?'

'The whole building is ours. I'll show you later. It's divided into a number of apartments. I have these two floors. Teo and Antonella have their space over there.' Ann gestured to the windows, which were framed with thick silk curtains, their folds blocking out most of the grey sky of the late morning. 'I have organized a light lunch for us and then . . . Well, Milan is a city that tries its damnedest to put on the worst front – hiding its treasures from anyone who doesn't know where to find them. It likes to keep secrets. But it's always good for shopping!' She stood up and walked to the windows. 'Look. Here. You wouldn't expect this, when you arrived?'

Katherine followed her, discovering below an enormous garden of gravel paths and sharp topiary. Trees were planted in vast terracotta pots around a pattern of small fountains and, beyond, there was another building, smaller but still a substantial property, all within the same stone walls. In the winter grey, the formality gave it an austere beauty. 'That is typical. Things are not what you first see. The façades are brutal.'

'That's extraordinary – a secret garden. You're right – I would never have imagined that when I arrived at this building. By the way, I didn't know Teo was coming out today, and on the same flight?'

Ann delicately removed something from her eye, blinking without any connected activity on her forehead. 'He told me late last night. You know children. They do their own thing. It's good that they are away from here for a while. Space.' She turned back to Katherine, her smile as manufactured as one of the many objects placed around the room. 'We all need space, don't you agree?'

'I'm only just getting used to not having Josh at home all the time. Space works both ways. It can free you, but you can find yourself so alone in it.'

'In our case, we need to be free. There is a lot of history here. The Fullardi family can be a heavy shroud. When we escape from it strange things can happen, but then we always return. Even the children.' Ann lit a cigarette, using it as punctuation to end the conversation. 'Come. Let me show you your room, and then we will eat.'

After lunch, and during what was left of the afternoon Ann walked Katherine through the streets of the centre, and the two linked arms as they swapped updates. The city was icy but in the expensive enclave in which they wandered, there was an atmosphere of cosseted warmth. The windows of the numerous fashion brands were unashamedly extravagant, with displays of exotic skins dyed unnatural colours, buttery leathers, creamy suedes, expensive large-cupped bras and insubstantial knickers. Although Katherine hadn't intended to shop for herself, Ann's pleasure was infectious and, in riffling through the rails, they rebonded.

Within moments of entering any shop, the two women would be greeted enthusiastically, and a manager would speedily bustle in at the chain whisper of Ann's name.

'It looks like you do a hell of a lot of shopping,' Katherine said to her friend as they ended the afternoon in one of the city's famous cafés, its careful display of dangling panettoni and trays of pastries as splendidly presented as a showcase in an expensive jeweller's.

'Oh yes, I'm a favourite on Montenapoleone!' Ann laughed. 'You know, since the crisis, so much has changed. Many of the best customers stopped spending here and now go over the border to Lugano to shop. They don't ask questions there. But now of course there is the problem with the Swiss franc.'

'Questions?'

'Yes. The government. You know, it's been crazy here. They question how much you spend on everything. They can tell from the shops. I'll explain. A woman, for example, she spends three thousand euro in Prada but she is *saying* that she only makes three thousand a month for the tax? Then the government, they say, how come you have this money? So these shops, they have a big love affair with people like me who just spend money anyway.'

69

Katherine noticed how the precise English Ann spoke when they were at school, came and went in her conversation, now she had spent so many years in Italy.

Ann waved authoritatively for attention. '*Due prosecchi,*' she commanded, without consulting Katherine, who was pleased to relax into being the dependent guest. 'You know, this is a small town. And the Fullardis have been here for ever. We no longer run the business but, even so, the name . . . It's still a big deal.'

'Isn't it weird to have a famous name that you don't have any control over?' Katherine asked. 'I suppose it was never yours really, though. It was Massimo's. But you still carry it around with you. And I suppose lots of people still think you have something to do with it. Like they must do with anyone called Gucci.'

'I'm used to it now.' Ann poked among the nuts in a small glass bowl without picking any out. 'When Massimo was alive I think, sometimes, he found it difficult. To see the direction the house was taking when he couldn't do anything about it. But, you know. In the end, it was good. They had to move out of the family-controlled, narrow mentality and they needed investment. Heaven knows what would have happened if the family had stayed in charge. Think of the wives and children, I always say when I hear any complaints from his brothers. We could have been in the poorhouse. Massimo's father knew all there was to know about leather, but next to nothing about modern business.'

'Why did you stay in Milan after Massimo died? Weren't you tempted to move?'

'I didn't know how I felt. As I said earlier, the family is such a big deal and to leave was, in a way, unthinkable. And, obviously, there was Matteo and Antonella. Their grandparents adored them and Milan was their home. It didn't make sense to move them. Yes . . . it was a bad time. You think that you know your life, and I discovered, in a heartbeat – literally – that I didn't. So I stayed and made my escape in my own way. The children have found it difficult at times, I know, but in the end, we have to look after ourselves.'

Their drinks arrived, accompanied by small plates of fat green olives and slim pale circles of bread spread with tomato paste and topped with slivers of anchovy. 'Now, we should talk of happier things,' Ann insisted, frustrating Katherine's desire to delve deeper. 'I only have a couple of days with you. Tell me about Rick. Is he a happier thing? Is he what you imagined?' she teased. 'Do you remember when we would sit and talk about what we wanted, and I said I would marry a politician, and you said you wouldn't mind your husband having some money but it was more important that he was kind and that you had kids. And somebody *handsome*. I remember that.' Ann sipped from her glass, producing a tube from her small clutch and drawing on the vapour hungrily. 'And you were going out with – what was he called? – Tim? Now he was an *angel*.'

'Tom. He was called Tom,' Katherine replied. Until then, she had forgotten all about him, with his treasured Raybans and his passion for the cadaverous Bowie of the Berlin period. 'That's clever of you to remember all that. Yes, I did think I wanted somebody hand-some. Rick's probably not exactly what I had in mind then. But when I think back . . . I knew pretty well immediately. I felt comfort-able with him in a way I don't think I had before with anyone. And I suppose I liked the fact that he made it clear he needed me. Wanted me and needed me. That did it. Of course, it's been a long time now and sometimes I expect we both wonder about what else there might have been out there but, all in all, it works.'

Ann laughed. 'Well, you got the money, too, no? The Tennisons, they are wealthy?'

'Well, they're not in the same category as your lot,' Katherine replied, deftly separating her husband's family from herself. 'But it's true. I have the kind of life I never expected. Sometimes I'm still surprised by it.'

By the time Angelo had deposited the two women back at Ann's apartment, the street was lit only by the yellow glow of a single street light. In London, at dusk, Katherine could look down into her neighbours' bright basement kitchen extensions or through the large windows of their living rooms, but any life on Via Santa Maria

Umbria was invisible. There wasn't a single chink of light from the shuttered windows the length of the street.

She was looking forward to an hour or so alone in her room before setting out for dinner. The apartment was decorated in a dense mix of styles: dark, overbearing Italian antique furniture was mixed with collectable pieces from the second half of the twentieth century; the rich brocades and velvets of the upholstery were punctuated with glass and mirrors. Everywhere, there were multiples: in her bedroom, eight porcelain plates hung above the writing desk; in the bathroom, a family of crystal bottles was ranged on a shelf. She recognized the design of the bronze palm table light in the living room and the tinted glass chandelier that hung from the ceiling in the hall. Back home, she had friends who spent hours at night, while their husbands slept beside them, bidding on Scandinavian auction sites for pieces like the curved chaise longue she had noticed in the drawing room.

Katherine undressed and lay on the bed in her bra and pants trying to decide whether to give into a short doze, run a bath or just flick through a magazine she had bought at the airport. The heavily shaded lights on the small bedside tables made reading difficult, or was it just her eyes? She was debating whether she could be bothered to find her reading glasses when she heard a knock on the door.

'One minute.' Katherine bounced off the bed, trying to remember where she had put her dressing gown, then gave up and ran to grab a large towel from the bathroom.

Teo stood outside, holding a large, leather-bound book. He walked into the room, with no apparent concern that he might be intruding.

'I thought you might be interested in this.' He handed the book to her and his eyes narrowed as he looked around the room. 'This used to be our father's study. It has a lovely view – over the garden and the Duomo in the distance. He had his desk here. In the middle.'

'Teo, I need to get some clothes on.' Katherine was all too aware that the towel, although large, was insufficient cover.

Teo deposited himself on the small sofa and opened the book. 'I know you are a calligrapher,' he said, 'and this is very special. It was done for my great-great-grandfather by some famous guy. Father always said . . . how do you call it? "A work of love on the page".' In spite of feeling underclothed, in order to look at the book with him, Katherine perched alongside him.

'This is very beautiful. A real treasure.' She touched the soft vellum; the colours of the inks – green, red, blue – were still vivid. 'Wait a minute,' she said. 'I want to have a proper look but I need to put something on.'

It was only once she had returned, her thin dressing gown pulled tight around her waist, that she was able to enjoy looking at the book. She couldn't understand the language of the epic poem inside the covers but she could appreciate the skill of the calligraphy, the detail of the illumination. She was close enough to Teo to notice for the first time the fine scar down the left side of his mouth. It was maybe an inch long, pale against his skin. The minuscule teethmarks of stitches ran its length.

'Can I keep it to look at properly later? I really should get myself sorted out.' She found his presence in her bedroom disturbing, and somehow more so because there was so little furniture she felt exposed. When he looked up from the book, straight at her and so close, she realized she was nervous about what he was seeing, that she wanted a sign of his approval.

He walked up to a wall, stroking the paper there, a faint fleur-de-lys pattern in olive shades. 'I think you are meeting Paolo tonight.'

'Paolo?'

'Ann's current man. She didn't say? Better than some. Better than –' He shook his head. 'I see you later,' he said. As he passed her he left a kiss so light, so quick, that she wasn't sure if it had been on her lips or, if it had, whether he had meant to place it there.

Alone in the room again, Katherine turned to the business of unpacking, pleased to involve herself in something practical. She pulled open the door of an ornately carved armoire in the corner of the room. It was stiff and the wooden hangers inside clattered together. It galled her that CeeCee's pronouncement, delivered as she and Rick were about to take their first holiday together, that you could tell the calibre of a hotel by the hangers, bounced into mind. The two dresses and a jacket she had brought with her hung lonely in the dark space.

She started to run the bath and called Rick, keen to hear his jocular familiarity. It would be an hour earlier there, nearly seven, which was probably not an ideal time to catch him, since there was an odds-on chance he would be in some meeting or other.

Just as she was about to ring off, he answered, sounding as if he had had to run for the phone.

'Hi. Just checking in,' Katherine heard her own voice echo. 'Can you hear me?'

'Yes. Of course. How is it?'

'It's fine. Where are you?' Something in his tone put her off telling him about what she'd been doing that afternoon, or about Teo's book.

'At home. I'm just about to go out. Bob Wallace is in town and he's doing dinner. Since I was on my own, I thought I'd go along.' Katherine imagined Bob holding forth centre stage at a table in some London restaurant his PA would have managed to book at the last minute. He'd be king of his orbit, his acolytes circling round him, and Rick would want to be in on the action. 'Hang on a minute!' Katherine heard him shout, 'Josh! Remember your keys, won't you?'

'Josh is there? What's he doing there with you? I thought he was at uni.'

'I don't know.' Rick didn't seem to think there was an issue. 'He just said he was down for the night.'

'Well, find out what's going on. He told me he had too much work on, and that was why he didn't come with me to Milan. I guess you'll see him in the morning.'

'Maybe not. I'm making that dash back to Paris for a meeting and it's a crack-of-dawn train. Didn't I tell you?'

'Don't think so.' The conversation wasn't going the way Katherine had anticipated. When she had pressed Rick's name on her phone, she had simply wanted to connect with home territory but, now that she had, it was failing to have the desired comforting effect.

'It sounds like you're in a rush, and my bath's about to overflow. I'll call tomorrow.'

'Great. Love you.'

Katherine went into the bathroom to turn off the taps, the water now scented with a mix of pomegranate and orange oil from a Venetian glass container. She stepped in, tying up her hair as she sank down. It was a little too hot at first, and the mirrored wall alongside the tub was covered in steam. Katherine scrawled a childish 'K' on it, before wiping the image away to reveal her reflection. Turning away, she looked down at her body in the water, her breasts pale, tilting to either side of her ribcage, her hipbones sharp, with the soft belly in between, her neck without any trace of the mottle she had noticed some of her more sun-loving friends were now showing. She'd never been a sunbather. Even though Rick, with his ruddy colouring, never tanned much, he liked to lie out on a lounger racing through a thick thriller, or walk around the pool in the heat of the day brandishing a cold beer as he held forth. She would rather be on the move.

Over the years they had discovered places that would suit them both, veering towards the familiar in the interests of keeping the status quo. Rick wanted his holidays to be stress free, with no nasty surprises. They had once spent a New Year in St Lucia, where Josh had befriended another boy of his age. As they shared an early-evening drink with his parents she had listened as the wife explained why they had put the children in an adjacent villa rather than take a family suite. 'Frank works hard, God knows, and when he's away he doesn't want to be woken at seven thirty by the sound of the Xbox, God bless them. Not that he doesn't love those kids. He does: they're his whole life. Everybody knows he's a real family man, but he needs his down time – a bit of relaxation when he gets away from the firm.' She looked admiringly at her husband as he gulped an umbrella-topped pina colada. As she listened, Katherine supposed Rick would like her to behave a bit more like this adoring woman. Several years later, she had read in the *Daily Mail* that Frank had been accused by his wife of hiding assets in the couple's highly acrimonious divorce. It was hard to believe that was now over a decade ago.

The blue dot on Josh's phone bounced merrily as he moved. He kind of liked seeing himself as a blob being guided to a destination along the empty street, tall white houses on either side. He'd been pretty sure that his dad wouldn't get on his case about tonight, and he'd been right. Rick had been laid-back when he'd found him unexpectedly at home. Generally, it was always after the event that Rick got in a state about how Josh wasn't *applying* himself; in real time, he was normally too into his own stuff to notice what Josh was doing. Mum was different. He knew that she had really wanted him to go with her to Italy, but he'd genuinely thought he had to work. It was only when he'd got Antonella's text that he'd figured he could hand his essay in *next* week. After all, it was only one evening.

He hadn't seen her since the fireworks. Sometimes, when he was making a cup of tea or sitting in the university library, he thought back to her look of fierce fury as she flung her fur on to the fire, and then her silence as they walked back to the house, as if whatever it was that had overtaken her had also gone up in smoke. He hadn't expected to hear from her – she was several years older than him and sort of in a different world. She reminded him of a stick of licorice, skinny, and with a strong taste of something completely its own. He didn't quite get why he kept thinking about her.

The intercom for Flat 3 hissed as it was answered, Antonella's voice crackling through the sound of the lock release. The door was heavy, and he had to step around piles of junk mail in the wide hallway – takeaway menus and pizza-delivery leaflets, local directories in cellophane wrappers, a posh sheepskin catalogue – as if nobody had been this way recently.

Most of his friends were living between university and their parents' homes. When Josh wasn't at university he was used to moving among these houses, turning up to exchange a couple of sentences with their parents in the kitchen, the usual stuff: How were things? Where were they going for the evening?

But this flat was a whole different scene: it was clear from the moment he walked through the front door straight into a glaring white sitting room. In the corner was some weird umbrella light with a silvery inside and there wasn't much else other than an L-shaped sofa and a low wood table, where Antonella and another girl were bent over a few lines laid out on a copy of *Vogue*.

'Hi, Josh. This is Alba.' Antonella looked up briefly. 'You like?'

'Sure.' Josh didn't do coke often – it was expensive and he wasn't that into it – but if someone was offering, he wasn't going to pass.

'So, where do we go? Do we get a cab?' Antonella asked a few moments later. 'Alba, you don't walk far in those shoes.' She reached for a small jacket made up of suede patches stitched together and pushed her arms into it, wriggling slightly. Her own feet were in plain black lace-up shoes. She had a short body that seemed to be almost an afterthought to her legs, which were almost straight from thigh to ankle in their black tights and a pair of black shorts. Josh checked out Alba's feet with their studded boots with spiky heels while their owner rooted around in a huge handbag, her black hair hanging over a denim jacket in a glossy plait.

'I told her you said this band was major. She's into music,' Antonella said, as if in explanation of Alba's presence. Josh wasn't sure he wanted the responsibility of whether Alba enjoyed the gig, but it was only a skittering thought, pushed off by the burn of the coke.

Antonella's phone rang and she answered immediately with a rattle of Italian. 'Teo,' she mouthed as the conversation continued. Josh looked around the room: three long, curtainless windows, a pale carpet, a bell jar on the floor in the corner with a stuffed owl inside. The emptiness made actors of the occupants, their gestures, movements and conversation highlighted by the lack of decoration. It made you feel like somebody was watching you.

'Do you live round here, too?' It wasn't the most inspired question, but Josh thought he ought to say something to Alba rather than both of them staying silent as they waited for Antonella to finish on the phone. His mum had told him that people never much minded what you said so long as you said *something* when you were introduced to them. Sometime, he was planning to test that theory out when she was nearby, making that *something* totally inappropriate but, for now, he was just playing it safe.

'No. I live in Milan.' Alba looked at him rather than her phone for the first time. 'Maybe I'm going to come to London for a bit. I can't decide. You know Milan. It is dead, but my friends are there. Though I have many here, too.' Josh considered this. He had no friends in other countries and, when he thought about it, until he went to university he hadn't known anybody outside London, unless you counted his cousins, who lived in the countryside.

'Yeah, Antonella told me that she knows lots of people here. How come there are so many Italians in London?'

Alba had returned to her Instagram feed. 'It's always been like that, I think. My mother and my father lived here when they were young.' She shifted her attention to Antonella, who was still on the phone but now standing by the window, tracing her fingers across the glass.

'Antonella. Come. We want to leave!' she shouted to her friend.

'We need to get a car. You fix it, one of you,' Antonella replied, before returning to her conversation. Josh was relieved to have something to do while they waited for Antonella to finish. He used Uber, pleased to see there was a driver practically on the street. The car arrived just as Antonella returned to them.

'Teo says he has just seen your mother at our house. You know' – she spoke to Alba – 'how our mother makes him crazy. He loves her, then he hates her. Then he doesn't know what he feels and he doesn't care. So now he wants to share with me how she drives him mad. I had to let him talk.'

The three of them crammed into the back seat of a dirty Prius,

Josh wedged uncomfortably against the door. Antonella pulled his woollen hat off, pulling it right down on her own head so that it covered her brows. On any other girl it would have looked ridiculous, but on her it looked kind of cool. She didn't have that swishy hair that would have stuck out. He imagined hers would just slide through his fingers like vinyl if he touched it.

The Belvedere was crowded. There had been a massive queue at the door waiting to get down the narrow, red-flock staircase and into the bar, and once you were there damp clothes from the evening's rain mixed with the smell of drink. The bar counter was packed four or five deep with everyone trying to stock up before the next band came on. Josh could see his friend Felix at the far corner with a couple of other familiar faces. For a moment, as he nudged his way through to them, he hoped the two girls would look at the crowd and make a run for it, put off by the smells and the scuzzy-looking venue. He didn't like having to look after them, now they'd arrived. Normally, the Belvedere on a Wednesday night would have been exactly where he wanted to be, he reminded himself. So what was so different tonight? They could leave if they wanted.

The buzz had been building for the past hour and was just reaching a peak of anticipation and impatience as the crowd waited for the lights to go down and shadowy figures to appear on stage, tweaking the amps, checking the leads. The band, Fire Circle, was bubbling under the radar but getting a massive number of YouTube hits, even though they hadn't yet been signed by a label. That might change, though, since Felix had told Josh the place was going to be jammed with scouts that night.

Josh had only met the band in the summer, although Felix had known Rollo, the lead singer, since they were kids. Rollo had been interested in some of the same Cuban music as Josh and, after the gigs, they'd often been the last two standing, walking around the city as dawn crept in. Rollo was nearly two years older than Josh, who, because of an August birthday, had always been one of the youngest in his class. He knew that Katherine often used this as an excuse, claiming that allowances should be made for him academically. It had been useful when he got crap exam results, but during the last year of school he was properly fed up with being treated as if he were not quite old enough. For anything. Hanging out with Fire Circle had made a difference. They were on a gap year ahead of him, and it was like he had a new life.

Antonella appeared at Josh's side and handed him one of the two plastic glasses she was holding. He flung names around in introduction without the sweat of specific allocation, shouting, 'Antonella – Felix – Jack – Alba!' and a couple of others that included a guy in a checked shirt that he'd met once before with Felix, and a short girl with a nose ring and denim dungarees who he didn't much like. They were spared the effort of any conversation when Fire Circle took to the small stage.

Josh's earlier nerves had evaporated, and he began to feel a kind of ownership of the evening, sensing immediately that the set was going to be good. Sometimes Rollo went off on a solo riff that took way too long, and he could lose the audience, but tonight the whole band were tight and confident, working well together and building the vibe in a really professional way.

Josh wasn't much of a dancer but, every now and again, he just liked to go for it, throw some idiotic shapes and lose it. Tonight, even with the coke and the whisky Antonella had passed to him, he found it hard to catch the wave and get into the music. Not that Antonella would have noticed – she and Alba were dancing together, wrapping their arms around each other and then separating for a shaman-style stomp before starting over again. By the time the band was into encores, Antonella had thrown him her jacket and was now wearing only a kind of cropped top. He could see the small silver bird that hung from her belly button and the start of a snaky tattoo that looked like it was going to run alongside the curve of a breast.

It was obvious that Antonella was amused by his attempt to

disguise his interest in her body, and she narrowed her eyes in a camp, flirty way before pulling him into their dance. The two girls shared him like a favourite toy, passing him back and forth, and for the rest of the set the room became only the sound and the space the three of them occupied. By the time the band wound up they were right up at the front by the stage, Antonella between him and Alba, her arms draped over the two of them as if they were the ones stepping forward to take a bow. As the audience cheered and applauded, Rollo, bare-chested and with sweat pouring down his face, looked down at Josh briefly as he stood there with the two girls. It was hilarious the way Rollo raised his eyebrows at the sight. Definitely impressed.

Earlier, Felix had told him that the plan was to meet afterwards at some girl's flat in Camden, and Josh was about to suggest this to Antonella when he felt her arm move from his shoulder. It could wait. He continued clapping. He'd always be one of the very last cheering the band before they walked off; he'd carry on for so long it had become a shared joke, a bit of a ritual. Felix came up beside him, his buzz cut beaded with sweat.

'Are you going backstage first?' Josh shouted above the pathetic end-of-the-show muzak that had replaced the live band. The lights had gone up a notch, too, to encourage another round of drinks. Felix nudged him, nodding his head in the direction of Antonella and grinning.

Josh turned to the girls beside him and saw them in a deep snog. Alba's fingers, covered in rings that snaked up to the knuckles, stroked the lower part of Antonella's exposed spine. He looked away, Antonella's jacket suddenly an unacceptable drag. He wasn't a servant. Everything had felt pretty good a few minutes before, but now a free-floating crappy feeling had taken hold and he wanted to get out for a smoke. As he moved towards the exit sign at the far side of the room he felt a hand on his arm. Antonella was beside him and took her jacket from him, chucking it on the floor before cupping his face in her hands and slowly pressing her lips to his, softly at first and then harder, opening him up and drinking him in. She tasted of whisky, and he could feel her sharp hipbones right up against him.

'Happy now?' she asked, moving gently away, linking arms with him to walk back to Alba, who, with her vague smile, appeared entirely unfazed by Antonella's defection. 'So. Do we have a party now?'

# Chapter Seven

When Katherine woke the next morning she spent the first few minutes of consciousness examining, as always, the previous night's sleep. She had a tricky relationship with sleep, regarding each night as a battle; it was so elusive, and she was always anxious that a strange room would exacerbate the problem. The linen was warm but crisp as she stretched her legs out across the bed, luxuriating in having no particular reason to leave it. She ran over yesterday evening in her mind. Ann had taken her to a nearby restaurant, where the panelled walls were hung with black-and-white pictures of film stars: the women of the period had perfectly lined eyes and stoles draped over bare shoulders; the men wore black tie. Ann had been greeted enthusiastically and escorted to a table in the corner facing out into the room.

'I know what's good here, so you should leave me to order. Are you feeling like fish? Or meat?' Ann asked as she waved the offered menus away. 'In Milan, I don't eat in restaurants so often. I have an excellent cook at the house, but I thought you would like to go out. Paolo is joining us soon,' she explained, at the same time nodding a greeting to a table of fellow diners nearby. 'He's an artist, and I know you will love his art. We must find a time to go to the studio. It has a totally original freedom about it. He is experimenting at the moment with work in a kind of silicone gel, but it is at an early stage. He says if it is a success he might cause a shortage in the supply for tits.' She massaged her own small yet defiantly firm breasts under the ruched fabric of her tight dress. 'I told him that most of the women in Milan already have all the silicone we need.'

'How long have you been together?' asked Katherine.

'Oh, it is several months now. You know, Katherine' – she paused – 'I think this really might be the one for me. I have kissed a lot of frogs, but I have a feeling that this is something special.' Katherine smiled at her friend, happy to share her hopes and wishing that it would be so. By the time Paolo arrived they were halfway through their meal. He hung his heavy coat on one of the pegs that lined the wall.

'I am sorry to be late. It was just at the moment, you know, when I had caught something, something really a little complex, and I had to finish. And then I felt dirty, and so I needed to take a shower.' His wavy grey hair, still slightly damp, curled at the collar of a white shirt, tucked into jeans. 'Have you ordered? Yes? So I think I will have the *tagliato di manzo*.' Ann moved her chair a little towards him, stroking his cheek before taking his hand in hers. He had clean, buffed nails and wore a large signet ring.

'So, what are your impressions of our city?' he asked Katherine.

'I've only seen a very small part of it so far,' Katherine replied. 'It feels very different to London, but I'm not sure why.'

'It *is* different. For an artist like myself, it is hard to work here. There is no recognition. It is a business city, not one for creative minds.'

'But you have wonderful fashion and furniture in Milan, surely? I thought it was a centre for design.'

'You know, it is very narrow in its horizons,' Ann interjected, backing up what Paolo was saying. 'You have to be big here to have any impact. It is, as he says, a place that is first for business. And Paolo . . . he is an artist. I have another home in Florence, and I think maybe we will spend some time there in the future. It's more – how should I put it? – more refreshing for the spirit.'

'Ann understands me very well. She is a wonderful woman,' Paolo volunteered, waving for the waiter to bring another bottle of red wine.

'We are lucky to have found each other.' Ann looked childishly pleased. 'I am still a romantic, you know, after all this time.' Katherine thought about reminding her that, when they were friends at school, Ann's down-to-earth manner and lack of girlish romance had made her stand out, but decided not to.

She had not immediately taken to Paolo, finding something petu-
lant and self-regarding in his manner, but Katherine had a policy of
being positive about her friends' partners. They were innocent until
proved otherwise. She despised the fact that so many people's
default position was cynicism, if not criticism, when anyone new
was introduced. At this age, surely they'd all learnt that you were
never going to win a battle against the object of a friend's affections
or lust. The best you could hope for, on the occasions when they
produced a real headcase – and there had certainly been some – was
to ride it out and be there to mop up the pieces afterwards.

She supposed it was easier for her to be generous since she and
Rick were still together after more than twenty years. All around
them, their married friends were breaking up at an alarming speed;
it was as if somebody was running along a shelf of pottery with a
sledgehammer. And then, for those who were still single, like Flo, as
the years passed, it was no easy task to insinuate somebody into the
medley of habits, preferences, allegiances and history that made
them all that they had now become.

And that was if you managed the initial sex. With Rick, sex had
become comfortable and comforting. Lying awake as he slept, she
would often remind herself that she was lucky to have somebody
who desired her, even if the act was no longer exciting. Occasionally, she was frightened by the idea that she would probably now
never know what another man might feel like, that the routines and
positions, the touches and words that she shared with Rick would
be the limit of her sexual experience for ever more. But then she
remembered how awful bad sex with somebody new could be.
How it could puncture your confidence and be physically upsetting
and, whatever it was like – bad *or* good – it most probably required
being seen naked by somebody other than a man who had long ago
stopped noticing the details of your body, with its unwanted folds
and mottles and stretch marks and straggly hairs. But looking at
Paolo – whose hand had now moved from the table to Ann's leg –
she guessed that sex wasn't a problem there.

★

Katherine's Christmas shopping list was extensive, since she had long ago taken on the task of buying gifts for Rick's extended family and work colleagues. When she began, the list had been considerably shorter but, now, finding presents for everyone had become a huge task, and she hoped to tick some of them off in Milan. Ann, propped up on a pile of pillows in the embrace of a dark-red dressing gown, sipped coffee and pointed her in the direction of the centre of the city, explaining that she could visit the Duomo and the new gallery of Italian art as well as the shops in the Galleria Vittorio Emmanuele and the surrounding streets.

'I'm staying here. I need to do a little organization for dinner tonight, and I have calls to make,' she announced, with the languor of one who has no compulsion to be seen to be busy. The ornately carved headboard rattled as she adjusted herself, moving the silver tray bearing a bamboo-handled coffee pot and milk jug from her lap and replacing it with iPad and phone. 'We will meet for lunch, and then I will take you to Paolo's studio on the canal. Call me when you are finished and I will send Angelo to collect you. You are sure you want to walk there now? It is so easy for him to drive you.' The idea of a stroll to the shops was clearly regarded as eccentric, but Katherine was looking forward to exploring the streets alone.

A weak sun had broken through the low cloud by the time she reached the Galleria, now loaded with several carrier bags and wondering whether she had made a mistake by rejecting the offer of Angelo. But she had enjoyed finding her way around the city, stopping off for a coffee at the bar of one of the many cafés where the Milanese stood at the counter to chat, and visiting the cathedral, where she lit a candle for her mother.

At the top of her shopping list was a briefcase for Rick. She knew he loved the traditional type with structured compartments. A different man carrying one might have looked fusty or pretentious, but there was something about Rick's lack of any deliberate style that saved him from this. He still had the air of somebody whose mother would exclaim with pleasure on the rare occasion she might find him wearing a suit. Josh was similar. Even though he and his friends all shared the loose jeans, sweatshirts and hoodies look, his were flung on without any consideration. She thought briefly of Teo: his style seemed an extension of his body and attitude, not something he put on in the morning. She wondered if he had always been like that. It was hard to imagine him as a small child.

Arriving at the Galleria, she stood for a moment to take in the sight of the beautifully arranged shops with their black-and-gold fascias, and the welcoming restaurants, where even in December, some tables were placed outside, under the magnificent glass dome. Half an hour later she had found the perfect briefcase, a deep walnut colour and lined in a soft, paler leather, as well as a dress for herself which she excused as an early Christmas present justified by Ann's party that evening.

The afternoon was dominated by a visit to Paolo's studio, where her suspicion that she would *not* love Paolo's art was quickly confirmed, and on their return her host retreated to her own quarters. Sitting on the stiff, high-backed sofa in her bedroom, Katherine looked at the dress she had bought, now hanging on the outside of the wardrobe. With its swirling paisley print and folds of fabric gathered at the waist, it wasn't her normal taste, which tended towards structured shapes and neutral colours. But, inspired by the more extravagant style of her fellow shoppers – the men in bright, knotted scarves and the *bella figura* of so many of the women – she had succumbed to its soft drapery, which had matched her mood that morning.

She leant forward to pick up the book that Teo had left. The leather binding was in extraordinarily good condition, the vellum pages bearing only the faint dimple of two hundred years of use. It was an illuminated poem of some kind and though the poet's name meant nothing to her and neither could she understand the words, that didn't detract from her admiration of the exquisite workmanship that had gone into the text and illustrations. She enjoyed working on poems, and several years ago had given Rick one she had chosen by Ted Hughes and carefully written out, commissioning a frame in the type of wood mentioned in one of the verses. Now she came to think of it, what had he done with it?

Despite having been told that people were invited for eight thirty, fifteen minutes later Katherine was standing alone in the first of a series of rooms in which the textured, dull gold fabric of the walls was picked out by the soft light from wall sconces. She had accepted a glass of white wine from a tray offered by one of the many staff who silently inhabited the place and was idly leafing through a picture book on the top of a pile when she heard voices. A couple had entered, talking for some moments as they surveyed the empty room before seating themselves together on a sofa at a distance, marooning her at the other end. She was grateful when Ann appeared, took her by the hand and walked her over to them.

'Giorgio, Flavia – you have met my great friend Katherine?' Their chatter in Italian became immaculate English as they shook hands.

'So it's a crazy time? Are you going to the di Carcini wedding next weekend?' Flavia asked Ann, bony limbs extending from a sack of deep-green velvet, her feet in the kind of thick platform shoes Katherine knew were fashionable but couldn't bring herself to wear. 'We have a wedding of the son of our friends near Rome,' she explained to Katherine. 'Everyone is asking why they do it at this time of year? When in the spring it would have been so beautiful in Sicily. Imagine Forzasimone for the wedding. It would have been superb. The place is made for weddings. So romantic there.' She made a moue of incomprehension.

'Flavia wanted to be at the lake next weekend with our family,' Giorgio explained, in the manner of a man used to injecting ameliorating addendums to his wife's statements.

'I don't know if I will go.' Ann reached for a cigarette from a silver box on the table. 'It depends a little on how Paolo is about his work. I don't want to leave him here alone. He is at an important stage. He told us last night, didn't he?' Her eyes travelled over Katherine's shoulder, scouting for new arrivals.

The suite of enfilade rooms filled quickly, guests moving between them and arriving finally at a fourth, where food was laid out on a vast round table: silver dishes of creamy pasta, truffled eggs, slivers of carpaccio dotted with rocket and Parmesan. Each dish was allocated its own white-jacketed waiter to spoon the food out as the guests formed an incongruous queue in their expensive clothes and jewellery, patiently holding out empty plates like children in a workhouse.

Katherine stood in line with Flavia, who had proven to be more amiable than she had at first appeared. She had strong opinions and gave an entertaining commentary on their fellow guests. They settled on a striped velvet sofa in one of the smaller rooms to eat.

'You knew Ann, when she was at school? Is that correct?' Flavia asked, peering at her plate to spear a leaf of rocket.

'Yes, we were great mates for a couple of years. She was a funny mixture of sporty and wild and made me feel very parochial. When she left London we kept in touch for a bit, but once she was married we kind of lost the connection. We had one dinner in London, her and Massimo and me and Rick. He seemed very nice. Quiet. Rather traditional. She was the one who kept the conversation going.'

'Yes, Massimo was a kind man. The family were not delighted with his choice of Ann – they would have preferred one of the Italian girls who they all would know, but he was crazy in love with her when they married. Giorgio was one of his closest friends, and he said that as soon as Massimo met her he told him she was the girl he was going to marry.' Flavia put her plate, still full, on the table beside her. 'But you know how the world is. Nothing is so simple. Things change. And then when everything came out after the crash, it was hard for Ann.'

'Yes, I imagine so,' said Katherine, frowning in what she hoped was a convincing display of shared knowledge. 'Did you know what was happening?' she asked. It was obvious that there was an aspect to the marriage which she was completely unaware of. And was now desperate to discover. She followed Flavia's lead in putting her plate aside.

'Of course,' Flavia sneered. 'We all knew. Ann knew as well, but she ignored it. It's not unusual for men like Massimo to have girlfriends, and Ann, she was sophisticated about this. She just didn't want to be humiliated in any way. The girl was Roman and so she wasn't on the doorstep, not in Ann's face, and it hadn't been a problem. But then when the bodies were found – and, oh, you know, there were missing clothes and such things – it was her nightmare. The family, naturally, asked the police to be discreet but even so it was very hard for her and made his death more complicated. And I think it changed Ann. Don't you?'

'I hadn't heard the whole story. Ann never said. But yes. She definitely has changed.' Katherine wanted to know more but wasn't sure how much she could ask. 'And Teo and Antonella – do they know what happened?'

Flavia placed a hand on her lap. 'What do you think? Those two know everything. They were very young – twelve? Thirteen? But people talk and children can always read the whispers, can't they? They have a sense when there is something that they shouldn't know. Yes, they discovered, and that was terrible, particularly for Antonella, who was unusually obsessed with her father. She had always been a little . . . extreme. Teo was calmer, with that cool way about him, but Antonella could be crazy. After her father died – and it was at a bad age for a girl, with the hormones and everything – she stopped eating. It was hard for years. Some people think that Ann didn't handle her very well – and of course then, a few years ago, the other situation . . .' Flavia paused dramatically. 'Then it was both of them who were causing major problems.' She interrupted her story to beckon across the room to a man who was heading in their direction. Katherine reluctantly took his arrival as a sign to move on, as the conversation took a different turn, about acquaintances she didn't share.

It wasn't long before Ann reclaimed her, steering her back to the dining table, where yet another course was being served. She would have been perfectly happy with just her original plate of food, but was not surprised to discover a whole different array of dishes: fillets of fish, several meats, small cubes of rosemary-speckled potatoes. She had often accompanied Rick to dinners with Italians for work and had become used to the enormous menus, which seemed quite at odds with the trim shapes of the hosts. Like many naturally slender women, Katherine lived in fear of losing this asset, and all her life had been careful about what she ate. She held out a plate for a portion of the fish.

'Come. You must meet Francesco. Do you know Montaverdi? No? Oh, that is his company – a wonderful, wonderful publisher. And Francesco, he loves women. He will think you are beautiful. I warn you' – Ann gave a girlish nudge to her friend's arm – 'he will make a play for you.'

Francesco was the kind of man Katherine immediately recognized as being hard-wired to flirt. Within moments he had seated himself next to her, and listened with a concentration that made her feel the cherished centre of his attention, despite the many other conversations, arrivals and departures that were going on around them. Although she understood that this kind of focus had little to do with her personally, he nonetheless succeeded in bathing her in a lovely glow of compliments. Katherine imagined he was around Rick's age; his dark hair was greying only at the temples and his face crinkled appealingly when he smiled, which he did a great deal of the time. They had been talking for a good while, his arm flung across the back of the sofa they shared when, across the room, Katherine saw Teo arrive with another boy.

'Ah, Teo.' Francesco followed her gaze. 'That boy has women of all ages – and many of them. He likes the game. Ann has great-looking kids. I remember when I could walk into a room like that and know people would be looking at me.' They watched as Teo leant, his arms folded, against an elaborate architrave, Doge-like in his reception of greetings, as if they were only his rightful due. 'I would cross the road, deliberately slow, and know that there were women and men in their cars watching me from behind the glass.' With a laugh, Francesco mimicked a cartoon wide-eyed driver at a steering wheel. 'I thought nothing of it at the time. Then, *boom!* . . . thirty-five, forty . . . we are less significant. And by now' – he paused for dramatic effect – 'we are ghosts.' His cheerful face indicated that he wasn't particularly concerned about this turn of events, if indeed he thought it really applied to him.

'I thought it was women who complain that at a certain age they become invisible,' Katherine replied, turning back to him and feeling his hand slide to lightly fondle her shoulder.

'Some, maybe. But not others. Anyway, this is not so for you.' The hand moved down to give her knee a reassuring squeeze. 'So, tell me, when do you return to Milan? Have we made a good introduction?' As Katherine answered that this was certainly the case, she noticed that Teo was looking directly at her. She turned to see if there was someone behind her, but there was nothing but a tapestry hung above a marble table, of a mythological scenario involving serious-faced cherubs, a waterfall and a young man with bow and quiver.

When Teo made his way over Francesco greeted him with a hug and a brief update on the result of that evening's football derby between Inter and AC Milan. 'I have been telling Katherine that she must come back to Milan now that she has discovered us.'

Teo crouched down by the pair. 'But we need her in London. You know she is looking after us?'

'I don't think that's quite the way it's turned out. Neither you nor your sister appears to need much looking after. Ann asked me to keep an eye out for them,' Katherine explained to Francesco, who, like Teo, looked amused at the idea, 'but that's not exactly necessary.'

'Did you visit Paolo's studio?' Teo pulled out a cigarette packet and, as he held it out to the others, Katherine realized it had been years since she'd been offered a cigarette.

'Yes, I loved the area around the canal. Do lots of your friends live there?'

'No,' Teo replied. 'What did you think of the art?'

'Teo, don't be difficult.' Francesco drew out the 'difficult' as a tease rather than a criticism. 'You know he is making your mother happy.'

'So. That is not news. My mother has been made happy by lots of men. It doesn't mean they are good artists.'

Confronted with the option of a discussion about Paolo's art or his and Ann's sex life, Katherine decided on the former. 'To answer your question, Teo, I thought there was something interesting in his ideas. It's probably got a way to go, but I was intrigued.' Paolo's silicone works were housed in a splendid studio space overlooking the broad canal. The canvases, spread with a variety of murky colours and textures, had been presented to Katherine by Paolo in a manner that assumed his originality and skill were givens, leaving Ann to enthusiastically explain why to her friend.

It was after midnight when the party broke up, the rooms suddenly emptying with a last noisy bustle of departure. Left with only Katherine and Paolo, Ann suggested a nightcap. 'After all, tomorrow you leave us, so we should have a toast,' she said, walking over to a crowded drinks tray under a large painting. Katherine agreed, unwilling to end the evening. Generally, she was one of the first to leave a dinner or a party, the next day's to-dos rattling in her head. But here, free of responsibilities and with an afternoon flight home, she felt like she had years ago, when evening could turn to night and then dawn, still freighted with possibility. Ann returned to the sofa with small glasses of a dark liquid she pronounced good for the digestion and placed herself upright on the sofa so Paolo could lie across her, his head in her lap as she stroked his hair.

Katherine excused herself for a moment, sure that there would be some hidden bathroom in the vicinity and discovering a jib door in the hall that opened on to a small dark-green space. Before going back to the drawing room she glanced quickly at herself in the mirror there, liking what she saw. She walked along the parquet floor of the hall, looking at the pattern of the different-coloured wood.

'There is the original sycamore, larch, oak and another wood I don't remember.' Katherine hadn't noticed Teo standing by the open front door.

'It's gorgeous. Where are you guys going?' asked Katherine, assuming that Teo's friend was ahead of him.

'To a bar to meet some people,' Teo replied. 'You want to come with us?'

Katherine had drunk enough to take the invitation literally. 'That's kind of you, but I don't think your mum would be impressed.' Their voices echoed in the high-ceilinged space. 'But thanks for asking.'

'No, I mean it. It would be good. I would like it,' he stated confidently, stepping forward and putting a hand on the bare skin of her arm. 'Are you sure you won't?' As he bent forward, Katherine was aware of having the opportunity to move back, but she didn't, wanting to see what would happen, letting him dictate the moment. Behind him the broad stone of the stairs curved downward to meet the chill of the late-night air, as the warmth of his lips pressed with a salty, smoky and utterly alive softness against hers. This time there was no disguising the deliberateness of his kiss, or her lack of resistance. 'Another time,' he said softly as he walked out, leaving her to close the door.

She looked quickly around, relieved to see the hallway still empty, and leant against the wall, trying to reorientate herself. The racing fizz was instantly recognizable, like the taste of a favourite sweet from childhood. But what had happened? It was simply a kiss.

Slowly returning to the living room, she adjusted her face into what she hoped was a casual smile, but the image of Teo's face – his long forehead, and pale eyes, his dark lips without any drag of years muddying their lines, lips that she had now felt on hers – ran on repeat before her. It was clear, as she sat opposite the couple, that the enthusiasm for a debrief had passed. Paolo, still prone, had his eyes closed and the gaiety of Ann's expression throughout the evening was showing signs of wear.

With promises that they would make the most of the next morning, they parted, leaving Katherine to walk to her room. Her bedroom had been arranged for sleep, the wall lights with their pleated damson silk shades had been switched on and the heavy curtains were drawn, as if she were in a hotel. She moved them apart to find another layer of thin white fabric shielding the window. As she looked down at the pattern of gravel paths in the garden below, she pulled up the memory of Teo's kiss, the pressure of his lips, allowing herself to indulge in that moment and the strangeness of simply being there. Alone. After some minutes she let the curtains fall back into place and started to pack. Not ready for bed quite yet. A kiss is just a kiss. Even from a boy only a few years older than her son. It was only when she had turned out the lights that she remembered to check her phone. She hadn't called Rick all day. After the previous night's unsatisfactory conversation, she was leaving it up to him to get in touch. There was no evidence of his having done so but glowing in a green text bubble above the +39 Italian prefix was a simple X. It was insane, she realized that, but the sight of it made her happy.

# Chapter Eight

*December*

The construction of Drayton Hall had begun in 1742, the substance and refined proportions of the building a demonstration of the Kendal family's successful trading with the New World. Olga had been amused when she had learnt of the house's nouveau-riche origins, aware of the parallels between her husband's immense wealth and the Kendals' fortune: both were based on similar exploitation of opportunity. Built around the same time as the great houses designed by Vanbrugh and Kent, Drayton came nowhere near the scale of a Castle Howard or a Houghton Hall but, in any case, Olga had excitedly commissioned Flo to compile a brief social history of the property.

'I want to give Alexander this when the house is complete. It's not the kind of thing he is particularly interested in, but he likes to think I *think* he is.' Olga tapped the side of her small nose knowingly. 'It will be an amusing record for us to have.' When she'd said it, Flo had noted Olga's manipulation of her husband with both admiration and curiosity. Although Olga was fondly able to reduce Alexander to the position of an indulged child, it was obvious that Alexander's presence, whether physical or otherwise, was always hovering nearby. While his wife gave the appearance of independence, it was an independence framed by the boundaries he had put in place.

It was freezing at the small kitchen table in Flo's flat, since the heating had only just come on, crackling and dripping as it moved around the skimpy radiators. The year had reached the point where any residual warmth from earlier months had completely disappeared and the scrappy pattern of the back gardens below was filled with skeletal trees and disregarded climbing frames. She'd already piled on two wool jumpers, a scarf and an old pair of socks before diving into the pile of books, coloured stickies jutting out of each one. Radio 6 was playing, a legacy from her last boyfriend, who had kept the mix of indie music and chat on permanently in the background, even as a soundtrack to their lovemaking. Not that they'd got anywhere near the love stage. She'd been surprised to find herself returning to the station after they'd split but, particularly in the afternoon, it made a nice change to Radio 4, which sometimes made her feel that she was getting old before her time.

She had discovered that, after the completion of Drayton Hall the family's fortunes had dipped, as their chief exports – wheat, flour and bread – became less lucrative. But, by that time, the house would have been furnished in the restrained and functional mode of the age, the general space spare, each piece considered. It wouldn't have been until the later Victorian era that the rooms would become more cluttered, a fact she thought Olga would enjoy. In the past weeks she had seen that Olga's attitude to the restoration and decoration of the house bore a similarity to the Kendals' approach: her interior decorator was charged with finding the exact pieces she had in mind and was very rarely able to persuade her to accept an alternative.

Flo's ability to refine ideas down to their essence stood in surprising contrast to her general fuzziness, as if all her focus had been directed to this one part of her, depriving the rest of any at all: her hair was wild, her figure unruly and general chaos surrounded her in her everyday life. When Olga had asked her to produce this study she hadn't really wanted to take it on, but Katherine had told her it was ridiculous to turn it down and reminded her that she was always complaining about not knowing where her next job was coming from. Occasionally, she regretted not having embedded herself more thoroughly in academia – teaching, for instance, which she'd considered after she'd got her PhD. It would have given her a more reliable income and structure, but she liked the freedom of her life, even if, occasionally, the unpredictability could be scary. Over the years she'd found there was usually some way she could earn a bit of extra cash – waitressing or helping out in shops; and recently she'd found she could get a useful sum renting out the flat for the odd night or week. She'd been lucky she'd been able to buy it, years back, when such a thing was possible for somebody like her. And she had only herself to support. Heaven knows what she would have done if she'd had kids. Sometimes she wondered whether there was a reason she hadn't quite discovered behind Olga taking her on for this project. But if there was, it was still unclear. And hers was not to reason why.

The previous day they had met in the Oblomoviks' London house. As Flo was telling Olga about the relationship between the park landscaping and the house, Alexander had entered the room.

'You remember Flo, Katherine Tennison's friend, who is helping me with Drayton,' Olga had said to her husband, who remained only just inside the doorway. 'Will you join us?'

'I am leaving now,' Alexander replied, with no attempt to recall Flo, or show any interest in her. 'I'll be back tomorrow evening. I may have Sergei with me for dinner.'

'Of course.' Olga followed him out of the room.

Despite the fortune that had been lavished on every detail, the house was a mausoleum, Flo decided as she sat, now alone, in the sitting room. Hanging from the ceiling was a crystal stalactite chandelier, its twin suspended just in view through the doors of an adjoining room. Thick black bookcases lined a wall, their contents piled horizontally in attractive patterns, the occasional book propped face out to show its cover. Everything was scaled up for impact. In a silver frame there was a photo of Bill Clinton with his arms around Olga and Alexander, all three grinning for the event's photographer.

Flo heard the front door close, and Olga returned.

'Alexander travels so much. He likes me to be with him but, on a short trip like this, it doesn't make sense. He will be in meetings and I will be bored. I've been to Montenegro before – several times.'

'What was your life like before you were with him?' Flo asked.

Knowing that Alexander had left, she felt able to ask a question she'd wanted to know the answer to since she'd first met Olga.

'It was different.' Olga leant back on the sofa, looking past Flo to the right, where the bookcases stood, in such a way that Flo also turned to see if the answer was to be found there. 'I had a very different life to this. But, you know, I prefer not to think about it. It is often the way that, when people change their circumstances, they don't look back, they prefer to see what might be ahead. I have always been someone who was determined. Even as a child I realized that you could have what you wanted so long as you were clever about how to achieve it. And that it made sense to have options. To not only . . . how is that saying? . . . have your eggs all together. The important thing is to decide what it is you want, don't you agree?'

'I've never thought like that,' said Flo. 'I see what's in front of me but I find it hard to look at the bigger picture. I've probably missed out on opportunities because I'm no good on long distance. I suppose that's why I feel safe when I have my nose in a book. Not literally, but when I can focus on what I'm learning and don't have to deal with other things.' Flo would have liked to find out what it had been that Olga wanted, but Olga gave a light laugh, dismissing the subject. 'Well, for now, Drayton is your book. Tell me what you have discovered for us.'

Olga's curiosity about and appreciation of Flo's research had rebooted her enthusiasm for the job and she'd been so absorbed in the books on her kitchen table that she was shocked to discover that Katherine was just about to pick her up for the opening of the gallery's Christmas exhibition. She rushed into the bedroom, where there was only just room for a double bed, a wardrobe and a large old leather trunk which served numerous purposes, although mainly as a surface on which to dump clothes. She peeled off and threw the sweaters she'd been wearing on to it, replacing them with a plain black dress and a necklace of miniature dayglo skulls.

★

The drive through the rush-hour traffic was frustratingly slow as the car crawled to the West End, where the city became glossy and twinkling in its seasonal finery, the large stores competing with extravagant window displays, the streets decorated with trees and sparkling lights. This small area of the city had become one huge Christmas bauble.

Flo could sense Katherine's tension. She always knew when Katherine was stressed: she had a way of turning her face sideways, tight-lipped and with a blank look. For some reason, Katherine always got worked up about these evenings and, over the years, Flo had decided that it was probably more to do with CeeCee's presence than anything else.

A few figures were visible through the windows when the car pulled up. Rick was at the far end of the narrower second room, in front of a small work, discussing it with a couple of people when Katherine and Flo went inside. Soon, the space was crowded with the usual mix of clients, journalists, dealers and friends, the mass shifting up a floor as each level filled. Katherine walked towards the stairs, listening to snatches of conversation floating from small groups like a radio scanning for a station. She found Olga in Rick's elegant viewing room on the first floor, tonight emptied of its usual furniture, the space dominated by two large canvases hung on opposing walls.

'He has wonderful taste, your husband. So many lovely things!' Olga examined one of the pictures: the thickly layered murky tones of a bedroom, a female figure sprawled on a lush tangle of sheets beneath the gaze of a man in a dark suit.

'Yes. He's very good at what he does,' Katherine replied, with a momentary rush of pride. She was pleased to hear him complimented by Olga: there was something about the woman, with her poised beauty and apparently impenetrable confidence, that made her want Olga to rate her as Rick's wife. Not to like her, she had no need of that. Katherine went on: 'He was a slow starter, but when his father died and he had to decide whether to continue with the gallery, he really went for it. Luckily, he has a remarkable visual memory, which helps. It's staggering what he can remember about pieces that sold, for example, even years later.'

'He has some good work,' said Olga, in a tone that slightly downgraded her earlier opinion. 'But, you know, for people like us, there is so much on offer. We are only interested in the truly great pieces, the museum-quality examples, and there are many of us chasing the same few. Alexander doesn't restrict himself to one type of art, and now I am looking at some of the newer British. It would be good to be a . . . pioneer.'

'Where did you learn about art? You seem to be very well informed. Not that there's any reason you shouldn't be,' Katherine added, not wanting to appear patronizing. But she did find it curious. 'I mean, I did History of Art at university and, of course, now, I've picked up quite a bit through osmosis, but I still regard myself as a beginner.'

'Oh, I picked it up, too.' Olga laughed. 'Before I married Alexander I was with a man who also bought art, and I learnt from him about how to buy and the way people collect. It was when I realized that you could be judged on the quality of what you owned, not just the quantity.' Olga gestured to the walls before looking across the room. Fred had appeared with Antonella and Teo. 'Your Fullardis have arrived,' she said.

Katherine turned to see the pair saunter across the room, their arms linked. She hadn't seen Teo since that evening in Milan and, after a couple of days with it replaying in her head, time and time again, the scene had eventually dimmed and, now, nearly a month later, it had lost the emotion that originally accompanied it. But as he approached she realized, with a mix of anxiety and delight, that whatever it was the kiss had provoked was still alive. Only moments before she had wished for appreciation as Rick's wife, and now she wanted to be someone entirely apart.

Fred followed behind the pair, talking to Sheila Weitzman, a woman wrapped in a billow of cream who Katherine knew as one of Rick's most long-standing and cherished clients. The two pairs arrived simultaneously and Katherine was grateful for the excuse to postpone speaking to Teo, greeting Sheila Weitzman taking precedence.

'Sheila. Great to see you. It's been forever, hasn't it? How are you? And Lou?' Beside her she could hear Olga speaking to Antonella, touching the girl's black leather jacket with interest.

'I am good. Lou is good. And we've just produced the third grand-child. Can you believe?' Sheila questioned brightly, inviting the answer that she couldn't possibly be old enough. 'Olga, I imagine you are interested in this?' She pointed at the painting closer to them. 'Lou has banned me from buying anything more at the moment. He says we have to think of the grandchildren and that paintings won't keep them in nappies and school fees.'

'Not for the moment. It's one of Rick's favourites, though, isn't it?' Olga announced, a hint of ownership in her voice.

Katherine couldn't prevent a frown of irritation creeping across her face. 'Not really. It's one of *my* favourites, and *I* want him to keep it, though Rick always says, "Stock is stock," so it's highly unlikely. He hasn't any special attachment to it.'

Antonella spoke for the first time. 'Perhaps Rick says different things to different people.' She looked at Olga without smiling, wiping away a strand of her hair that had fallen in front of her face, so Katherine noticed for the first time the slightly drooping lid of a lazy eye. It gave the impression that she saw something fractionally different to what others might.

Sheila Weitzman adjusted the cashmere that was swathed across her substantial bust. 'Well, of course. All gallerists say different things to different people. They're like hairdressers. They tell their clients what they want to hear.' She looked pleased by her analogy. 'Olga, we must have you and Alexander for dinner in the New Year. Katherine, you and Rick, too. I'll fix it. Now, I should go. I'm joining Lou at Wigmore Hall.'

They watched her departing figure, surprisingly brisk as she sped away, stopping on her route to speak briefly to Josh, who was near the stairs. His important client now departed, Fred was free to approach Antonella. He'd spruced up for the evening, exchanging his usual rumpled checked cotton shirt for a white one, and wearing dark trousers and a pair of camouflage-print trainers. Before joining Tennison three years ago he had considered taking a job in one of the auction houses, but he hadn't really been able to see himself as one of those guys – grey suited and soberly tied, that smiling eagerness, the deferential stance, honed for their role of professional suitor.

'So would you like a drink?' he offered.

Antonella looked at Teo. 'And would you?'

Teo shifted slightly in his coat. 'I'll follow you in a few minutes.' He watched them collect Josh before the three of them returned to the ground floor.

Katherine spoke. 'This exhibition is really the start of Christmas for me. It's sort of the firing gun. "We're off!" What are your plans?' Neither Olga nor Teo leapt at the conversational opener with any enthusiasm. Teo declared curtly that he hadn't decided and Olga's answer was similarly vague. Katherine thought of the large Christmas tree that was being delivered next week, which would stand in its usual place near the window of the living room, decorated this year in her scheme of silver, white and red, and of CeeCee's traditional lunch at Charlwood, its format unchanged for years, and couldn't decide whether she felt reassured or stifled by the predictability of it all.

'I'll leave you two.' Olga opened the clasp of a slim velvet clutch to take out her phone. As she did so, a small, white object fell out and both she and Katherine bent to retrieve it. Katherine got there first, picking up the card, and noticing on it a doodled heart and arrow. It reminded her of the heart Rick had carved on a tree early on in their relationship and how they'd remarked that their initials, 'KW' and 'RT', were easy to carve, unlike the curves of an 'S' or 'B'. Olga took the card and scrunched it up before replacing it in her clutch with a snap, clearly unwilling in any way to acknowledge Katherine's amused smile at the childish heart. She moved away.

Now left alone with Teo, who was standing beside her, and closer than before, Katherine could feel sweat beading on her upper lip.

Keeping her eyes on the room rather than him, she was unwilling to move away but uncomfortable staying where she was.

'Let's go and see what's happening downstairs,' she said. She was determined not to mention the last time they had met. Teo showed no inclination to refer to it either, but put a hand on her shoulder before she moved to lead the way.

'Does everyone leave the city at Christmas?' he asked. 'Milan becomes very empty.'

'Is your mother spending Christmas there?' Katherine enquired, imagining that Teo would join her.

'I am sure she would tell us if we asked. But we haven't cared to. Perhaps . . .' Teo stopped on the staircase, pressing himself to the wall as other guests made their way up the pale oak steps. '. . . Perhaps we could see you if we are in London?' It was the last thing Katherine had expected him to say. Squashed against him and simultaneously nodding and smiling at the parade of faces passing them, she couldn't decide how to respond.

'We go to Charlwood for lunch on Christmas Day,' she managed to reply. CeeCee enjoyed asking new people to this occasion, and had once reprimanded her for referring to them as waifs and strays. 'Such an offensive term,' she had said. 'We all know that visitors from outside the family make such a difference. I prefer to think of them as the spice of the meal.' CeeCee would have no problem with Antonella and Teo being there, but Katherine might well do.

They reached the bottom of the stairs and Teo left to join Antonella, Josh and Fred, who were smoking on the pavement outside. Katherine's feelings of confusion were amplified when she noticed that Olga was with Flo at the far corner of the room. For so many years Katherine had allocated Flo the role of being her personal safe house, and the sight of her in such enthusiastic conversation with Olga whispered betrayal. She knew she had introduced the two, but she hadn't intended them to have a friendship which excluded her.

Katherine scoured the room for Rick, finding him near the centre of a group of men. The numbers had thinned a little, as the guests who had dropped in out of duty had moved on, leaving a chatty core who were happy to indulge in the good white wine that was being served. She caught his eye, and was grateful for the inclusive smile he gave her as she made her way over to him, keen to weigh anchor in the harbour of their marriage.

The next morning Rick poured himself a third cup of coffee as he scrolled through his emails. He looked up as Josh, rubbing his eyes, walked into the kitchen on the way to the fridge, where he spent some moments staring at the contents before closing the door without appearing to have found what he wanted.

'To what do we owe your presence at this early hour, Josh?'

Josh looked pityingly at his father and crossed to the sink to fill a glass with water, which he drank in one gulp, immediately refilling it.

Katherine, standing as she turned the pages of a newspaper, walked over to her son and gave his face an affectionate stroke.

'It was good to have you there last night. Where did you go after?'

'With Antonella and Teo. We ended up in some massive house. I played a bit of pool.'

'Where was it?'

Josh shrugged. He walked over to the window and looked out. It had been a strange night, and he still hadn't decided what he felt about it. A robin was balanced on a bird feeder Katherine had hung from an ornamental tree near the house.

'I remember this time of year when I was your age. You never knew where you'd end up in the evening. It's one of the things I loved – the sense that anything could happen. There was something about Christmas that did it – the number of parties, I guess.' Josh's look managed to convey how unlikely he found this: his mother, now so organized and unspontaneous, enjoying ending up in some random place. 'It's so rare there are surprises now,' she continued, thinking of the round of seasonal drinks she and Rick would attend in the next weeks, the women using the opportunity to adopt the style of the Hollywood housewife, with waisted dresses, velvets and costume jewels, the men sizing up the quality of the alcohol served. Katherine followed her son's gaze to the garden.

'I wonder what's happened to the parrots. They seem to have left us now it's winter. It's been weeks since I've seen them.' The fact that neither Josh nor Rick was likely to have a view was no reason for her not to go on. 'Here in London people regard them as exotic vermin. Certainly the home team scarpers when they arrive. Look at that robin today.' She cheerfully produced this convenient evidence, the garden free from the glittering interlopers. They all three peered at the small bird balancing on the metal feeder. 'Flo told me that during the 1930s the workers on the banana plantations – in Colombia, I think; anyway, somewhere like that – were poisoned by a pesticide they had to use. They began to feel ill really very quickly, but a lot of them carried on because they were paid extra if they did, kind of danger money. After a few months their skin began to turn blue, they lost their sense of taste and their appetite and, eventually, lots died. The other workers, the ones who weren't infected, called them the Parakeets, *los Pericos*.'

'Hmm. Thank God for the jolly robin,' Rick returned, stroking Katherine's hair amiably as she went to sit alongside him. 'That's a classic Flo piece of information.'

Finally having decided to eat a bowl of cereal, Josh placed himself at the opposite end of the table to his father.

'I asked them to Christmas lunch,' he announced.

'Who?' Katherine asked.

'Teo and Antonella. They said they didn't want to go back to Milan. They probably won't come, but I thought it might make CeeCee's more fun. CeeCee likes to have tons of people around, doesn't she? She's often told me to invite a friend if I want.' He paused to place an overloaded spoon of milky flakes into his mouth.

'Well, it's not my lunch. Rick, what do you think?' Katherine asked as she opened a cupboard full of baking trays. She waited for his reply, feeling herself unable to judge whether, if everything were equal, which it most certainly wasn't, the Fullardis would be welcome at Charlwood, and simultaneously despising herself for her faint disappointment that Teo had also discussed this subject with Josh. It made it more obvious that the natural relationship should be between those two. Not between her and Teo.

'Rick,' she asked again, the contemplation of the baking trays giving her little comfort, 'what do you think?'

'About what?'

'About Antonella and Teo coming for Christmas lunch. Didn't you hear? Josh has invited them to Charlwood.'

'If you want to invite them, Josh, give CeeCee a quick call and check it's okay. I'm sure she won't mind. I can't say they're my favourites, but there are so many of us we can dilute them pretty effectively.' Rick drained his cup as Katherine watched her son, in a bright-green T-shirt and baggy pyjama bottoms, still hungrily spooning in the cereal. It didn't seem so very long ago that she was the one with the spoon, tempting him with stories to have another mouthful. The whole scene had a disconnect, this tableau of domesticity in front of her.

She wondered if her son fancied Antonella and supposed that he must do, and then acknowledged for the first time that Teo had infiltrated some part of her, a singing, trembling part that had been smothered once she had met Rick and made the decision that he, with everything he represented, was to be her future.

'By the way, darling' – Rick's voice brought her back to the moment – 'here's the name of that book I know Fred would like for Christmas.' He put a scrap of paper with the name scribbled on it down on the kitchen counter.

Katherine looked at it and added it mentally to her list. 'That reminds me,' she said. 'Last night Olga dropped a piece of paper on the floor with a heart and arrow scribbled on it. You wouldn't imagine Alexander to be the heart-drawing kind, would you? It makes me think of him in a different light.'

Rick walked towards the thermostat. Its reading was a frequent subject of discussion during the winter months. 'I could swear this room isn't anything like twenty-one degrees,' he remarked. 'It's way more than that.'

'Alexander Oblomovik drawing hearts? You're kidding!' Josh pushed the now empty cereal bowl away from him.

'Love moves in mysterious ways.' Rick turned back to them, waving his arms like a spook, his face a cartoon figure of gloopiness.

Katherine walked over again to look at the robin, which was still pecking at the food and had now been joined, in apparent harmony, by a sparrow.

'There's something I find odd about Olga,' she said. 'I can't put my finger on it. Last night, she was chilly to me, almost patronizing, and then when I saw her talking with Flo she was all girlish laughs.' Katherine scrunched her face as if she'd just tasted something unpleasant. 'I mean' – and she shifted her voice down several notches to mimic Olga's – ' "It's one of Rick's favourites." Like, I'm not your *wife*?'

'I'm sure she didn't mean it as an insult,' Rick replied. 'Olga's just Russian. They're different. They simply don't think like you or me.' He walked towards the garden doors. 'It's baking in here. Let's get some air in the place.' He pushed the glass doors open with a noise that scattered the feeding birds. They flew off into the grey sky.

# Chapter Nine

Katherine had learnt of her mother's death during a weekend with friends in Norfolk. Josh was very young and a group of them had taken the children out to a harbour wall for crabbing; they had just returned to the house when Rick phoned to break the news. Juliet Wilson, on a short holiday in Istanbul, had, as far as they could tell, simply walked into a busy road looking in the wrong direction and had been hit by a container lorry. She died instantly.

Katherine's brothers immediately flew out, but it had been decided that Katherine should stay where she was. There had seemed no point in returning to London, and she had spent the night sitting out in the walled garden watching the tide come in under a full moon, the white sails of dinghies bobbing up into view and then disappearing as the water ebbed. As the sun rose Josh appeared in his pyjamas, running across the grass towards her and flinging himself into her arms. The need to calm his acute anxiety after having found her bed empty was an effective balm, and the baton of motherhood now finally passed.

Her mother's death had left Katherine more than ever implanted in her husband's family; she had wanted to be embraced by the Tennisons when she was first with him, but now she found the family oppressive at times, and never more so than during the Christmas period. As a teenager, she had usually spent Christmas with her mother and stepfather, relieved at no longer having to divide herself between parents once her father had left the country to start a new life with a much younger American wife. Although she missed her father, the long holidays in his airy, low Californian house with its swimming pool and lemon trees were a compensation. Cindy, her stepmother, was the kind of light spirit who took her to have highlights in a salon and booked her in for a bikini wax before a day's shopping in the big local mall.

'It would be nice just for once to be able to spend Christmas Day here. Do our own thing,' Katherine said to Flo on the phone as she sat fiddling with a loose piece of wool on a crewel-work throw.

'Well, at least Charlwood's just down the road. You don't have to bed in for days,' Flo replied. 'CeeCee's just the necessary evil in your world.'

'I guess.' Katherine realized that Flo's supply of sympathy for her annual complaining session about Christmas at Charlwood had been exhausted. 'When are you back?' Flo always returned to her mother for the holiday, generally returning with reinvigorated guilt over not living there in Ireland near her.

'I'm hoping to make the thirtieth. It's when I've booked the ticket, but there are gales forecast. If I get back later it won't matter, since Olga's leaving any day now. I'm pretty up to speed with every-thing, anyway, but it's strange how she seems to like me to be around a bit. I guess I'm amusing to her – a weird specimen.'

'She clearly likes you more than she does me. I get that bleak Siberian stare most of the time.'

'You probably expect too much from her and she feels competi-tive. Maybe she's jealous of you.'

'What would I have that Olga could be jealous of?'

'I don't know. I'm just saying. But there's something about how established your life is, the status, that she might envy. She's very aware of the way some people feel about the Russians – that they're responsible for the crazy property prices in London, philistines only interested in the size of their boat. Anyway, I like the woman. And I'm learning quite a bit myself about the period. I've never really had much time for the Georgians, but now I'm a little bit in love with them. Give me a pier glass and a tea set and I'm yours. Imagine tea pots being status symbols. It's kind of fascinating.'

The conversation did nothing to diminish Katherine's irritation at Flo's intimacy with Olga, and she ended the conversation snap-pily with a 'Call me over the break' before returning to her study.

The Reynolds family tree had to be couriered to Julia Reynolds today, in time for a presentation over the holiday. She took a last look at the scroll. Generations of births, deaths, marriages, divorce, all given their slot in immaculate copperplate. The hopes and expectations, tragedies and triumphs of each person reduced to their name on a chart but also preserved for posterity. As Katherine carefully placed it inside a cardboard tube, surrounded by bubblewrap, she felt her usual sadness at the end of a long piece of work. The hours spent in that room focused on the paper in the front of her, with its demands of total concentration, were liberating in a way she was sure Rick wouldn't understand.

Rick could see her at their usual table as he walked past the bar, the high stools occupied by figures leaning into the marble top, platters of seafood being carried high between them. The restaurant was packed, as always, but this lunchtime the atmosphere had an end-of-term festivity. He was planning on going into the gallery on Monday, but today was the last day before Christmas for the rest of the team, and he could tell it was the same for many of the lunchtime crowd around him.

Rick's passage across the room was interrupted by glancing acknowledgements to other diners. Just after he had stopped to congratulate the well-fed figure of an acquaintance on the birth of his first child, he felt the vibration of his phone. Unable to resist checking it, he pulled it out of his pocket quickly, glancing at the unnamed number and a small texted image. He pressed on the picture to fill the screen, and there was Olga. She was lying on a fur rug, wearing an outfit that could be thought clichéd but was no less erotic for it – her breasts were compressed and offered up in a tight, black basque, her legs were crossed in black stockings, the darker tops pressing down on her flesh. It was unquestionably her, but the pose, like a Vargas girl, all perky and brassy, the wide-eyed come-hither expression and the stuff she was wearing wasn't her at all. He had almost reached the table now and had to jam the phone back in his pocket, inconveniently excited by her sending it but wondering who had taken the picture. It hadn't been sent from her usual number.

CeeCee was sitting with a glass of white wine before her when he reached the table, moving at a measured pace to allow him to enter his mother's zone rather than dwell in the disturbing one provoked by Olga's text.

'You look a touch *distrait*,' CeeCee commented as he took his seat on the banquette beside her, shuffling himself into the corner spot and stretching his arm out against the leather seat back behind her.

'Really?' Rick picked up the menu. 'I've no idea why. I'm absolutely fine.' He looked quickly at the list, more as a way to deter conversation than out of curiosity; he already knew what he would eat. 'A dozen of the Merseas?' he asked, for form's sake. 'Does that sound good?' This pre-Christmas lunch had, like so much seasonal activity, become a tradition. They would share a platter of oysters and she would order sole off the bone while he would toy with the idea of fillet steak and then plump for the sea bass, since he knew he'd be ordering the white wine she preferred. His mother had always had a strong head and, unlike most of the women he knew of his own age, enjoyed a drink at lunch.

'I notice Alan's sitting there on his own. Do invite him over to join us for a drink. He was always such a fan of Michael's.' CeeCee gestured across to a well-known novelist seated in the corner.

'He's probably waiting for someone,' Rick replied, noticing that he sounded remarkably similar to Josh when he was asked to do something he found intolerable: the same flat mumbling, as if by making the answer hard to hear the original request would disappear.

'No. I don't think so.' CeeCee took a sip of wine. 'He was at the table when I arrived and he's already ordered. Go on, darling. I would love to have a few words with him.'

It was, Rick thought, astonishing, the way in which his mother was able to fucking do his head in. It was par for the course: he'd only been in her presence for about five minutes and she was at it.

He didn't enjoy being a messenger boy; he had nothing to say to Alan, and he was pretty sure he wouldn't agree to come over and join them. The guy was notoriously rude and difficult.

The exchange held no surprises for Rick, the older man scarcely raising his eyes from the notepad on the table when Rick arrived and replying shortly to the invitation that he was busy, making no attempt at a polite refusal.

'He says thank you for the invitation but he has to finish something he's working on,' Rick informed CeeCee on his return, while CeeCee flashed a broad smile in the direction of the author, who hadn't been able to restrain himself from a quick look to see how his message had been received.

'You know, he *used* to be the most attractive man,' CeeCee commented. 'I always thought he might be gay, even with that conveyor belt of wives. He has that catty wit. And those moods. He'd turn on a dime, Nancy told me, when they were together. Of course, volatility can be engaging. But then Nancy herself has always been a little difficult. It's what happens when you have a first-class brain but no intelligence.'

Rick decided not to question what she meant by this and instead concentrated on attracting a waiter's attention. By the time the oysters arrived and he had finished a glass of the Meursault they both liked, Rick began to relax. After her initial, demanding behaviour, CeeCee was on more appealing form, commiserating over a particularly good gouache that had slipped through his hands at Sotheby's earlier in the month and even contributing a shrewd idea as to who might be selling an almost identical one in the near future. He knew she felt he fell far short of his father in terms of intuition when it came to art, but he also knew that his father would never have made it today. The business was so much bigger, so much more complex, and required a different kind of nous. He would, just once, have liked CeeCee to recognize that, in this at least, he was the superior of the two.

Although CeeCee had spent little time with him and his sisters as children, she had remained a determining figure in all their lives. A shrink, he often thought, would no doubt have something to say about their response to the early distance between them which, rather than having made them reject her, had resulted in them being unusually available for her.

He watched as his mother shook a careful drop of Tabasco on to an oyster before delicately lifting it from the plate. CeeCee did not invite thoughts about her age, which she carried with an admirable insouciance, only impatient when she was unable to do something quite the way she could at thirty. If he viewed her impartially, she looked pretty good. Katherine was often fretting over wrinkles, pulling her skin as she looked in the mirror and asking, 'Do you think I ought to get work done?' He didn't have much of an opinion either way, but now he was looking at his mother he doubted that Katherine was going to age as well as her. Not a thought he was likely to share with either of them.

The picture of Olga on his phone came to mind; he imagined the curve of her hips and, though he hadn't spotted it on the picture, the dark mole he knew was inside the top of her left thigh.

'I'm sure you know that Josh asked if he could invite Matteo and Antonella for Christmas lunch? Of course, I said that would be delightful,' said CeeCee.

'Yup. He told us. Between you and me, I think he's got a bit of a thing for Antonella, but I doubt he'll get anywhere. He's probably not even going to try. Sometimes it's better just to dream.' Rick laughed at the thought. 'But then you can't second-guess what your kids do, can you?'

CeeCee looked up at the waiter who had arrived to take away the empty platter of oysters.

'They were simply delicious,' she said, dabbing at her mouth with a napkin. She turned to her own son. 'I don't know about second-guessing, but I've always felt I knew what you were going to do. Your emotions would flitter across your face like a weather map and we could always tell whether the clouds were about to descend. Your sisters were much more complicated.' She ran her fingers along the stem of her wine glass before adding, 'And it was always difficult for you to conceal anything from us. I'm not sure that people ever change.'

Rick took this as a reference to the drug habit he'd had before meeting Katherine, which neither of his parents had ever referred to outright but which he knew they were aware of.

'I'm looking forward to seeing what Mrs Oblomovik has done at Drayton,' CeeCee continued, looking straight at her son, although her expression was veiled behind the tinted frames she always wore. 'She's an interesting creature, isn't she?' Rick was grateful for the arrival of the sea bass and sole, allowing a short break in the conversation while the table was adjusted for this next course. He didn't see how CeeCee could possibly know about his affair with Olga, but he had learnt not to underestimate her channels of information. If she had guessed, or heard something, she probably wouldn't confront him with it. That wasn't her way; but she would like him to be aware that she knew. So long as he managed to keep it private and within clear boundaries, she would regard condemning him for it as far too provincial.

'Olga? Yes. She is a certain type.' Rick leant over for the salt, seizing the similarly housed pepper by mistake and then exchanging it after seeing the first black speckles on his fish. 'I've got to know her a bit this year since she's become interested in some of our artists. She does most of the buying. Alexander is more of a silent partner. You know' – he stopped for a moment, as if an idea had just struck him – 'they're a good example of how buying patterns have changed. A lot of people like them have totally abandoned the silo mentality. They've exchanged specialization for more of a mix.' He wondered whether this attempt to move the conversation away from Olga to the safer subject of general buying habits sounded as unconvincing to his mother as it did to him.

'That may well be true. Patterns alter but, in the end, it's a remarkably small pool that everybody fishes in. And, being small, we all know so much about each other. I always used to warn Michael there was no such thing as a secret. You must remember that everybody shares any secret with at least two people, usually

115

their husband or wife and their lover.' She laughed at the memory, helping herself to the side portion of steamed spinach before offering the small bowl to him. 'You see. I'm right. Nothing does change,' she commented lightly, as he shook his head in refusal. 'You never did enjoy spinach.'

As Rick left the restaurant he pulled his collar up against the whip of the wind. Usually, he felt a lightness at having ticked the box of that particular lunch, but today that was replaced by an anxiety at what his mother might have been suggesting about his having an affair with Olga and, in some way he couldn't quite figure, that picture on his phone.


He had no intention of wanting to make trouble in his marriage and he was sure that Olga felt the same. Nothing Olga had ever said indicated that she wanted to leave Alexander. Although he wasn't a great one for analysing these things, he imagined that she regarded him as an occasional treat, as he did her. Of course, he had wondered what had drawn her to him in the first place, but what was the point of getting involved in the whys? He imagined that he was just another object in her collection.

He looked at the picture again. From that angle, it couldn't be a selfie. It must have been taken by somebody else – unless it was some elaborate timer set-up, which seemed unlikely. Then he noticed that her hair was different. Not substantially, but it was definitely not the way it was the last time they had met. He was sure a woman would be able to pinpoint what had changed.

He wanted to have his head clear when he got back to work, not buzzing with that picture, so he resisted taking his phone out to look at it again, or even to read his emails, as he walked back towards the gallery, an after-work crowd of smokers and drinkers already gathering at the pub round the corner. But just before arriving, while he waited to cross the road, he gave in. Clicking on his messages, led by one from Katherine about a drinks party the following evening, he looked at the photo briefly, before putting his phone back in his pocket and then taking it out again to text Olga on the number they usually used. 'What a picture. Where's it from? Wish I was there x', he typed, then pressed send, watching the words fly into their little bubble on the screen, at the bottom of a string of such bubbles he and Olga had exchanged.

Walking into the bright warmth of the gallery, he joined Fred, who was seated casually at the far end of the room talking to Sophie, a long-haired intern on her last day. Fred shuffled some papers pointlessly and put his mobile away as Rick appeared.

'How's tricks?' Rick asked. 'Any action?'

'Nope. We were just chatting about gap teeth. I've never seen a bloke with a gap tooth, have you? No. Really. There's all those models with them, like that Swedish or Danish one. The blonde where the gap kind of says I know I'm pretty but I'm not perfect.' Fred warmed to his theme, watched with interest by Sophie. 'But guys? Can't picture it.' He shook his head.

'Katherine has a gap. I've always liked it. She wanted to get it fixed but I stopped her.' Rick scratched the side of his face as he thought about it. 'No. I guess I agree. I can't think of a guy. Anyway, what's with the gap-teeth discussion?'

'It's as good a subject as any,' Fred replied, shifting from a sprawl into a more workmanlike position. 'Is there anything you want tidied up before the end of the day? Oh, and by the way, Katherine called. She said she wanted to talk to you about some drinks thing tomorrow night.'

'Yes. I know.' Rick, unreasonably, felt hounded by Katherine chasing him all over the place about this drinks do. He heard the *ping* of a text and, leaving Fred and Sophie, walked towards the stairs to read it.

'What picture? What are you talking of? x.' It had been sent from Olga's usual number. He clicked back into his messages and looked again at the picture of her. What the fuck? Was she having him on? But he knew she wasn't joking. She just wasn't the type to joke. If she had one flaw, it was that she lacked much of a sense of humour.

The original excitement he'd felt on seeing the image had now morphed into something much less pleasant, a sense that, inside his skull, somebody was pulling a string tighter and tighter and it was in danger of snapping. He moved his head, partially in the hope of stopping the tension increasing, and partially as if, by looking around, the answer might present itself. But the work on the walls was no help, and all he could think was if she said she didn't know about the picture, then she didn't. So where the fuck had it come from? Who had sent it?

Under the duvet, in the company of his laptop, Josh was running calculations on the condition of his room. If he got up, Mariella could come in and clean, which would relieve the admittedly small but nagging issue of the mess. But he didn't want to leave his warm bed right now.

The other night he'd been round at Antonella's, and when she was getting him a vodka he'd seen how she kept her shoes instead of food in the kitchen cupboards above the counter. They'd sat for ages on the huge mattress on the floor of her bedroom, where she rolled joints in her lap, taking noisy drags before passing them to him. He liked the way that she was so thin she could fold in on herself like an origami bird. Beside her, he didn't feel lanky or clumsy, but protective. Which was pretty random, since Antonella didn't appear to need protection and, if she did, there was Teo, who was like some kind of weird bodyguard, never far away.

He found it hard to really get a handle on their relationship. She would talk about him all the time. Once, she mentioned a girlfriend of his and her face got tight and mean as she described her: 'a little lizard of a girl. She had that skin, you know, that is *steeeeky*' was how she put it, adding, 'Teo, he has lots of girls, lots of women, but they never last with him. He throws them like tissues, all crumpled in the bin.'

Every time he was with her he found himself more drawn to her. It was more than liking the way she looked, which he thought about a lot, even though he'd always had a thing for blondes – unless you counted Jen, who he often made out with at parties but who had a boyfriend in Paris. His girlfriends bore no resemblance to Antonella. Their rooms were cluttered dens of girldom where he would trip over the leads of permanently plugged-in hair straighteners and struggle to make space in the mess of make-up and tangles of jewellery, pink Oyster-card holders and Caitlin Moran paperbacks to roll a cigarette or put down a bottle of beer. But then, it wasn't likely that Antonella was about to be his girlfriend.

She played with him, though, and every now and again there was just a moment when it looked like he might have cracked it. She would do something like rub up against him, or snog him, or lick his neck with her rough tongue like a cat, and he would think he might just be able to push it a bit further. But self-preservation kicked in and he didn't want to jeopardize how close he had got and then find himself knocked back. A week ago, when he was lying awake in bed unable to sleep, he had devised an Antonella app in his head, where he progressed through levels of exploding black balloons. He would gather points based on the amount of chaos caused, which would lead him nearer to her, the final goal.

When Teo had come home he had walked straight into her room, ignoring Josh completely, and told her she had to get herself together to go out. 'He keeps me under control,' she said, obviously enjoying that idea. Teo seemed to be the only person she would listen to. He had heard her talk about her mother, or one of the lecturers on her course or some other luckless character who might have made an attempt to get her to do something, and he knew how she would argue fluently, but with a complete lack of logic, against their plan of action. But with Teo she seemed to positively enjoy his authority, even as she mocked 'Papa Teo' before he left the room. She hauled Josh up to dance with her, wobbling on the mattress, her long toes like claws, finding a balance as he staggered clumsily.

Josh had hoped they might invite him to join them. He waited for Antonella to tell Teo that he was coming, too, but once she'd pulled a floppy black hat down on her head and was heading for the front door, he realized it wasn't going to happen. Instead, they'd parted on the doorstep and he'd walked towards the tube, messaging Felix to see what was going on. They'd met at their usual pub, where Rollo was with some girl who was obsessed with him. The place was full and noisy, helpfully dimming the disappointment he felt about not being with Antonella, but even so, everyone seemed dull and familiar. When he was around her he felt different, and it was a different he liked. He knew a guy at university who was doing Psychology who had this theory that at any point in time you became the person you were then, and everything that happened was because of the alignment of particles at that point. When Josh was with Antonella the particles, whatever they were, adjusted in a different way and he was a more interesting person, one that was more like her and intrigued to see where random roads would take him. 'Come on. You have to make things happen. Take the chances. You never know what's over the cliff if you don't get right to the edge,' Antonella had said to him only the other night, and he had agreed. What was the point of only doing things when you knew where they would lead?

# Chapter Ten

As she woke on Christmas morning Katherine moved closer to Rick lying beside her, briefly appreciative of the warmth and familiarity of the marital bed and his woody, sweet smell. She gently touched his chest, running her hand down to the soft pile of his genitals, neither movement intended for anything other than confirmation of his presence. There had been a desultory attempt at sex the night before, when he had reached between her legs for a few minutes and nuzzled around her mouth. As he stroked her she'd considered whether to go along with it, but in the end she was dry and leaden and sleepy. 'I don't want to waste you,' she had excused herself. 'Let's save it for tomorrow.' Rick had amiably moved away, only adding a light, 'You don't know what you're missing,' and had immediately found the companionship of the autobiography of a polar explorer a perfectly adequate substitute.

The previous day Robert had arrived from Charlwood to collect the presents, so that the display of gifts under CeeCee's tree could be organized before everybody arrived. When her grandchildren were small they would stand outside the double doors waiting for them to open, and then rocket into the room squealing over the enormous stacks of colourfully wrapped shapes. Now all of them were nearly past that stage, the youngest about to turn twelve and unwilling to be the only member of the pack still showing any excitement at the sight, but CeeCee, nonetheless, liked to continue the tradition of the great reveal.

Rick shifted in the bed, emerging from his dream. 'Happy Christmas,' he whispered, wrapping an arm around Katherine and rubbing his face in her long, loose hair, which, when they had first met, he loved to brush. They spent some time lying like this, and months later, when Katherine looked back, she remembered that time, the weight of Rick's arm across her waist and his breath on her neck, as the last moment when their marriage still looked the way it always had.

By the time Antonella and Teo arrived at Charlwood the piles of presents under the tree had disappeared and the tsunami of wrapping paper had been disposed of. While some members of the gathering – Josh, for example – had received exactly what they had wanted (in his case a new fifteen-inch retina display MacBook Pro and a substantial donation to his bank account), others, like his cousin Amy, carried around with them a dull disappointment on discovering that the Miu Miu handbag was in pale blue rather than pink. The overall glut had prompted comments by several of the parents that, really, there were a ridiculous number of gifts and that next year there should be a moratorium. Yet saying that reminded them they were now becoming old, remembering how churlish such a pronouncement had sounded when they were children and *their* parents had said such a ludicrous thing.

Rick was in the process of distributing coupes of golden champagne as the Fullardis arrived. Antonella had changed her look dramatically for the occasion, pulling her hair back into a tight chignon and wearing a white sheath dress with a black fur-trimmed bolero. With Teo following in a formal black suit, the pair looked as if they had just walked off a Fellini set as they came over to greet Rick.

'Heavens. You look very chic, Antonella. I'm not sure I would have recognized you.' Rick handed her a coupe as he spoke, which she accepted daintily, taking the fine stem between finger and thumb. He turned to her brother. 'Teo, happy Christmas. You managed to time it well. I imagine the roads were empty. We've just finished the *disgustingly* huge unwrap.'

Josh came back into the room from a cigarette break outside the kitchen. His own dark-green shirt showed the hand of Mariella's ironing and his trainers had been exchanged for black slip-ons. Cee-Cee was pretty relaxed about what was worn on Christmas Day, but

Rick always went on about it being important to look as if you had made a bit of an effort. His father must be pleased with Antonella's appearance, Josh thought. Standing beside his father, who was rocking, the way he did when he chatted to people at parties, bending at the knee and grinning more than was necessary, he suddenly felt uncomfortable about Antonella and Teo being there. He knew he had invited the pair and was looking to them to inject a bit of difference into Christmas Day but now that they had swooped in, Antonella almost in disguise, he wasn't at all sure what to do with them.

They remained in a silent tableau by the fire as Katherine watched from across the room. Until the gallery party, she had imagined that she had successfully parked Teo's kiss in a part of her memory from which it could occasionally be brought out for a quick look and then be put back, having provoked little other than pleasant curiosity. But that night she had realized she was kidding herself and it had meant far more than that. It was uncomfortable for her to see Teo bang in the centre of Rick's family, and his presence highlighted her incipient but generally well-smothered feeling that she, too, was an interloper here. Until this moment she had felt a hundred per cent present in the affectionate yet intricate tensions of the family, but now it was only Teo who was in focus, consigning the teenagers, lying in a heap sharing stuff on phones, and Rick's sisters Charlotte and Emily and their husbands, conversing politely with Amelia and Jerry, to background noise.

'He's an extraordinary-looking young man, isn't he?' CeeCee said to Katherine as she watched him. 'I have always thought that real beauty is transcendent. You can't *not* notice it, nor the trouble it so often brings in its wake. She's got something different' – she gestured at Antonella – 'allure, definitely.' As she spoke she checked her watch impatiently.

Outside, the sky was a December white brightened by a weak, cold sun. On the terrace a few small birds explored the mossy cracks in the paving for potential food. 'Ah, Robert. Are we ready for lunch?' CeeCee asked, spotting her aide in the frame of the door.

'Yes, Lady Christabel,' he replied, moving around the room to herd them down the long hall and into the dining room. CeeCee positioned herself at the centre of the long table, glancing at the place cards on either side.

'Jerry, you're here' – she knocked on the table – 'with me . . . and Teo, you, too.' The rest of the party shuffled around the table looking for their spots, the younger members hoping that they might be seated together, their faces tensing as they discovered their allocated adult dining companion. While CeeCee had believed in the segregation of her own children when they were growing up, now she was a grandparent she took great pleasure in mixing the generations: it pleased her to think that it would be her grandchildren's experiences at Charlwood that taught them social skills for life.

Rick patted his niece Amy's back in cheerful commiseration as he pulled out a chair for her beside him, and watched, amused, as Antonella found her place next to Jerry, his splendid girth contained by a dark-green waistcoat, and on her other side his youngest nephew, Tommy. He always thought the seating at these meals was like a jigsaw puzzle where a piece was missing. The picture was doomed to be imperfect.

A long table had been set up under the windows and an enormous turkey, skin golden and legs trussed, was being carved by Robert. When the guests drifted over to help themselves to slices of the meat and all the trimmings Katherine found herself standing next to Teo.

'Josh is delighted you're here today. It's made it much more interesting for him than being with the usual cousinhood. Of course, he loves them, but it's always exciting to have someone new.' She hoped with this statement to distance her own feelings about his presence.

'And you?' Teo asked. 'Do you like me here?'

'Well, of course,' Katherine said. 'Of course. Gosh, that's some bird, isn't it?' Seeing that Teo didn't even bother to pretend interest in the size of the turkey, she continued, determined to force herself and the conversation on to neutral territory. 'What would your usual Christmas hold? Would you spend it with your mother?'

'Normal Christmas. Let me think. Normal.' Teo sneered. 'I don't think we have had a normal Christmas for many years. When our father was alive we generally spent it in the countryside with all the family. In Italy it is Christmas Eve that is the big event. But then it changed. And pff . . . since . . . well . . .'

'Well?'

'I don't want to talk about this.' He took her arm with a smile that relieved momentarily the burden of his strange beauty and the underlying tension that always seemed to inhabit him as they moved to the serving table.

By four o'clock lunch was finished and, generally sated, the adults conversed politely in the manner of those who would prefer to be relieved of doing so. A doze, a walk, a flick through Twitter or Instagram: all were tempting alternatives to the business of conversation as the curtains were drawn against the encroaching dark and the fire was topped up. Katherine was happy to see Josh chattering in a crowd, and Antonella appeared more relaxed than usual, and was obviously making an effort to be friendly.

CeeCee alone appeared unaffected by consuming the vast meal and suggested a race version of charades. Despite there being a number of attempted refuseniks, two teams were drawn up, and a list of clues to be acted out, by CeeCee, with the aid of Mel, Charlotte's youngest, who was drafted in to provide 'the contemporary references I won't be so strong on'. Mel happily agreed, spotting an opportunity not to have to participate in the kind of competitive activity her older sister, Amy, particularly enjoyed.

Rick hadn't welcomed the task of trying to explain the game to Antonella, who had been allocated to his team, imagining that she would be antipathetic to the task. But he had been surprised.

'Me. I love to act. It is one of my talents.' She struck a mannered Audrey Hepburn pose, extending her arm and lengthening her neck with a prim smile. 'We have played these kinds of games before. Teo, maybe he is not so happy. But look' – she drew Rick's gaze over to where Teo was sitting beside Katherine on a sofa, his arm stretched out behind her – 'I think he is fine. Super-relaxed.'

The first few charades took a long time to be resolved as the teams were getting into their stride, with noisy objections about cheating and barracking over the methods of mime used. By the third, Voldemort, Rick's team was slightly in the lead, with Rick ingeniously acting out a French death for *mort*. The next was 'I Kissed a Girl', which Mel had suggested and CeeCee had enthusiastically included. It had been Josh who had guessed Voldemort and therefore was charged with enacting the song title for his team. He weighed up whether to use Antonella or Amy in the mime and, although he would have preferred to use Antonella, at the last minute he bottled and grabbed his cousin, planting a kiss on her bright-pink lips. Across the room, Teo was acting it out for Katherine's team, and had bestowed his kiss on her, leaning down to her for possibly a fraction longer than the audience might have expected had they been of a mind to analyse. But the demands of the race overtook any such thoughts as the title was guessed and Katherine jokingly volunteered, 'Gosh. I am delighted to have qualified as a girl. Thanks, Teo.'

The game ended when Rick's team victoriously shrieked the discovery of Picasso, and slowly the guests broke apart, with Josh leading one group away and Rick excusing himself for a short kip.

Katherine found herself alone in the drawing room, only the crackle of the fire left in the vacuum after the noisy game. She briefly considered joining Rick in their room before discarding the thought in favour of a moment to herself. By the standards of their usual Christmases, this one had so far got high marks. She didn't hear Teo until he put a hand on her shoulder behind her. Turning to see who it was, she was startled to see him standing there.

'Come,' he said, lifting her from her seat with a strength she was surprised by.

'Come where?'

'Ssh – just come with me. I have something to show you.' As she followed, Katherine was keenly aware of the sound and movement of each footstep that was taking her nearer to some unfamiliar place. The house was silent, its many rooms allowing people to disappear easily, and the long hall was empty, with only the crackle of the fire, as Teo led the way through a door at the far end. They walked past the immaculately tidied kitchen. She wondered how Teo had found this part of the house, where the staff worked, and which, although there was no green baize door, was rarely seen by visitors. He turned left, drawing her into a room with him. Katherine knew this was a spare bedroom used only if the rest of the house was full. There was a single bed with a flowered quilt, an armchair and chest of drawers, in contrast to the huge bedroom where Rick was at this moment sleeping, surrounded by all their clothes and gifts. The only light was from the lamp outside the small window. Teo took hold of her and unzipped her dress in a swift move, peeling off her underwear to leave her standing naked while he examined her.

'This is how you should always look,' he said softly. So this is how it feels to be unfaithful, Katherine thought briefly as they kissed, his clothes falling from him without clumsiness or fuss before they moved together to the bed. There was not a second when she considered moving away, although for a few moments it was as if she were hovering above, watching, just as she began to feel Teo moving inside her, his slim body so strange to hold, his skin smooth like air, his long hair falling across her face until he lifted her hand to hold it back, laughing with her as they rolled over on the narrow bed.

It was only several hours later, once she had heard the roar of Antonella and Teo's departure, after the remaining guests had consumed a dinner of cold cuts on laps and she had noticed that Josh was definitely stoned or drunk (it wasn't quite clear which), that she acknowledged what she had known since that moment in Ann's hallway in Milan. What had happened was no surprise. It wasn't a decision, it wasn't a question, it was simply how it was. And, seated in the living room surrounded by the Tennison family, Rick in the corner, fiddling with that phone of his, she was certain that it would happen again. And, despite the fact that, for every reason possible to contemplate, she and Teo together was obviously wrong, it had felt, and still did now, completely and utterly right.

Rick heard the *ping* of his phone as he was compiling a forkful of cold ham, salad and curried rice from the plate on his lap. They always had a cold dinner on Christmas night, left by CeeCee's staff in the kitchen. Although only CeeCee lived a life staffed up to the hilt, the touch of Petit Trianon lifestyle didn't escape him as they fended for themselves that evening – rummaging around for the cutlery, carrying platters into the dining room, delving into the unfamiliar contents of the pantry for chutneys and mustards. By breakfast the next morning Robert and Tina the cook would be back in service, the kitchen returned to a country the other side of the border.

He waited until Charlotte had moved away from beside him, taking their plates back to the kitchen, to check the message. There it was again, the unfamiliar number and '1 attachment' in a box. He clicked on it, knowing what it would show. This time, Olga was entirely naked. Her skin was pale and she was slightly arched towards the photographer so that her torso was stretched taut. Below, there wasn't even the thin strip of pubic hair he was used to. She was on her knees on that same fur, looking at the camera yes, but with no trace of the excitement that came into her gaze from time to time when they made love. Like the previous photograph, this was clearly posed, and he noticed, when he pinched the screen to enlarge it, that her skin had the slight pixellation of some kind of reproduction. He shut the image down quickly, jabbing open one of his news-feed apps while he gathered himself. Something was going on. No question about it. That picture had no place in this part of his life. Clearly, someone was out to get him.

# Chapter Eleven

## *January*

Low pressure had hung over the country for weeks. If it didn't rain it drizzled, and it was hard to remember that there was any other type of sky than one filled with dense cloud. It was the kind of weather that made some people lose the will to live, or at least start Googling winter-sun breaks in an urgent need to banish the SAD they complained of with tedious and predictable repetition. But Flo wasn't bothered by it. If anything, she preferred the moist, grey blanket that covered the country to piercing hot sun, to which her pale skin was unsuited, and which made her cross constantly to the shadowed side of a street. As Flo and Olga walked through the murky sludge of the Drayton parkland, the grass, sky, trees and horizon were uniformly drab.

'I think next year I will make sure that we are not here at this time,' Olga remarked, her usually clear and bright eyes emerging a little red and watery from her furry hood in a face tanned from her recent holiday. 'Next week Alexander will be travelling and I thought of joining him but then, because of the work here, I felt I should stay. Anyway, he will be in Moscow half the time and that is no better. Worse. My friends say it has been terrible there the last few weeks.'

'You're becoming English, talking about the weather,' Flo replied, negotiating a muddy trench on the perimeter track of the parkland stretched out behind the house. She looked over to where an ornamental pond glimmered like a dirty coin at the foot of a gentle slope.

'It's not true. That thing they say. That the English talk always about weather and their dogs.' Olga was setting a brisk pace, her boots kicking up mud as she trod. 'The weather is talked about *all the time* by people who travel a lot. It's no matter where they come from. When I was a girl stuck in Moscow, nobody talked much about weather. So it was snowing? So it rained? It wasn't interesting.' She turned to check how close behind Flo was, continuing as she saw her trailing by only a few paces. 'But once my life changed and I travelled I realized that everybody talks about it. If they can fly out, and if the weather will cause a delay. If the boat will be able to anchor, or the helicopter can land. Look at a wealthy man's phone and check out his weather apps,' she went on, now well into her theme. 'You know. It's like boats. Alexander and many of our friends love to be on their boats. These are men who can organize everything in the world. They are used to getting what they want when they want it. But when it comes to the wind and the tides, they can't have everything. So they get stuck in places. Schedules get chewed up. I used to find it odd, but now I think it's part of the appeal. Something they can't control offers a kind of freedom. Nature is a relief when everything else is something . . .' She stopped for a moment to look back at Drayton, the pale stone clear against the dreary sky. '. . . Something that you always feel you have to get right, to do better.' She took a packet of mints out of the deep pocket in her coat and offered one to Flo. 'The dogs, though . . . that may be true. The English are mad when it comes to their stupid dogs.'

Flo pulled the hood of her jacket up to stop her hair blowing around her face and took a mint. She had started the day with a sore throat and a thick head and, during the walk, the inevitable runny nose had started. The strong mint was welcome. 'That's funny. I'll take your word for it, although there's something about wind and tides and moons and all of those natural phenomena that does have an order of kinds. It's just not one that can be controlled by money.'

The pair had spent the morning going through some of the research Flo had compiled for Olga. She had put together a collection of images she thought Olga would find useful in her renovation of the house, trying to come up with small details that would interest or amuse her. The majority of the building work in the central portion of the house had been completed and fireplaces were now reinstated, windows reglazed, plasterwork occasionally replicated. It was possible now to see the huge house as it was going to be with its new owners, a mix of Georgian details and oligarch lifestyle. Where the original servants' quarters had been, a cinema was in the process of being installed, with deep leather chairs and a silver popcorn machine, and in the opposite wing a pool and gym had just been put in, their style identical to that of those found in a luxury hotel anywhere in the world. In some areas, however, Olga had become obsessed with period authenticity, and that morning she was excited by the insistent shade of blue paint on the screen which Flo explained had been popular at the time the Kendals would have moved in.

'Surprising to use a strong colour, but I have always loved colour. That rail, though, would be a problem for the furniture I have in mind,' Olga remarked, scrolling through pictures of dado rails. Flo was impressed by Olga's decisiveness on every point. It didn't matter what the subject, her face was never furrowed by troublesome consideration.

Flo's approach to almost every aspect of life was the complete opposite. She was acutely aware of the many alternatives that could be brought to play in any decision, and it haunted her if she didn't feel sure that she had examined all the possibilities on offer, and even those that weren't. Due diligence was her forte but, invariably, when she finally plumped for a certain course of action she still felt it might be the wrong one. She found Olga's alternative modus operandi relaxing but it was something she was able only to observe rather than adopt.

After several hours, Olga proposed a walk before they set off back to London. By now, Flo had become used to the way in which, in Olga's life, whatever was required appeared immediately so, when freshly cleaned walking boots were lined up in a row in the as-yet-uninhabited house, she no longer asked about how they had come to be there. During her months in Olga's company she had realized that a defining characteristic of being rich was that it was unnecessary to wait until you needed something for it to be available.

'Do you know how long Antonella and Teo stay in London?' Olga asked, just as the house came back into full view, its classical proportions demonstrating the same sense of dominance over its surroundings as had its owners for more than three centuries.

'I've no idea. Why?' Flo looked up from the ground where, as usual, she had been focusing her eyes for most of the walk, only seeing the landscape around her when she stopped moving.

'I was just thinking of them and wondered whether the situation they have with their mother will ever be healed.'

'I'm not in that loop. I know they're all fucked up about her, but that's not unusual when it comes to mums, is it?' Flo shouted into the strengthening wind as the distance between the two of them increased.

'No, Flo, it's different. You don't know the story?' Olga stopped to wait for Flo to catch up, clearly not wanting a syllable to be wasted of what she had to tell. 'Okay. So you know their father was killed in a car accident. Did you know about the naked girl in the car?'

'Yes. Katherine told me about it and how it had been hushed up at the time,' Flo replied.

'Of course, it was difficult for Ann. The damage to her self-esteem was huge. Remember: she had always been the outsider. She was this Belgian girl when the family had wanted a traditional Italian wife for Massimo – and, in the end, everybody knew about the girl in the car. They say that she changed after that and slept with everybody.'

Flo nodded, unwilling once again to say that, so far, this wasn't news to her. She could tell that Olga was keen to deliver fresh gossip. 'Katherine did say that she was pretty out there when she was at school with boys and sex. Even at sixteen.'

'Anyway.' Olga made it clear she had no interest in Katherine's claim to earlier information interrupting her tale. 'After her husband died she had all these men in and out of her life, like that circus lover I told you about, and at some point, maybe five or six years ago, her man at that time was really bad news.' Olga generally had a very measured way of talking, rarely altering her tone, no matter what she was saying. It could be misleading if the listener wasn't concentrating, as the timbre of her voice bore no relation to the content, but in telling this tale she spoke so fast the words spat out. 'They were all staying in the house in the countryside. Ann knew the family didn't like her to take her lovers there, but often she ignored them and this man was staying when Teo and Antonella came for the weekends. By this time, Massimo's mother had died and so she probably thought she could do as she wished.'

When she stopped for a moment, Flo asked, 'How do you know about this?'

'I'll tell you in a minute.' Olga sounded impatient. 'But this is the important part. Teo learnt that this man – the boyfriend – was making moves on Antonella. She was what? Sixteen? Seventeen? There was an enormous fight between him and the guy, and Teo was badly beaten – you know the scar he has by his mouth. That was from this fight.' Olga produced this emphatically, as evidence to back up her story. 'But when Ann learnt about what had happened, about the fight, she believed the *guy*, not Antonella. She was like, "Oh, you are *fantasists*. You *exaggerate*. You two, you *always* cause me problems." She took the side of the lover, and she kept him there. Can you believe it? And the kids had to stay there with him in the same house until sometime later, when he left her for some other crazy woman. Imagine.'

'Hold on,' Flo said. 'I'm confused. Did he rape her? And why would a mother behave like that?'

'This is where there are different stories. The guy apparently said that Antonella was totally out of it and came on to him and he pushed her away, and Antonella said he came into her room when she was asleep and she woke up and he was fucking her. And that this was not the first time he'd tried it. He was always feeling her up, she said.' Olga mimed the gestures of a hand stroking her breast and trailing her thigh.

133

'So Antonella told her mother about it?'

'No. She tells Teo, who, like I said, had this huge fight, and then it all came out because he had to go to the hospital to be stitched up. So, for the first time, even if Ann had suspected something about this guy, it was now in her face. Apparently, since their father died the kids were always like this' – Olga clasped her hands together in a double fist – 'and Antonella blamed her mother for his death in some way. Irrational, of course. And then, when he was found dead with his girlfriend, it can't have made Ann feel so good.'

'It's kind of hard to imagine anybody making a move on Antonella that she didn't want. She seems so impenetrable, but I guess she was younger then.' Flo tried to imagine Antonella as a teenager, without her carapace of cool. 'How *did* you learn all this?' Having delivered her anecdote, Olga had started walking again and the grey of the sky was turning to black around the east where the parkland met the road.

'There was a Milanese couple in the Maldives after Christmas. We were together for dinner one night and we were talking – you know how it is. They had a daughter with an eating disorder and, in the clinic, she met Antonella, who was put there after this all happened. Antonella was mega-damaged, they said. She told their daughter her mother was a waste of space and a total coke-head. But they also said people took different sides and not everyone thought Antonella was completely without blame. How could you want to stay with the guy, though? If it were me, I wouldn't want him in the house.'

'Poor girl. Who was he?' Flo asked.

'He was a loser. No money, no job but, apparently, great looking. Arm candy.'

Flo compared this description to that of Alexander Oblomovik. He had lots of money, was successful, powerful and definitely not arm candy. As the daylight had almost entirely drained from the afternoon, the puddles and ridges in the path were increasingly impossible to spot.

'I am pleased that now we have electricity,' Olga commented, looking over the park to where the ground-floor windows of the house glowed like the toothy mouth of a Halloween pumpkin.

Inside, Flo removed her muddy boots, propping herself against the wall and wedging the heel of first one and then the other into the mouth of a bronze armadillo placed there for the task, while Olga disappeared in the opposite direction, to the room where they had been working earlier. Flo's black biker boots, the toes now faded to a scrubby grey, were lined up at the side of the hall beside Olga's elegant brown leather ankle boots, but she left them there, enjoying the freedom of her socked feet. She looked up to the curve in the staircase. When the house was completed, Olga planned to have a round table underneath it and had already shown Flo swatches of the leather she would be using for the visitors' books, their rich damson covers embossed with a gold 'Drayton Hall'.

Flo looked towards the main door, trying to imagine how it would have appeared centuries back. When Mr and Mrs Kendal returned from their afternoon stroll they would have found the candles lit, the light sparking off mirrors and cut glass everywhere. But then again, perhaps at this hour they would already be preparing for dinner in the newly introduced space of a dining room. The timing of that era's domestic lifestyle had been dictated so much more by natural light than was now the case.

She had no idea where Olga had gone. Turning to where she had last seen her, Flo peered into an antechamber to what would be the new dining room for which Olga had commissioned a table to seat thirty when it was at its full length. It was easier for Flo to imagine the life of the Kendal family in the house than to envisage how it would be occupied by the Oblomoviks. The hours she and Olga spent together rarely touched on Olga's life. Even after several months, she didn't feel she knew much about the couple's existence together, and it was hard for her to picture them here, marooned in their island of treasures. The house was unimaginably huge for two people.

She moved to the far end of the dining room and from somewhere nearby heard Olga's short bark of a laugh, followed by her low voice and then the laugh again, this time nearer. Underneath her feet the floor was warmed by an elaborate underfloor-heating system that must have cost more than the average family home. The unlit room allowed her to see outside, the light pollution of the local commuter town making it easy to discern the shapes of the trees and the arch of a stone bridge at some distance even in the dark.

'If we are going to meet I need to leave immediately, so we must stop talking,' Flo heard Olga say. 'I can be there by seven, but we won't have much time. I'm sorry. I would change the plan, but it wouldn't be wise. Even an hour would be good, yes? Have you missed me?' It couldn't be Alexander Olga was speaking to in this sweet, uncharacteristically flirtatious way. In any case, she had just said that he was away travelling. 'Oh Ricky!' Olga exclaimed, more loudly, as if she had caught a thought just before it disappeared. 'I have a little present for you.'

Before she could stop herself Flo sneezed twice, noisily. Unwilling to be found in such close proximity to where Olga was talking on the phone, she ran back through the hall to the study, grateful for the muffle of her socks and the new wood floor. In its original form it would have creaked with every step she made.

She was alone in the study for some minutes, gathering her books and putting them in her black canvas bag, closing down her laptop and checking to see what she might have left behind. Her cold was gathering momentum, making her feel leaden. She was just about to grab some toilet paper from the lavatory to blow her nose when Olga reappeared.

'Are you ready to leave? I had no idea of the time, and I need to get back to town,' she said.

'Sure – let's go,' Flo managed to say, before another pair of huge sneezes shook her and left her needing to wipe her nose with the sleeve of her jumper. Olga looked at her for a moment before saying, 'Ah. So it was you sneezing just now?'

'Sorry?' Flo's main wish at that second was for some tissue paper, as she felt another sneeze coming on.

'Sneezing. I heard a sneeze earlier, but it was the other side of the house.'

'Oh. Yes. Probably. Can you excuse me? I need to get some tissues.' As she left the room she saw herself in Olga's eyes: lumbering away in an oversized grey jumper, her hair wild and her disproportionately small feet that she was aware sometimes made her look as if she might topple over.

On the drive back, Olga sat next to the driver in the front seat, unlike on the journey that morning, when she had sat next to Flo in the back, touching her arm whenever she wanted to make a point and chatting eagerly. When they reached the motorway and she still hadn't spoken, Flo decided to say something – anything would do – working on the premise that to stay silent would make it more obvious she knew Olga had been speaking to Rick.

'That was a good day. I really enjoyed it, and I reckon that in the next few weeks I should have a nearly complete draft for you.'

Olga didn't answer. Flo could see that her profile was set hard, despite the soft, round nose and the curve of her cheek. She leant back against the seat and closed her eyes, allowing the heaviness of her head to take over after hours of trying to ignore it. There was nothing she could do. It would have been easier if Olga were not so obviously freezing her out, the easy amity gone and replaced with what? Boredom? Fury? Guilt? She realized now what Katherine had meant by finding her cold. But Katherine, she was sure, had no idea about anything else.

As Rick walked into the club two girls behind a long table were greeting the man ahead of him, their bright smiles disguising any trace of what they might really think.

'Good evening, Mr Tennison,' the darker haired of the two greeted him, while her companion checked an iPad.

The club was a new addition to London, designed to combine the qualities of a traditional gentlemen's club – entitlement, status, a prime location – with something more stylish and modern. The membership fees were astronomical but the international wealthy would happily pay twice the amount to be able to hang out where the famous came to be safe from the intrusive eyes of people who weren't wealthy or important enough to be able to sink into the deep leather armchairs or place heavy crystal tumblers on shagreen-topped tables.

Rick had reserved a position in the corner of the room near the garden. It was six thirty, still in the *cinq à sept* zone which Rick's father would speak of, waving his cigar as he joked about these legendary hours when Parisian men visited their mistresses. He wondered how many of the other drinkers in the room, either seated at the bright bar lined with colourful bottles or huddled in couples at a table, were, like himself, rendezvousing with lovers.

Meeting Olga in such a public arena was a bluff. Nobody would go to the club if they didn't want to be noticed, since the whole point of the place was to be seen by people who knew you or who you knew of. And after noticing who that might be, they would no doubt tell their friend, wife, colleague later that evening or, more likely the next day, that they'd run into you there with X or Y. Rick pulled up some artworks on his iPad and put it on the table in front of him to act as sufficient decoy should anybody question (which they wouldn't) why Rick Tennison of the Tennison Gallery should meet his client Olga Oblomovik for an early-evening drink.

Although Olga never spelled out the need for caution, he had once or twice seen a look that made it clear that she was fearful of Alexander discovering their relationship. Occasionally, he wanted to know why she took the risk, but when they were together he just wanted to indulge in the excitement and pleasure her body brought him, and he didn't want to waste their limited time approaching a subject he was certain she wouldn't want to discuss. After all, in his previous affairs, when he had been asked the same thing, the conversation that followed had held very little allure.

The crowd that evening were standard issue, casually but expensively dressed, in cashmere hoodies, denim that had come so far from basic utility wear it had now become a luxury. The style announced that they were their own people, not bound by convention, although, equally, they conformed to a new norm. The only group in the room wearing suits and ties were – what? From Singapore? Malaysia? Korea? Even Rick's navy sweater and chinos appeared staid compared to the T-shirts and trainers of many of the men, with their tinted shades and careful stubble.

He leant back in the chair, watching a group of women posing together for a group shot. Their long, blonde hair, winter suntans and camera smiles were checked on the phone by each before agreement was reached. He guessed that the picture was being posted, reaching a network of other women probably smiling somewhere else into somebody else's smartphone. Who wanted to see that you had scrambled egg for breakfast and that your kids looked cute on the beach in Mustique? It didn't do it for him. But Katherine loved Instagram, scrolling down with an amused smile, every now and again offering him a look at something she hoped might entertain him, like a mother hen handing out a morsel to a chick. At any rate, it was obvious the phone ban in the club wasn't working.

Olga arrived as he was about to check his own phone. He stood immediately to show her where he was, placing a friendly kiss on both her cheeks before they sat. It was the first time he had seen her since before Christmas, before he had received any of those texts. He briefly wondered if the present she had referred to might have to do with them. She was slightly tanned, which made those eyes of hers even brighter than usual. Before he had met her he had never thought a woman could have eyes the colour of sapphire. He wanted to touch her, drink her, fuck her, eat her, but instead they ordered drinks – a martini straight up for him, water for her. He had forgotten the effect of her beauty. How, like pain, it made everything else irrelevant.

'I haven't been in this place for months,' Olga said, with a glance around the room. 'Before they opened and they were looking for members we were asked if we wanted to become . . . what do you call it? Founder members? And I thought, why not? It could be kind of fun. But since then – we had a dinner here once last year – we don't use it. Alexander isn't comfortable here, for some reason.

I think he sees too many people he does business with, and it's not relaxing. But I should come sometime with girlfriends. It's a pretty room.'

'Mmm. Not as pretty as you, though,' Rick replied, about to touch her before moving back. 'No.' He laughed, and gave her a pleading look. 'I can do better than that, can't I? But not here. It's difficult being here with you, just sitting in these chairs, when I want to be doing something completely different.' He leant in again towards her. 'When are we going to be able to meet properly?'

'We've only been here for a couple of minutes. Be patient. We'll work something out,' she replied with amusement.

'I thought you might like to have a look at these. You might be interested.' Rick passed her his iPad.

Olga looked at a few images. 'It's possible. This one maybe. I think you mentioned it before.' Olga had picked out a picture of a large bronze, twisted like a glorious pretzel, mounted on a black plinth. 'I was at Drayton when you called earlier. With Flo. I'm not sure how much longer we will be working together – she says she's nearly finished.' She pulled her hair back from her face, exposing a row of small diamond shapes running down the rim of one of her small ears: stars, a crescent moon, a heart. 'Flo . . . Is she trustworthy? Discreet?'

'I imagine so.' Rick assumed that the question was to do with concern about security around the house. 'In fact, she's probably the most discreet person I know. They're new, aren't they?' Rick asked, pointing to the studs.

'Yes. How observant you are. I got them done in New York when we were flying back. Alexander wanted me to go with him rather than come straight back to London. It was only for the day. I had nothing to do and so this woman who does the piercing with the stones came to the apartment. It was something to pass the time.' She smiled. 'Alexander thinks they look cheap. But' – she gave a shrug – 'they're fun.'

Rick slowly picked up his phone, jabbing at the screen.

'I guess I should show you these.' He scratched at his eyebrow, as he so often did when he needed to concentrate. 'I was going to just delete them, but then I thought you should see.' Shifting his chair a little closer, he spoke quietly, although the chatter of the crowded room ensured privacy. 'Look at this – the first one.' He held out the phone, showing the picture that had arrived before he had lunch that day with his mother. Olga took it and looked at herself on the screen for only a moment before asking, 'And the others?' She glanced at the next images, each with an unnatural pose, the nudity enhanced by the conventionally tacky accessories. Looking at them now, Rick could see he had been right: her hair was different, it was obvious now. In the pictures, she had a kind of fringe whereas now, here, it fell evenly either side of her face to her shoulders. 'I've been getting them at random intervals since before Christmas,' Rick said.

Olga sighed and briskly handed the phone back to him. Watching her, he realized he had been relying on how she reacted to get a lead on his own behaviour. Embarrassment? Surprise? Anger? Any of these he had been prepared for, but not the chill that had instantly replaced the flirtation of only moments before.

'So?' she asked, shifting her chair back from him.

'Well, I kind of thought it would be me saying, "So?" to you. Do you know the pictures? You must do.' Rick felt unsure of the best line of questioning. 'Did Alexander take them?' he offered lamely, adding quickly, 'Not that it matters.'

Olga's expression made it clear that this suggestion was completely ludicrous. 'Yes, of course I know them,' she said. 'The question is why do you have them?'

Rick was silent as he considered his options. It was the first time he had been confronted by this side of Olga – those sapphires, now sharp and unforgiving; the lips that had trailed his body with delightful languor at one moment and urgent sucking and biting the next, now firmly closed in a manner that was both defensive and accusatory. As they sat across from each other in the crowded bar, he felt hopelessly wrong-footed and confused by her reaction. He had expected Olga to explain the pictures to him in a charming, possibly embarrassed manner – telling him the circumstances that had led her to be photographed in this way, maybe teasing him a little. They could have joked about it. He could have asked her to dress up for him in that stuff next time, just for a bit of fun. But it was clear that this was not going to be the direction of play.

'When the first one arrived, I was meeting my mother for lunch,' he explained. 'Actually, I thought you must have sent it for a joke. It was in that week before Christmas and I was in a rush. I had a quick look, got all excited and put it away to look at later. Then I texted you and you said you didn't know what I was talking about so, when the next one arrived, on Christmas Day, I was like . . . what the fuck? And then the others dropped in. Look, darling. You have the advantage on me. You at least know what the pictures are.'

'Keep your voice down,' Olga hissed. 'Yes. I know them. They are old. They were taken before I married Alexander and they were published in some magazine. It was just a job. I left that life a long time ago. Of course, I knew they were around, and now you can find almost anything if you dig deep enough for it.' Although Olga was answering his questions, she was obviously furious. 'So the pictures, they are not important. But who sent them? And why? That's the problem. That's what's important.' Rick realized then that it was not just anger but fear that he could hear in her voice. She stood up.

'Where are you going?'

'I'm leaving. I don't want to discuss this here.'

'We can go somewhere else. No problem.' Rick followed her to the stairs, passing the table of men in suits, who looked appreciatively at Olga, but it was obvious from Olga's speed that she had no intention of staying in his company. Inside the club he couldn't touch her to reassure her, but once outside he took her arm quickly to halt her. He wanted to hold her, which was the only thing he thought might calm her down.

'Look. I feel as bad as you about this, but let's not panic.'

'I am not panicking. But I am telling you to find out what is going on. My husband is not a man to anger. Someone, somewhere, knows about my relationship with you and is sending us this signal. How do I know they aren't going to inform him? You do understand, don't you? You have to find them and stop this.'

She walked towards her car, across the street, without looking back at him, and within seconds she was hidden from him by the tinted glass as the car sped away.

# Chapter Twelve

Katherine loved the river. This afternoon she was leaning against the stone wall of the Embankment, looking across at the new buildings that lined the southern bank in a display of uninteresting modernity that she felt let down the churning swathe of the Thames, with its rich history and continual ability to intrigue. Across the water she could see the green tidemarks on the wall beyond the huge, industrial barge anchored by a giant's rusty chain as a smaller, working barge passed on its stately progress east.

'Once, I saw a shop dummy, naked, stuck in the mud, like this,' she said, raising one arm in greeting, the other firmly holding on to Teo's hand, even though the demonstration would have been more effective had she not. 'For a moment I thought it was a real person. I always think that if I lived on the river I would never be bored.'

'We used to have an apartment in Florence near the river. When we were teenagers we had parties on the roof and we would dance right on the edge, high above all the tourists. You would see them looking up and staring at us, and we knew they were waiting for one of us to fall. But it never happened.' Teo turned away from the water below them, which was swirling in mystifying patterns near the bridge. 'Let's go. It's cold now and' – he held out a hand, squinting into the sky – 'it rains.'

They had spent the last hour at Tate Britain, a gallery where Katherine was immediately comfortable, unlike Tate Modern, which made her feel stupid as soon as she entered the huge, dehumanizing proportions of the Turbine Hall. She had been pleased when Teo sounded enthusiastic about her suggestion of checking out the older Tate, as she had worried that it might appear too much like something a parent would suggest.

Although they had managed to spend time together in bed in his flat, they would also meet occasionally without having sex, which Katherine, in a way that she acknowledged was entirely irrational, felt added a small, really minimal, justification to the whole business.

She had spotted him immediately on the stone steps of the museum. It was early afternoon but he still looked as if he was waking up to the day as she approached, unsure, as she always was at first, of how to behave once she was with him. But as they walked around the series of rooms that housed so many familiar works of art, and he stood just behind her, nearly touching her but inches away so she could feel the heat and delicious pull of desire, exacerbated by the hush of the place and the watching guards, she knew he felt, if not exactly the same, then something similar.

Teo had a real and informed interest in art. Although he didn't speak a great deal as they moved through the rooms, when he did he managed to tell her something she hadn't thought of herself. If she compared his thought process to Rick's, even, Teo's was unquestionably the more intellectual. She was surprised by the strength of his opinion on the contents of the different rooms, the juxtapositions and choices made in the display. He had stopped for some time in front of a Paolozzi bronze, his head tilted to one side and chewing his lip. 'My father had one of these,' he said eventually, returning from where he appeared to have briefly escaped.

Katherine had been fascinated by Turner's self-portrait – the generous lips, winged brows and short hair of a colour that could have been blond but was possibly prematurely grey. He would have been, the adjacent caption read, aged about twenty-four in the picture – a similar age to Teo, yet already a known phenomenon as an artist. It made her feel better about the age gap, but she didn't mention the thought.

She had expected to be swamped in guilt and confusion over the relationship. When she wasn't in Teo's company she couldn't imagine being with him, could never conjure up what it felt like, as she could with Rick, her husband's companionship and body so ingrained in her that she scarcely had to think about his being there.

But as soon as she was with Teo the strangeness evaporated and she entered a sealed world where it was natural, easy and she could recognize feelings of her own she had forgotten ever existed.

The first time the two had met after Christmas she had taken a taxi to a pub where she and Flo used to hang out in the years before she had met Rick. She didn't like the idea of having Teo in her car, which was impregnated with her daily life: driving Josh to the station, dropping Rick off at the gallery, crossing London for Pilates, or visiting friends who would no doubt be both horrified and fascinated by what she was doing.

Even after downing two tepid gin and tonics in the hope that her nerves would soften, they only increased when Teo placed her behind him on his motorbike and raced back to his flat (empty of Antonella, he assured her). Speeding through the dark streets, her hands clamped around his waist, her legs having to straddle the wide seat, had shot her with adrenaline. When they had arrived at the flat her legs were shaking, a combination of the bike and panic about whether the sex would even be possible again, and now, six weeks later, she had come to regard that same taut feeling as part of the excitement of the affair. But she had to admit she really didn't enjoy the bike.

Teo took the umbrella she produced from her handbag, opening the white polka-dotted fabric, and held it high above them as they walked from the Embankment wall to the bike, his other arm around her waist.

Katherine hadn't intended to bring Teo to her house that afternoon but when he had parked just around the corner he had asked, for the first time, 'Can I come in? You know, just for a few minutes. I would like to see where you do your writing, your work. I promise you, I will be super-good.' It had seemed churlish to refuse.

There was no sign of Mariella when they walked into the kitchen. The housekeeper had usually left by this time but, occasionally, she was still there, folding clothes or rearranging items in the downstairs pantry or, in good weather, standing in the garden looking at the birds. It had been she who had first spotted the parrots, nearly a year ago now, when the early spring light had made their colours so conspicuous on the still-bare branches. She had complained about all the broken egg shells she had found spattered on the paving, their viscous insides sticking on the stone until the gardener arrived and cleared them up the next day. Mariella did a lot around the house, but she didn't regard cleaning up an avian foetus massacre as part of her job description.

Katherine climbed to the top of the house, Teo behind her, quickly passing the rooms that led off the wide landings in between, and ignoring her and Rick's open bedroom door. When they reached her long, low space Teo marched to the slanted board where she was working on the initial lettering for a book plate, looking at it briefly before moving over to the shelf where she had arranged her inks, enamel mixing bowls and brushes.

'Do you spend a lot of time in here?' He leant against the wall, his arms folded, just as he had those few weeks back at the party in his mother's flat, with the same assumption of a right of ownership over his surroundings.

'It depends.' Katherine had been about to perch on the arm of a soft old chair, its faded chintz regarded as unsuitable for display downstairs, but instead she remained standing, a little galled by his casual appropriation of a room which she had had to brace herself to bring him to. 'Sometimes I am here for hours. I lose track of time. Sometimes I don't come in for days. I usually find calligraphy totally absorbing so, when I start and it's going well, I don't want to stop.'

'Why do you do it? Do you make money?'

'Not much,' Katherine admitted with a smile. 'It's not the cash machine that drives the Tennison lifestyle. But I cover my costs, I reckon, and, luckily, I'm a kept woman.' She regretted the last words, which she had lightheartedly used many times during her marriage but which, in the current circumstances, had a nasty ring. 'The point never was to make money. It's something that I suppose suits my personality. There's nothing random or sloppy about

147

calligraphy and I find it interesting to make things work out. It's almost scientific in a way – you work with proportion and space, even the weight you put on the pen and the flow of the ink.'

Teo had picked up a thick, short penknife with an engraved bone handle.

'This is good. Where does it come from?' he asked, pulling out the three blades and bending the smallest gently with his thumb.

'Originally, calligraphers made their own pens. It's where the word "penknife" originated. Some people still do. I saw that knife a few years ago in the medina in Marrakesh and I thought it was beautiful, although it's not an original.'

'Have you ever made your own pen?'

'Is it likely? I just like it as an object.'

'Can I have it?' He flicked two of the blades back into place, leaving the large one extended. 'A little present to keep. A memory of you.'

They both knew she would agree. Katherine was constantly surprised by how, in this relationship, she was the needier partner. If he asked for a memento, of course she would hand it over, flattered that he might want it. The inequality was unusual for her. She had never behaved that way with boyfriends, and it was the very opposite attitude which, she realized, had appealed to Rick. When they met he had responded to her coolness and distance but, with Teo, she was almost craven.

He walked over to her, taking her wrist in his hands and bending to kiss it before . . . before touching the knife lightly to the lines that circled the flesh.

'Take it. Although you do know it's meant to be bad luck to give knives as a gift?'

'It won't count, since I asked for it,' he replied cheerfully, lifting her arms above her head, still holding the gift, and kissing her.

It was Teo who broke away first, tucking the knife into his jacket pocket.

'I have to meet Tonne. I must go.'

Katherine attempted not to show her disappointment. In spite of her unease at him being in her house, she hated this moment of parting. She always felt his immediate absence as a physical with-drawal, until time passed and she re-entered her real life.

Something about him being in the cocoon of her study made her ask the question that she had previously avoided. 'Antonella. What does she know?'

'What does Antonella ever know?' Teo replied unhelpfully. 'You mean about this? We don't talk about it. She hasn't asked me any-thing. And I haven't discussed it, but if she did, then I would tell her. I never lie to her.'

'But you can't do that, Teo. You musn't tell her. Are you crazy? This really is something that nobody must know about. I've never done anything like this before in my marriage and I don't really understand why I'm doing it now. You'll only be with me for a short time and, if nobody gets hurt, I've convinced myself, for some rea-son, that I can manage it. But if Rick or Josh learnt about us, it would be terrible. You don't have those sorts of ties, but surely you can understand that?'

'My tie is to my sister. *You* must understand *that*.' Teo sounded exasperated, his usual languor replaced by an impatience at being confronted like this. 'If you have one of us, you have to deal with the other. It has been this way for many years now. Together, we survive. It was something important that we learnt. That's what's important to me. And to her.' He raised his hands quickly then dropped them by his side. 'It's your choice.' He left the room, and ran down the stairs and out of the house into the ugly light of the late afternoon.

Katherine went down and stood in the gloom of the drawing room, the familiar shapes of the furniture waiting to be ignited by light and people. It felt like a ghost room, a shadow theatre in which she was the only solid presence – the arrangements of flowers, the careful display of artworks, the large, colourful cush-ions and the two low coffee tables felt as insubstantial as props on a stage set. She turned on a light switch and unfolded the tall shutters against the heavy rain.

★

Later that day Katherine attempted to persuade herself that Antonella probably didn't know about her relationship with Teo, and that, at worst, if she did, she wouldn't want to hurt her brother by causing trouble. It was by no means a convincing scenario, but it was the best she could come up with.

By the time Rick returned home she had made herself forget the conversation she'd had with Teo and instead focus on the evening ahead with Lou and Sheila Weitzman. Katherine had a soft spot for Sheila, who had followed up her suggestion of dinner with an invitation and, in the new year, a *pour mémoire* specifying a 'strictly casual' dress code.

When the invitation had first arrived and Katherine had mentioned the dinner to Rick, he pointed out that it seemed a great idea from the safety of six weeks' distance, but he would put money on the fact, when the evening eventually arrived, they would wish they weren't going.

Once, when Katherine had complained to Flo about feeling that she and Rick got barricaded in by too many social events, Flo had flung back at her that it was a high-class problem, and she didn't want to hear her complain of yet another party. It was one of the few occasions when there had been a real sense of social separation between the friends, and Flo's rebuke rang in Katherine's head whenever she, like tonight, was underwhelmed by the prospect of the evening ahead.

Just yards from the heavy traffic of the Finchley Road, the wide street where the Weitzmans lived was patrolled by a sole private security guard. It was only once you were behind a high hedge that their red-brick mansion with its white-painted woodwork was revealed, in the glare of security lighting. As they turned into the gated forecourt Katherine and Rick could tell, by the cars already parked, that they were not the first guests to arrive.

'I wonder how many there'll be?' Katherine said, as she waited for Rick to turn off the ignition. 'Do you remember, last time we thought it was going to be a big dinner and there were just six of us.'

'Yup. It doesn't look like this one's going to be like that. Anyway, let's get on with it.'

Inside, the house abandoned the architectural expectations generated by its external appearance and opened into an enormous room, constructed by means of expensive and complex load-bearing structural engineering, that bore more resemblance to an art gallery than a living space. Rick guessed there were about twenty people there, maybe slightly fewer, as he accepted a glass of champagne from the tray offered to him. Lou Weitzman waved from across the room. He took Katherine's arm and they walked over together to where the older man was chatting.

Lou's own taste in art was strictly Modern, and in both this house and their place in Provence, there were Auerbachs, Hodgkins and several Bacons, impeccably lit and beautifully hung. Sheila, though, had developed a passion for the YBAs and newer contemporary artists and, here in London, a tortured iron figure by Tim Noble and Sue Webster projected its shadow meaningfully on the wall opposite.

'Katherine, Rick – good to see you. You know . . .' Lou introduced them to the two men he had been talking to, the crinkle-cut, grey hair on his head reaching only to their shoulders. But what he lacked in height Lou more than made up for in legal and financial acumen, and Rick had often had reason to be grateful to the passionate acquisitiveness and advice of both Weitzmans.

'Sheila and I have just returned from Berlin, where it's really all happening nowadays. If you want to make discoveries, like my dear wife and I were able to make – what, forty years ago now? – well, you can't do it here any more. The time has passed. Berlin's the place.'

The group continued to praise Berlin, not only for the artists but also for the beauty of the Tiergarten, the still-forbidding architecture of some of East Berlin, and the impressive achievement of the Holocaust Memorial.

'For Sheila, that was a very, very moving experience, even this time. And we have visited it often before.' He looked in the direction of his wife, a millefeuille of expensive indigo-dyed linen. Rick had forgotten that his mother had told him the previous week that she had also been invited to dinner and now, as he joined Lou in looking over at Sheila he could see CeeCee seated in one of the groups of chairs in the corner, a man kneeling to talk to her as she looked benevolently down on him.

'Sheila and I are very fond of CeeCee,' Lou remarked. 'Some of our first pieces came by way of your father, and we had some good times together back then. It was a different age, though. Whole damn different thing. Now it all moves so fast, and even old pros like us get swept up in the speed of everything. Anyway,' he concluded, taking a sip of what Rick knew would be water – Lou Weitzman never touched alcohol – 'our time is up. We have all we could want, and more. Leave it to the new kids.' And with that he gave Rick a companionable pat on the back.

By eight forty-five the guests had been placed at the long marble table, shipped in one staggering piece from the quarries of Carrara. It weighed so much that the floor had had to be reinforced before it could be installed. Lou would proudly announce this to anyone who was a first-time visitor to the house, adding that it was kind of interesting to know that they were dining on a table that came from the same place as the Pantheon, and, seated some way down the table, Rick guessed that was exactly what Lou was now telling Olga. He hadn't seen Olga or Alexander during the pre-dinner drinks and it was only as Sheila had led the way into the dining room, at the back of the house, where a wall of French windows gave out on to a floodlit garden, that he had realized the couple walking slowly in at the head of the rambling procession was the Oblomoviks.

Until now he had had no problem finding himself in the same place as Olga in the company of her husband. But tonight, following their last unsatisfactory meeting he had to admit that the sight of her beside Alexander had blown his usual insouciance.

He turned to talk to a pretty, dark-haired woman beside him – probably a few years younger than Katherine – whose name was vaguely familiar. As they chattered on, he attempted to blot out the anxiety that was manifesting itself as a sharp pain in his lower back. Several years ago Katherine had told him as they were preparing to go to a business dinner that she had spent countless evenings sitting beside men who showed absolutely no interest in her life and relied on her to provoke conversation with questions and then to show appropriate enthusiasm at their replies.

'It has occurred to me to drop into the conversation that I am a murderer with a particular penchant for eating men's balls, just to see what might happen, but it would be too depressing to learn that they probably wouldn't even hear me say it,' she had suggested wearily, anticipating the evening ahead.

After that, when he remembered, Rick made a conscious effort not to be tarred with a similar brush, and immediately showed a calculated interest in his neighbour. The woman next to him this evening, he quickly learnt, was Lebanese, as was her husband, Hakim, and the couple, with their young daughter, currently divided their time between Paris and London. She preferred Paris, but her husband's business was based in London. Most of all, she would have liked to live back in Beirut, but it had been impossible for them for years now and she was worried that her daughter might never know what it was like to live there. He found her easy to listen to and liked the way she announced this fact without any kind of emotional drama.

Even taking into account Katherine's admonishment, he just couldn't take those women who got all worked up about something and then expected him to get equally worked up about it. Of course, it was true that women didn't have the monopoly on being dull but he did feel that he'd had his fair share of nutters sitting beside him over the years, banging on about this and that.

Katherine spent the earlier part of the dinner talking to Alexander Oblomovik. When he had immediately placed not one but three smartphones on the table in front of him, she had braced herself for competing with a screen, but she had found him a great deal more engaging than she had expected.

'You must be longing for the work at Drayton to be finished,' she suggested, deciding not to mention her connection with Flo, who she felt was unlikely to have made much of a dent on Alexander's consciousness.

'Yes. We're hoping it shouldn't be too long now. Olga has made the restoration of the house her business, and I am proud of the work she is doing. She has learnt so much so quickly. I travel all the time and she has had to take on this big job alone. But she is a determined woman.' His voice was not unfriendly but, as with his wife, the lack of emphasis in his speech left the listener to judge which were the most important comments. He looked across the table to Olga, who was talking to Lou with a softness Katherine wouldn't have expected. Katherine was also surprised that he remembered Josh from the bonfire party.

'Does he have a career that he is interested in?'

'Of course not,' she replied with faux exasperation. 'Are you kidding? Everybody knows that I adore our son but even his most devoted admirer couldn't claim that he has any direction. He's still young, though. Did you have any idea at that age?'

'Since I was fourteen I was working. By twenty, I had bought a couple of companies.' Alexander, she noticed, had eaten all the foie gras on his plate but had left the salad leaves that surrounded it. 'So yes, I had a plan and I followed it. And I had a wife to support.'

'You were married before Olga?'

'Yes.' Alexander's reply didn't invite further questioning, but Katherine pressed on.

'And where is she now?'

He shrugged. 'Somewhere she is able to access her bank account, that's for sure.'

'Did you have children?'

'No. If we had, then maybe it would have been different, but there was nothing to keep us together. I worked all the time. It was hard for her, now I look back. But it was for the best – I met Olga.'

'And would you like kids now?' Katherine was doing decidedly better than she had imagined she would.

'Yes. Very much. That is a reason for the new house. It would be a good place for a family. So' – he smiled in a way that brightened his whole face – 'we are trying.'

The thought of Olga and Alexander trying was the point at which both decided to move away from the subject and, shortly after, each other. For the rest of the meal Katherine addressed herself to her other neighbour, Hakim Samoni, the husband of the woman seated next to Rick.

It wasn't late when they left, their host having risen at the end of dinner to announce that coffee would be served and then he would shortly retire; Lou considered an excellent evening one that allowed guests to be free by eleven. Rick switched on the radio as they drove back to catch the news on the hour.

'I'm pleased we went,' Katherine said. 'I hadn't expected to enjoy it, but I got Alexander and he was kind of surprising. There's something about him which makes him nicer than he appears.'

'Really?' Rick's response was not, she knew, a real question, and she suspected that he had only half heard, listening instead to retail predictions and the detail on the last goal of the Chelsea–Liverpool match that night. But she continued to download her thoughts on Alexander, thankful that the evening had provided a good distraction from her afternoon with Teo.

'Yes. On one level, he's absolutely what you might expect. Like, he told me he had built a business by the time he was twenty, he's been married already, and he made it clear that he didn't care where that poor first wife is now, while also telling me that he gives her money. But there was something about him that was softer and more human than the walking breeze block he appears to be. He's very proud of Olga. Adores her.'

'Ah . . .' Rick was grateful for the familiar chatter of the news-caster, as he found himself unable to produce a suitable response. During the course of the evening he had had to accept that not only had Olga not returned his calls for weeks but that she had done nothing at the Weitzmans' to throw him the slightest indication that she was about to do so. He had been really enjoying his affair with her and felt a childish injustice at it being messed up through no act of his own. It wasn't fair. Just those fucking awful pictures.

'Yes, and he says they're trying to have a kid,' Katherine continued. 'She's much younger than him – I mean, he must be about your age, don't you think? – so she's got time. But he's getting on and, suddenly, I felt a bit sad for him. All that money and no kids.' She opened the window for some air, looking out as the large houses of the Weitzmans' neighbourhood gave way to long avenues of anonymous mansion blocks. Teo and Antonella's flat was just a few roads away, she realized, then continued her analysis of the Oblomoviks as a diversion from that thought. 'I wonder where they met. What the story is. Olga's definitely got a past, but then, by all accounts, they all have. Of course,' she corrected herself, 'we all have a past, but you know what I mean. You get a sense there's been quite a bit of reinvention going on. In a way, I envy that. It would be interesting to start all over and see what you might be.'

Rick kept silent for a moment, then asked, 'Didn't you say the Fullardis lived around here?'

'Yes. I believe so,' Katherine said, unable to ignore the fact that she could see the dark window of Teo's bedroom just across the street and that she desperately wanted to know where he was right now and who he was with. Instead, it was her turn to listen, as her husband recounted his conversation with Serena Samoni.

Rick woke early the next morning, although he would hardly call it waking, since he wouldn't really describe the past few hours as sleep. Olga's attempts to become pregnant had circled his brain as he skated on a veneer of semi-consciousness. By six he had given up on the prospect of rest and had left his bed and Katherine, who was coiled on one side in what he assumed was contented slumber.

The garden was still dark, with the rooftop chimneys opposite just emerging in the dawn. Generally, on a weekday, Mariella would organize breakfast for them (currently, a revolting-looking green juice for Katherine and a boiled egg for him), but she didn't clock on this early and his tiredness craved a carb hit. He made coffee, searching through the coloured foils of the pods for the strongest blend, but his hunt for fresh bread or a croissant came to nothing. Ahead of him was a demanding day, and he was now regretting that he'd told Katherine he could drop her off on his way in to work, since he would now have to wait until she was ready to leave.

Rick was not a man who found leisure easy, particularly when it was unscheduled. Faced with an unexpected couple of extra hours in the morning he mentally riffled through the time-filling options – some yoga stretches, another couple of chapters of the still-unfinished polar-expedition book, the *FT* download, and opted for the last over the immediate checking of his emails. He looked quickly at his phone and decided to text Olga so that she would be reminded of his existence as soon as she woke, if only as a text presence: 'Aching for you. You looked so beautiful last night. Call me.' As soon as he had pressed send, he felt better. At least he had done something to make him feel that their relationship still existed.

The action had nothing to do with his affection for Katherine; he knew he loved her in a way that needed no such activity to confirm it. When she came downstairs, as she surely would, her face free of make-up and with slightly puffy eyes, hair already brushed and her bare feet poking out beneath her dressing gown, there would be the same pleasurable recognition there always was. It wasn't something he wanted to lose or jeopardize, but that morning, as the daylight crept in, the only thing that really mattered was whether Olga would call.

Katherine opened the bedroom curtains an hour later to look out on the rectangles of light popping up in the houses across the garden as the day came alive. The fact that the other side of the bed was empty meant that Rick was probably wishing that he hadn't offered her a lift to get her colour done. It was rare that he left the bed before her, unless it was for a flight or a particularly early breakfast meeting, and she knew that he would be resenting being awake too early and impatient that he now had to wait. She pulled on a pair of jeans and a sweater rather than the dressing gown she normally wore for breakfast and massaged moisturizer around her eyes and above her brows in the faint hope that the rejuvenation promised by some Dead Sea mineral would actually occur. In the kitchen Mariella was surrounded by the army of bottles and packages containing the ingredients that made up Katherine's morning smoothie. From her expression, it was impossible to gauge what she thought as she threw them one after the other into the blender, knowing that the cost of a week's ingredients was close to what she earned in a day.

'Have you seen Rick?' Katherine asked.

'He had made his own breakfast already when I arrived, though he said he couldn't find the croissants.'

Katherine shared a look of exasperation with Mariella as she sipped from the large glass of liquid Mariella had now poured and went in search of her husband. She found him in his study on the first floor. When they bought the house they had wondered if it was going to be too large for the three of them. But Rick had rightly pointed out that nobody had ever suffered from having too much space and, within a year of moving in, at times the house felt as if it weren't quite big enough.

Rick's study was where he kept all the things that Katherine found, for one reason or another, inappropriate for the rest of the house. The walls were hung with his personal memorabilia: rugby-team pictures from his school days in which, as a teenager with an open face and thick, springy hair, he stood three away from the cup-bearing captain; a framed poster of the Knebworth line-up from 1979; a couple of watercolours an early girlfriend had painted on safari in Kenya; and several childhood drawings by Josh. On the wall of shelves to the left of his desk were biographies, books on art and several hardback thrillers, but also a tangerine gonk with dangling woollen legs he had brought back from a rugby match in South Africa and a line-up of miniature sports cars, their remotes long consigned to the bin. He liked to closet himself in here playing stadium music through Bose headphones – REM, Red Hot Chili Peppers, Nickelback – the kind of stuff that let you mentally crowd-surf. It was a different world to the tasteful rooms which his wife had put together, or the restrained and carefully curated showcase of the gallery.

'You must have got up early. I didn't hear you,' Katherine said at the door, looking at her husband's back, in a faded ikat dressing gown.

'Yes. I had a terrible night. I don't feel like I've slept at all.'

'Do you remember when we never talked about how much we had or hadn't slept?' Katherine spoke fondly. 'Now we're always banging on about it. One or other of us.'

'Let's be fair – it's normally you. And it's normally you complaining about the way I crash so quickly – how do you put it? – my barely contained narcolepsy?' Rick closed his laptop and turned to his wife, faintly surprised to see her dressed. He checked the time. 'Christ. I've been up for hours, messing around, and now I'm about to be late.'

When the weather was fine Rick liked to walk to the gallery. The forty-minute head-clearing march through the park was a positive plus in the day, but it had rained heavily every morning that month and this morning was no exception. Katherine ignored Rick's angry commentary on the crowded roads, lines of buses and delivery trucks. There was no point in engaging with him on the question of whether the guy in front was a total moron, or how another idiot had thought it a bright idea to place a fucking three-way light at a particularly busy junction. She thought of calling Josh to say hello, but eight thirty in the morning was no time to expect him to greet her cheerfully.

The *Today* programme was interrupted by Rick's phone ringing over the hands-free Bluetooth as, undeterred by the oncoming traffic, he attempted to overtake a row of buses. Katherine glanced at him to see if, in spite of this demand on his concentration, he was going to answer and was pleased to see he was ignoring the call, especially given that a crash with a number 9 bus appeared an imminent possibility.

She waited for the radio to resume but instead a voicemail

followed. 'Hello, Ricky. Got your message. Call me.' Olga's voice was unmistakable. Rick fumbled at the phone control on the steering wheel and continued to look ahead.

'Was that Olga?' Katherine asked, unnecessarily, holding out her fingers in front of her as she considered whether to get them painted a bright colour like turquoise or one of those trendy sludges at the hairdresser's.

'Yup.'

'"Ricky"? "Ricky"? What's that about?'

'I have no idea. But I was trying to get to work in one piece with all these crazed madmen on the roads so it wasn't a good time to speak. I'm trying to interest her in a couple of lithographs, which is probably what she was phoning about. I'll call her when I get to the gallery.'

Months later, Katherine asked herself whether hearing those few words was the moment she suspected that there was more than a business relationship between Olga and her husband but, at the time, she simply asked the question, without suspicion or particular interest. Later again, she wondered what she could have been thinking.

A few minutes later she gave Rick a quick kiss goodbye, then slammed the car door shut before running into Thomas Spensley, the salon that had maintained her 'natural' blonde for the past decade. She was one of the first customers. A man was having his short back and sides trimmed, his sallow skin and neat stubble poking up from the salon's high-necked gown, which reduced all clients to the same unattractive species. Flo had once suggested that the robes were designed that way so that hairdressers were not only empowered by wielding the scissors but also by dressing their victims in a garment that had the same enfeebling and humiliating qualities as a hospital gown or prison uniform. The only difference was that you paid a fortune for the privilege.

'Just pop yourself here for me,' a junior cheerfully suggested, gesturing at a leather chair in front of a wall of mirrors. 'Want any magazines?' Ron, Katherine's shaven-headed colourist, appeared at this point, his trousers hanging loosely below his hips. Katherine enjoyed the ritual of the salon. The fact that nothing unexpected ever happened. She knew that Ron would ask her whether they were doing the usual as he combed through her hair, picking out strands and considering the state of play.

'Looking good, Katherine. Looking good,' Ron said, as he always did. 'When the weather gets a bit better we might brighten you up a bit, but we don't want you looking too brassy, do we? Don't want you going all Russian on us.' He lowered his voice conspiratorially and dropped the strands of hair he'd been examining.

Katherine thought of Olga's hair, which nobody would describe as brassy and which had a gloss that was now impossible to achieve on her own, no matter how many vegetable rinses and conditioning treatments Ron directed when she was shampooed. She tried to remember if she had ever heard anyone refer to Rick as Ricky before, and felt sure she hadn't. It sounded very odd, but then not much surprised her about Olga.

Ron possessed a wide and vocal range of opinions and Katherine was amused by listening to his take on Angelina Jolie, or Nick Clegg, or fracking (all unremittingly hopeless), or Sky Atlantic, or Steve Coogan, or a referendum on Europe (wouldn't hear a word against). His flow was unstoppable, so it wasn't necessary to contribute much as he daubed the chilly paste on to her hair with a balletic brio, the apparent randomness of the application serving only to demonstrate his expertise.

When he'd finished she sat within the pleasant heat emitted by a contraption placed next to her and tried to read a magazine, but she found herself once more thinking of Teo. Through the years of marriage and motherhood, she had given herself completely to being a mother to her son and a wife to her husband. The calligraphy certainly occupied her, but her immersion in it rarely, if ever, stayed with her once she had left her workroom. Until the appearance of Teo she had hardly questioned her commitment to all this, or her early marriage and lack of a real career, but now, as she whirled around in a kaleidoscope of desire and anticipation, she began to ask whether what she had felt was contentment or whether it had simply been blind acceptance. Perhaps the difference was small. Perhaps it didn't matter much either way, but staring at herself in the hairdresser's mirror, her hair covered in an icy caramel paste, her face not so different, but with the softening jawline and the sag between her eyes to remind her how her mother had looked before she died, she felt determined to keep hold of what Teo offered while she could. He made her feel a different person, somebody who was looser and sweeter and utterly alive in her skin, and when he touched her, or even looked at her in a certain, wanting way, she felt extraordinary. Rick didn't even come into it.

# Chapter Thirteen

*April*

Sprawling on the sofa, Josh pointed one of the remotes at the television. He had been channel surfing for a couple of hours in his grandmother's house with the curtains pulled against the bright sun that had encouraged the rest of the group out on a walk he had no interest in joining. CeeCee's television was smaller than the one at home but at least she had Sky and she was talking about joining Netflix. First off, he'd had a quick scan of what was recorded, storing up the option of a David Attenborough documentary on water buffalo if there was nothing else worth watching, but since it was Saturday, there was football.

Watching the footie was about the sum of Josh's athletic output. Unlike Rick, he wasn't at all athletic and throughout school had done his best to avoid sports, even the cricket that his dad was so keen on him playing. He had always found it easy to make friends but he hated the jocular camaraderie of the changing rooms and the stresses of team spirit. The only sport he had shown any interest in was fencing, in his early years of secondary school, but that had dissipated after a few sessions. When he signed up for it he'd imagined himself as a swashbuckling, piratical character, but his experience in the school gym lacked any connection with this person of his imagination and, after a term, he had packed it in.

The television room was small, furnished for use by the grandchildren. The chairs were patterned in a dark fabric that had survived quite a few spills and stains, and the room had a cosy feeling in contrast to many of the other rooms. CeeCee had always been good about letting the children watch as much TV as they wanted, which, when he was younger, was one of the good things about visiting.

That, and the fact that she always kept thick, white, sliced bread for toast and sandwiches, unlike home, where his parents thought sliced white was the food of the devil and only ever had a kind of brown bread that tasted like cardboard.

During the whole of the spring term Josh had been distracted by thoughts of Antonella. To be fair, his Geography course was probably more interesting than he had expected and he had even quite got into a module examining the environmental impact of building stadiums on subtropical cities. But although he had his work and a group of friends, he couldn't deny that he was a bit obsessed by her. There was a small part of him that dared to hope that if he could just do that extra thing – though he had no idea what – he just might get her. She wasn't so far away. He could see her stringy hair falling over her pale shoulders, where the bones jutted sharply, and the mismatched pupils of her eyes. He could hear the way her voice, with its emphatic lilt and speedy rattle, would deepen when she teased him, making him feel as if he were someone who really meant something to her. When she messaged him or Snapchatted, it wasn't the same as when his other friends did. He got messages all day long, as they all did, but when there was something from her it was like she pressed a button and he lit up. The effect didn't last long, though, and then he wanted to hear from her again.

He'd only agreed to lunch with his grandmother on condition that Rick would make sure he was back to meet up with Antonella in the evening. There had been a bad moment when she'd texted him that she and Teo were going to a party in Milan that weekend, but then there'd been some drama or other and she'd said she was going to be around after all. Josh took a gulp from the Coke can at the foot of the sofa and checked on the Liverpool–Arsenal match, just as he was made aware of the group's return from their walk by the chatter from the other end of the long hall and the noise of Roland crashing along the wooden floor. He waited for one of them to come and fetch him – it would probably be Mum – but it was Rick who appeared in the doorway, looking at the television, lured by the chant of the afternoon's results.

'What's the Chelsea score?' he asked, depositing himself on the tightly upholstered arm of the sofa before sliding down with a crash beside his son. Josh broke the news of Chelsea's last-minute defeat by Spurs. Josh and his father shared a loyalty to Chelsea, but Josh had also formed a kind of relationship with Crystal Palace, whereas Rick was *obsessed* with Chelsea. At uni, Josh ramped up his attachment to Palace since Chelsea was such a predictable posh London club to support, and he'd also kept quiet about the visit he'd once had with his dad to lunch in the directors' box at Stamford Bridge before the match. Afterwards they'd sat with a whole bunch of other guys watching the team lose.

'What time do you want to leave?' Rick asked, hauling himself from the sofa. 'I think we'll come with you, so you won't need to catch the train. We're kind of done here now, and Katherine would probably like to get back, too.'

'Whenever,' Josh answered, but kept his eyes on the screen. 'I said I'd meet up with Antonella about eight.'

'Okay. What are you two doing tonight?'

Josh shrugged. He had no idea what they would do, but it would be interesting whatever, because just hanging out with Antonella was bound to be interesting. And even if he had known, he wasn't likely to share the information with his father. One of the good things about uni was that he didn't have his parents always asking him, with a mixture of curiosity and concern, what he was doing, where he was going. He didn't ask them about their stuff all the time.

'Why don't you switch the TV off and come and have some tea with us? Then we can leave.' Rick padded off, shoeless, down the hall.

A few minutes later Josh reluctantly followed his father, going into the small dining room, where a tempting array of food had been laid out, as if a large lunch hadn't been produced only a few hours before. Small rectangles of cucumber sandwiches, a large, golden-crusted pork pie and a glistening ginger cake sat on the table, and CeeCee was pouring from a large china tea pot whose weight threatened to snap her thin wrist.

'You should have come out with us, Josh,' she remarked as her eldest grandchild appeared. 'We had a good walk. Still,' she continued, 'I am sure you enjoyed yourself. Tea?'

Josh watched his father carve a considerable wedge of the pork pie, dabbing up the crumbs that fell with a finger and dropping them into his mouth before making headway on the pie itself.

'I gather the Oblomoviks have had trouble with permissions for the gun room over at Drayton,' CeeCee commented as she placed a cucumber sandwich on a china plate.

'Have they? Katherine, you'd probably know about that?' Rick addressed his wife.

'Why would I know anything more than you? You're the one who's in contact with Olga,' she replied, in a tone that she quickly realized sounded snappier than she had intended. She followed it with a more convivial, if still tart, 'Oh, you mean I would hear from Flo? No, she hasn't given me an update recently and, anyway, she's got nothing to do with that, or stuff like the cinema and the gym. I think they've got some kind of spa area being built too, though. It appears Olga likes her little comforts.'

'Did you see that story about them the other day?' Josh spoke up. 'There was a picture in the paper of them standing together at some party. Don't know what it was saying – I didn't read it. They kind of spook me out. He looks weird, like there's something evil about him and she's . . .' He crammed a piece of ginger cake into his mouth without finishing the thought.

Katherine spoke, ignoring her son's dramatically negative opinion: 'I didn't. Did you, Rick?' She looked across at her husband.

Rick rubbed his hand over his chin in a vague way and shook his head before addressing CeeCee. 'Mum, we should be leaving soon. We promised to get Josh back for his date.'

Josh looked crossly at his father for using the term. It wasn't a date.

CeeCee either hadn't heard Rick's suggestion about leaving or had decided to ignore it. 'Josh, that's very interesting. Why do you consider Alexander Oblomovik evil? Now I have come to know him a little, I find him a rather *simpatico* character. He certainly has a good eye for business. My own opinion is that Olga is the more complicated of the two.'

Josh rocked back in his chair with a snort of laughter. 'Sure,' he said.

'What's so funny?' his mother asked. 'And watch the chair, please.' She had been telling him not to rock back on chairs since for ever. But had he ever fallen off or broken the chair? No.

'Nothing.' Josh pulled his phone out from his pocket, his bent head clearly conveying that he had no wish to add anything more. He busied himself checking Twitter for comments on the Chelsea match.

'I'm sure Josh has reasons for his amusement but, obviously, he doesn't feel like sharing them with us all. Now, who would like another cup of tea before you leave?' CeeCee took control with a small smile, bracing herself in the high-backed chair. 'Rick, I wonder if you could go and have a word with Robert? He wanted your thoughts on the broadband here. He thinks we should change providers. I'm well and truly out of my element in these matters and told him to speak to you.'

'Dad's pretty crap when it comes to all that,' Josh contributed. 'We've got snailband at home. I know' – he qualified the accusation before Rick could defend himself – 'that you've got the top rate and whatnot, but I tell you. It works way quicker in my room at uni.'

CeeCee looked at the two in a manner that discouraged any more time being spent on the question. She favoured what she called debate rather than argument, as long as it ceased as soon as she found the subject uninteresting or unpleasant, the former of which applied to a discussion about broadband.

By the time the Tennisons were making their way out of the grounds of Charlwood, the early-evening sun was adding soft shadows to the fields in the distance and a glow to the crowds of daffodils that lined the drive. Sitting behind his parents, Josh watched his mother looking silently out of the window. He had plugged in his earphones and was playing around with the 2,745 songs on his iPhone, regretting some that had failed to make the download from his computer and were uselessly hovering in a cloud rather than being available for the journey.

The earphones insulated him from his parents' conversation, which he imagined was about CeeCee – it normally was after they'd spent some time with her. It was obvious how manipulative his grandmother was and how she wound them up, but, at the same time, when his father was with her, his usually confident, joshing figure came over all defensive and sulky; he got worked up over small things. You could even see it in the way he played with Roland, as if it really mattered how he chucked the ball for the dog to chase. It was strange because, in general, it was pretty hard to get to him, and he always seemed as if he could deal with anything that might happen. Josh didn't think he'd ever seen his father really hurt about something. Annoyed and impatient? Yup. He was always yelling about some random thing or other, but as soon as he stopped shouting the story was over. It was Mum who got silently wounded over stuff, which meant that you had to ask her what the problem was and then you'd be stuck having to deal with a conversation about it when it would have been easier if she'd just said so at the start. All things considered, he'd rather deal with his dad.

The thing about Antonella was that Josh was never completely sure they would meet until he was there in the room with her. He had got used to the way that they would make some kind of a plan – or at least he thought they had – and then, if she wanted, she would cancel right up to and over the last minute. He'd get a text, or sometimes a call, where she'd ramble on about how she had to do this and had to do that so maybe she'd call again in a few hours and they could see what was happening. With anyone else, he would find it infuriating and wouldn't bother but, with her, well, he'd go right to the end of the line, and then some.

It was nearly eleven by the time he was propped up on the mattress at her flat. She was pulling out clothes from the cupboards that ran along one side of her bedroom and flinging them dramatically on to the floor, covering the white carpet in a mess of fabric that was now creeping up to her ankles.

'So, what do you think?' She posed in front of him in a vest and black jeans. He had just seen her bending down to pull the jeans on, dragging them over her plain black knickers with a wriggle, watching him watching her in a way that was impossible for him to read. In a way he'd reached the inner sanctum, but that was partially, he knew, because she needed an audience.

Antonella held her cigarette carefully away from her body while she adjusted her top, then handed it to Josh to hold when she couldn't get the drape right with only one hand.

'It looks good,' he said, on automatic, as she turned to look in the mirror on the inside of the cupboard.

Even so, she made an exasperated noise and, ignoring his approval, tore off the top, furiously dragging it over her head and reaching back into the wardrobe, her small, bare breasts with their surprisingly broad spread of nipple like stains on the pale flesh. He could count her ribs, but he decided it would be cooler not to carry on looking while she found something else to put on. Her cigarette burnt low between his fingers.

'Do you want the rest of this?' He held out the remains, standing up to go into the living room to find an ashtray when she didn't reply. From the bedroom, she shouted, 'So, Luca, he's a crazy guy, really. But he has good parties. Francesco is bringing this crowd he met filming in Rio. And Josh, he says there are all the models . . .' She appeared in the doorway in another outfit, doing a shimmy samba. 'Fun, yes? The models, for you?'

Josh was used to Antonella flinging names about without caring whether they meant anything to him. It didn't matter. The way she talked, it wasn't as if you had to say much, or even *could* say much. She liked to riff off things, moving from one thought to another seemingly without any connection, and he was happy to listen, dropping in the odd comments so that he wasn't totally silent. Even then it was more about what she heard in his tone than what he actually said.

It was hard to imagine Antonella on her own because, although she did most of the talking, she liked a continual chorus of appreciation: 'Yeah', 'Sure', 'You got it' and, if she was in the right mood, a lot of laughs. He'd noticed that if nobody was listening to her she would get pissed off and start talking louder, moving closer to you to grab your concentration. When she did this, her lazy eye became more obvious. With any other girl, it would have been a nightmare but, somehow, with her it worked and she could make you do what she wanted. He saw her do it to others, too. It wasn't just him.

Antonella put on a Euro-disco remix before plopping herself down on the sofa beside him. She fiddled with the top that she was now wearing, an intricate black bandage that exposed slices of bare flesh as she moved, then jumped up again.

'Teo said he'd come with us. So where is he?' She jabbed out a text, looking down from the long windows to the street.

'Maybe he'll meet us there. That would be okay, wouldn't it? When did you last hear from him?'

'He is so unreliable now.' She sounded spiky and cross, and was biting her lip. 'You know, things are changing with him. He used to look after me, but now . . . I'm not so sure. We were like this.' She wound her arms around her body, stroking herself in a gesture of protection and desire.

'When we were young, after my father was killed, Teo was my guardian. He said he would always take care of me. You know' – she turned towards Josh with a look of desolation he had never seen before – 'I wouldn't be alive if it weren't for Teo.'

'What do you mean, you wouldn't be alive?'

'Josh, you have no idea what it is like to be us. You are here with your little family and you think it is all all right – yes? You think, really, that you are safe. And you don't know how it can be when – *bang!* – something terrible happens. Like it did with our father and the crash. And then with my mother, who was such a bitch.' Her words were speeding up frantically, threatening to overrun her. 'Yes. You could say she did the normal things to look like she cared, but I never thought she did. She never made me feel her love. And then, when she was with that guy who raped me, and she didn't believe me. It was the end.'

'Whoah! Hang on. I don't know about this. I don't know any of this. What man raped you?' Josh wasn't sure whether Antonella wasn't strung out on something she'd taken before he arrived; he was so used to her being a drama queen. Someone had raped her? It didn't totally surprise him to hear her say it, but he didn't know whether it was true, or her version of the truth, which was more like a collage.

'He *raped* me!' Antonella shouted. 'Don't tell me you don't believe me. It's what happened. I was seventeen, and I was in my bedroom in the Tuscan house. I didn't want to eat with the others and I had gone to bed early. I remember it so clear, even now. It had been a hot day. There was a dinner outside. I could hear the sound of everyone through the window and I felt sad that my father wasn't there. He loved to eat in the garden. Long tables, candles. Every time it was possible we would eat outside. And, for some reason, that night, it got to me. So I was lying on my bed in the room – just lying. It was empty. I mean, I was empty – I didn't want to be with anyone. There was a knock on the door and I heard it open and the footsteps. At first, I guess I had my eyes closed, I thought it was someone my mother had sent with food. They were always sending me food.' She spat, mimicking, ' "You must eat something, Antonella. Why don't you eat something, Antonella?" '

As she told her story she walked round the edge of the sitting room, banging the walls, three times in each spot in a furious ritual. 'I felt someone on the bed and opened my eyes, and it was Giancarlo. I can see him now in a black shirt with the buttons open and the black hair, like some crap gigolo. He sat there and started to stroke me. I sat up and shouted at him to get out, and he didn't move. There was now music outside, too, and I knew they wouldn't hear but, anyway, I was screaming, but only for a moment before he pushed me down and he put his big fat hand over my mouth and felt me with his other hand. He said I needed somebody like him to take control of me and then maybe I would come to my senses. And then he raped me – I smell him now. I feel him pushing into me. I couldn't stop him. I couldn't stop him. In a way, maybe, I didn't care. It was easier. I was empty.' As she came to the end of her story, Antonella's words had begun to slow, her pacing, too. 'I kept quiet at first, because what was the point? It was easier. But then I told Teo, and then he told our mother and, of course, Ann didn't believe me. She said someone would have heard if I shouted. She said I was making it up to move the attention away from not eating. But Teo, he fought for me. He was my hero. That was before.' At this Antonella flipped back to her annoyance at Teo not having returned to the flat. 'Now I don't know what he is. Shit. Where is he?'

Josh had listened with a growing sense that, this time, Antonella was telling the truth. He had never seen her so unhappy before. She'd been angry and irritable many times, incandescent on occasion, but he had never before felt that he should put his arms around her just to soothe her – even though that had fuck-all chance of succeeding. But before he reached her she had reverted to her original spiky irritation, and it seemed like the wrong thing to do, as if, having told him, she didn't want the experience dwelt on any longer. He wished that Teo would come soon, since it seemed the most likely way that the Antonella who had started the evening, the one that was filled with fun and flirting, the one that made him think there might be something brilliant just around the corner, would return and replace this version.

She came and sat down next to him on the sofa, stretching her legs over his knees and again fiddling with her clothes and pinching her arm a couple of times before pulling her top tighter and then pinching her skin again. She levered herself closer so that she was nearly on top of him, her eyes like pools of thick gelatine, so dark that the pupils were scarcely visible. Their shoulders touched as she handed him her phone.

'Look. It's funny, yes? We should send it. How much do you think she got for this? I think now, with her name, it would be a whole lot more, yeah?' The screen had another of those pictures of Olga. Like the others, it was pretty weird and old-fashioned. It was tame, really – nothing like the porno stuff he was used to. But, all the same, he couldn't pretend that this picture of an adult he knew posed in that 'have me' way didn't make him feel uncomfortable. It wasn't that he was embarrassed, exactly, but he didn't want to see this stuff. It was kind of like seeing Flo with nothing on. Well, okay, a bit better than that.

'How come you didn't send this one when you sent me the others?' he asked, handing it back to her, and playing for time. After Antonella's revelation just now, he didn't want to upset her any further.

'I did. I don't know. What does it matter? I found another. But, come on, let's send it. Now.' Her face was right up against his, and she moved her lips along the edge of his hairline, reaching a sensitive spot just above his ear. 'Have you got the phone with you?' she asked.

'No. I don't carry it around with me.' Josh thought about where the phone might be; it was one of Antonella's cast-offs, which she'd given to him so he could send the pictures anonymously. He knew it was in his room somewhere, but he hadn't used it for a bit. He wouldn't have minded by now if he'd lost it anyway and this whole game stopped. It didn't seem funny any more. It hadn't seemed that amusing ever, to be honest.

The whole thing had started as they were leaving the party at the gallery. Antonella had asked him if he wanted to go with her and Teo, and Teo, as usual, hadn't really seemed to care whether he came or not. Fred had run up and said he was going to join them when he'd locked up. Josh had seen in the way that Antonella had been behaving with Fred, twining herself around him, teasing him and generally shining her headlights on him, that he was going to be the one who got her attention that night. It was kind of funny watching Fred trying to behave like he was working and concentrating on the guests and looking after them when you could tell he was loving a bit of the Antonella treatment. But Josh didn't want Fred muscling in on her, and he'd kind of hoped Fred would get a better offer or, failing that, get the address of the place they were going to in Notting Hill wrong.

Antonella and Teo knew millions of people. There were all these Italians in London who turned out to be some kind of relatives of theirs and, also, wherever they went, people just noticed them, as a pair with this kind of cool. They would walk into a room and you could see everyone check them out. It wasn't anything they did; it happened before they had done anything at all. But they knew the vibe they gave out and played up to it, acting like they were super-close to each other and sometimes even dressing like they were twins.

At the house they'd all gone down to one of those basements that tunnels under the garden, where there was a room with a pool table, some socking great plastic sculpture in the corner and the massive sofas all those sorts of places had. Far down a corridor there was the glimmer of blue and a faint smell of chlorine.

He'd played one round of pool with some guy who didn't speak much English but was an amazing shot and had beaten him in no time at all, and when he left the table Antonella was sitting with Fred in that private way she had. It was still pretty early, but he didn't much want just to hang around and watch, so he was thinking of leaving when Antonella ran up to him and kind of pulled him upstairs, to a room with no one else in it.

'Don't go. It is only starting, this evening, and we are going to have fun,' she said. 'It won't be so good if you aren't here. No. For real. Fred's not the same as you. I just wanted to ask him something about an idea.' She kissed him, and he remembered how her mouth moved first like a feather and then slowly, sucking. This time, he thought it might be different and something might happen, but then she moved away, just a small distance, so that he was still right in her zone but they weren't touching.

'Hey. Look at these,' she said, and pulled out her phone. She showed him the pictures of Olga, maybe four or five, turning the images horizontally and vertically, pinching them in and out, leaning right into him as he looked so that he could smell that smell of hers and see the little crust of spit on the side of her mouth when he looked up from them.

'Hysterical. It's Olga, right?'

'Of course.' She grabbed the phone back and looked at the pictures, smiling.

'What are they? I mean, where did you find them?'

'Oh. It wasn't difficult. They were just on the net. They must have been published sometime. For sure, a few years ago. They're probably something she doesn't want to remember now. But, you know, pictures haunt, don't they? Like those tribes in Africa who think if someone takes your picture they've captured your soul. And now pictures don't disappear . . .'

'Yeah. Classic.' He wasn't at all turned on by the pictures, and wasn't sure how he was meant to react, but Antonella seemed ridiculously pleased with herself. The room must have been somebody's study and he felt jumpy, nervous that somebody might come in any minute and find them there, two random people looking at this stuff.

'So, I had an idea. And you' – she stroked his sleeve, wearing the smile he had come to recognize meant that she expected to get what she wanted – 'and you are helping me.' She pulled him to her. 'So the pictures are funny, right? And I think your dad he has a bit of a thing for Olga? You know he fancies her? For sure. So why don't we give him a thrill and send him the pictures, but we don't say who they are from? It's like, a game.'

'What do you mean, Dad fancies her? Where's that come from? She's a client of his, that's all.'

'Oh, Josh. Are you a little boy? A *teeny-weeny leetle* boy? You know your parents. All parents, they fancy people. They are alive. They aren't just parents looking after the little Josh. Making the cake, buying the presents. Reading the story. They aren't always caring about you. You have to be so stupid not to see the way your dad looks when he sees her.' Antonella pulled a grotesque, foolish face to illustrate her point, making Josh laugh for a moment, but the way she was talking to him, as if he were that child, was doing a

175

good job of stripping away any of the attraction he'd just thought she might feel to him. 'Olga. She's a babe. She knows how to play men. I'm just saying your dad is a man. Come on,' she continued, holding the screen away from her a little as if she could admire the image better from a distance.

'So what do you want me to do?'

'Well, it will be fun if he doesn't know where they come from. I thought you could send him the pictures at clever moments. So that they pop up totally random, and he does not understand. You can use one of my phones so that he doesn't know the number. Right?' In the moment it took before Josh gave his reply, Antonella added with her dismissive shrug, 'You know, if you don't want to, if you don't find it funny, Fred will do it. He'll get it. He gets me. He really gets me.'

Of course Fred gets you, Josh thought. We all do. It didn't take an Einstein to work out that this was one of her challenges. There was a part of her that hadn't grown up, that liked childish things. The second she was told she couldn't do something – like smoke somewhere – she would do it, just to prove a point. If you said no, she would say yes. He'd already learnt that.

So he said yes. For now. After all, it *was* pretty funny and, at the end of the day, what was the problem? He didn't want Antonella to think he was somebody who wouldn't do anything risky, and how risky could it be? His parents were totally together. They weren't like some parents, who were always having affairs, and their kids were left rolling their eyes, like they didn't care, waiting till it passed, which half the time it did and half the time it didn't. No, they seemed fine, and his dad would probably just find the pictures a bit odd and have a bit of a laugh. He wondered if he'd mention them.

'Okay. I'll give it a go.' It was worth agreeing to see the respect on Antonella's face.

'Yaaaaay. Geeenius,' she cackled.

'Does Teo know about them? The pictures?'

'Of course he does.'

'And about sending them to my dad as a joke?'

Antonella didn't reply. Instead, she opened the door, holding his hand and pulling him with her as she ran down the stairs back to the party in the basement. Fred was still on the sofa, now talking to a girl in a bright-green jacket and tiny skirt who must have just arrived. He watched Antonella walk over and sit the other side of him, in a way that squeezed the competition on to the far edge.

By the time Teo finally returned to the flat, Antonella had calmed down. The idea of texting another picture had acted like a Xanax in taking the edge off her mood, but still she paced the room, unable or unwilling to settle, constantly checking the slim diamond watch on her wrist which she always wore, even though she'd told Josh she didn't care about time. It caged you in.

Months back, when Josh had first visited, the echoing emptiness of the flat had felt wonderfully free, as if the space had so few traces of occupancy and none of history that anyone could be anything in it. When he went to other people's places, girls had normally tried to make a home. They would put a few flowers in a vase, or there was a smell of something someone had cooked up in a big batch and a mess in the kitchen. But as far as Josh could see, the kitchen cupboards that weren't housing Antonella's shoe collection had never been put to any kind of domestic use. Tonight, however, although nothing had changed, the flat felt different. Maybe it was because nothing *had* changed. But rather than being a space where things happened, it felt the opposite, claustrophobic and lifeless.

The sound of Teo's bike outside the house drew Antonella to the windows, and she opened them out on to the small balcony with a crash and shouted into the dark, silent street. 'So you arrive! Now! You are so late. What happened?'

She continued the tirade as he came through the front door.

'You make me wait here for you. You know I want to go with you tonight. Francesco, Luca, they expect us together. I don't want to be alone.'

Josh was shocked by this display: her shrill tone, the pointless accusation, the yelling about him being late when she herself didn't know what it was to be on time. Teo's hair had been flattened by his helmet, which he now threw on to a chair. He had cut it shorter and it seemed darker and had a wave that softened the strong bones of his face. In contrast, Antonella's hair had grown, and reached well below her shoulders in ropey tendrils she was now twisting round her finger.

'Come on. We can go?'

'Antonella, calm down. I need to change. I won't be long. Why are you so crazy tonight?'

'Crazy? I am not crazy. It's you who are crazy.' Teo left the room, shutting the door to his room noisily.

'*Scusi*,' Antonella muttered, bowing theatrically then running into her own room and returning with a black feather jacket with huge sleeves that made her look like a raven. She turned to Josh as if to say 'We're off!' but didn't go anywhere.

When Teo came back he was barefoot and carrying a pair of leather shoes, a tube of polish and a chamois leather. He sat on the edge of the sofa and started to apply the polish in a methodical way, slowly and with great concentration, rubbing each area thoroughly before moving on to the next.

'Oh, now you polish the shoes, Teo! You say I am the OCD girl but you are the obsessive. I wait for you to go to Luca's and now, you go rub rub, rub rub.' She imitated the movement. 'Enough. You try to be our father. It's too late for that.' Antonella turned again to Josh. 'Our father, he did this with his shoes all the time. We watched him clean them together and he would let Teo do the polish at the end. So now? He is the baby again. I do not believe it.'

'I won't be long, Antonella. Take a pill or something. Or I'm not coming to the party.' He took the penknife Katherine had given him out of his trouser pocket, running it in a slow, deliberate movement along the join between the leather of the sole and the shoe, scraping out the small deposit of polish that had gathered in the crease and spreading it on the cloth.

'Is that Moroccan? The knife?' Josh asked, grateful to have an excuse to say something rather than stand there like the cipher he felt reduced to. 'Mum has something like that. They used to use them to carve the calligraphy tools, although I don't think she's ever used hers.'

Teo carried on with what he was doing, which had by now ceased to have any real purpose and was more of a tick, as if he were feeding worry beads through his fingers, running the knife in a single curve around the side of the shoe, hesitating at the tip before swooping along the other side. It was clearly driving Antonella mad.

'Of course,' Antonella said with a sly glance at her brother. 'She gave it to him. Didn't she? Didn't she, Teo? Your *girlfriend*.' She pronounced the word as if it tasted poisonous, adding, 'So there you are, Josh. Remember what I said before. Parents are just other people. They do their own thing. Has she written your name in ink on your skin? She did on Teo. Here.' She made a slicing movement across her collar bone. '"T E O", with all the curls and everything. What do you call them, Teo? The sherrifs?'

Serifs, Josh answered silently. There was a noise in his head that he couldn't identify and he felt his face burning.

'What are you saying, Antonella?' he managed.

'He fucks her. It's weird, isn't it? Your "mum" and Teo.' Antonella used her fingers as mocking inverted commas.

Josh looked at Teo, hoping he would tell him that this was just another one of Antonella's stories. That she shouldn't make so much stuff up. Teo was holding up one of his shoes. He examined it and then placed it precisely on the floor.

'You know, Antonella, sometimes you are too much. Say too much' was his restrained comment.

'So is it true, Teo? You and Mum?'

Teo looked up from the shoe and raised his hands: *mea culpa*.

Josh couldn't even start to process the thought of his mother with Teo. It was so far away from anything he could imagine that he could only hear the words, he couldn't conjure up any picture. And in any case it was a picture he had no desire to view. It was all some ridiculous tangle – his mum, Teo, Antonella, the photos, Olga, his dad: all this shit he'd been thrown. Was some of it his fault? Any of it? He had no idea. Antonella was more than capable of making stuff up. Teo hadn't denied it. But if it was true, it was insane.

Antonella moved up to him and put an arm around him. 'It's okay. Don't look so sad. We have a party to go to. We will take care of you.'

He pushed her away. 'I don't want to go anywhere with either of you. You're so . . . you're just *sad*.' As soon as he hit the street the blast of fresh air made him throw up, the taste of the evening's vodka lining his throat in a vomity burn that didn't feel bad. The Tube was shut, and he started to walk home through the empty streets, only an occasional car passing. In the distance the sound of a train continued for ages, and Josh wondered what train could take so long, and where it was going. He plugged in his headphones, aiming to fill his head with music so he didn't have to think about stuff. But he couldn't stop thinking about it.

And what about the pictures? Those pictures he had sent his dad as a joke to tease him about a crush – and all the while his mum was being screwed by Teo and he, Josh, was being played by Antonella for all he was worth. He stopped for a moment to send a message to Felix, relieved when, in a matter of seconds, he felt the buzz of a reply. 'Sure, mate. Call me when you get here and I'll come and let you in.' Home was not a place he was going tonight.

# Chapter Fourteen

*May*

When the book club had been formed – could it really be four years ago now? – none of those who had gathered to enthusiastically discuss *The Time Traveler's Wife* had expected that they would now be meeting in Katherine's living room to talk about their twenty-fifth book. Technically, it was their twenty-sixth, but they had unanimously agreed that Tessa Forrester's last nomination should be ditched when, after about a week, none of them had thought it worth investing the time in. Anyway, shortly after her book was abandoned, Tessa's husband was transferred to Credit Suisse in Zurich and took the family with him, allowing her to escape the small but nonetheless hurtful indignity of having introduced the one failure to the group.

The club consisted of the six founding members and two more recent additions: Julia Hernandez, the opinionated American wife of a hedge funder and, today, for the first time, Serena Samoni, who, since the Weitzmans' dinner, had launched a determined and ultimately successful social assault on Katherine. They had been visiting a furniture dealer's one morning when she had almost pleaded to be included in the group. She explained, with an honesty Katherine couldn't help being touched by, that despite all her efforts she was finding it hard to make girlfriends in London. In Beirut, much of her social life was centred around other women and she wasn't used to the loneliness she so often felt here with Hakim's frequent travels. When Katherine had put the request to her fellow members the only person who had objected to Serena's inclusion was Julia, until then the newest member, claiming that Serena 'just wanted to be everywhere' and concluding, 'It's kind of tragic.'

Flo was mostly indifferent to the make-up of the group, but she liked the way it made her read fiction and her role, allotted by unspoken but unanimous agreement, of keeping the discussion moving along and preventing the conversation getting bogged down. That was her contribution, since the rota of meetings held in turn in the members of the group's homes was never going to include one in her single-bedroom flat, so she took seriously the responsibility of conducting a rewarding discussion.

It had been several months since they had last met, partially due to everyone's diary commitments but also because the book to be discussed, Orhan Pamuk's *The Museum of Innocence*, was quite a doorstopper. Katherine was pleased that the living-room seating allowed a large number of people to sit close to each other and chatter. In the last year the group had agreed to skip the sit-down dinner that was originally part of the deal, as everybody was trying to eat less and, truth be told, juggling everyone's current intolerances and regimes made catering a nightmare. Dinners were for when they were with their men and, left to themselves, it was a treat not to have to do the whole meal thing and be able just to nibble on almonds and kale crisps.

They had all more or less completed the book, although Serena admitted she had read it when it was first published, along with both Pamuk's earlier *My Name is Red* and *Snow*. This gave her an edge.

'I guess because I come from a different culture to most of you I am struck by how his work deals with displacement and loyalty and what it means to be part of a culture,' she said, tucking her long, black hair behind her ears.

'And class. It's also about class, isn't it?' added Flo. 'And the pressure of conforming to the mores and patterns of a group is something that Pamuk is concerned with. Since he wrote it, of course, Turkey has been struggling more than ever with a lot of the preoccupations that Pamuk deals with here.'

Serena was perched on the edge of the ottoman, a slight thing in a pair of jeans and a silk shirt. 'Tradition and loyalties and conforming to expectations are subjects that are often written about in Middle Eastern literature. But all the ideas are just as relevant here. It's easier for me, as an outsider, to see that.' She was obviously pleased that on her first appearance she was able to bring to the table a personal insight the others were unable to provide.

The group nodded in general agreement, Julia riffling through the colour-coded stickies jutting out from the pages of her copy of the book and opening it at a fluorescent orange one.

'You know, this is all true. But, hey, dudes! It was also a great love story, no?' Julia's petite build and blonde pixie crop would have led her to be described as elfin, were it not for her substantial bosom, which she generally highlighted with a taste for tightly belted dresses. Her voice had the dominance of a Southern cheerleader. 'This is a man who is tormented by a girl he loved and thought he'd lost. Right? When it comes down to it.'

'Well, it's certainly a story we've heard before,' Flo agreed. 'There are so many writers who have dealt with the question of "unsuitable" attachments. Flaubert, Tolstoy, Wharton . . . it goes on and on. But I would argue that is secondary to the other points he is making. What do others feel?'

The discussion continued, the addition of Serena encouraging each woman to behave more in character than they might otherwise. Just as siblings rarely deviate from their designated persona in a family, each had forged an identity within this forum.

'But he is doing his best to keep things going, surely?' Katherine contributed as they discussed Kemal's infatuation with the shop girl Füsun and his engagement to the socially appropriate Sibel. 'It's not like he wants to give up his existence. Not really. He cares about his life, his world, Sibel, his family, his friends. But there's this pull.'

'Yes.' Julia leant forward, folding her legs under her to become a neat package. 'It's always interesting to see who cares about that stuff and who doesn't, with all the break-ups going on now. Like, some people and – let's face it, generally, it's the guys – they just meet someone and *wham*! That's it. The whole family silver goes out the window. The houses, the kids, the old friends. They trade it in for the new model with the boobs. And yes' – she moved her hands in a dismissive gesture – 'I know what you're thinking. But you know it wasn't like that with Matt and me. He was in a dark, dark place, and if I hadn't come along, who knows . . .' Her lips tensed to demonstrate the depth of her concern. 'And Matt and I have really put a lot of time into his kids from that marriage, even though – call it as it is! – Claudia has *not* made it easy for any of us.'

It wasn't unusual for the meetings to veer off in this direction, aspects of the text leading enjoyably to an opportunity for the women to discuss their own lives.

Katherine couldn't stop her mind wandering. Rick was in Vienna, which was fortunate, since she had committed to hosting tonight's meeting long ago, but if she'd realized earlier that he would be gone she could have used the opportunity to be with Teo for a whole night, something they'd only achieved once before. She had considered cancelling the book club, but allowing seepage from the relationship into the rest of her life was something she had promised herself not to do. It would mean a frightening degree of contamination.

Julia was the first to break up that night's meeting. 'I don't know about you guys, but I am *wiped*. It's really good for me to concentrate on this kind of thing and not be thinking about Matt and the kids, but it takes it out of me in a different way.'

'Things you aren't used to are usually exhausting,' Flo suggested. She had enjoyed the discussion and had been interested in the dimension Serena brought to the group. 'Personally, I find knocking up scrambled eggs for one far more tiring.'

Julia's small laugh acknowledged her renowned excellence as a cook. Since she and Matt had been together, she had made it part of their USP that she did the cooking for their many dinner parties herself. She had a special fondness for dishes that were served individually, in the earthenware ramekins she'd had shipped over from her mother's house in West Virginia (all four dozen of them), or the china shells that daintily housed the seafood Matt loved.

There was the usual protracted huddle in the hallway as everyone got ready to depart. Katherine stood in the door and watched as Serena walked to her driver, who was waiting in the Range Rover outside. Flo was still in the living room and had just poured herself another glass of wine when Katherine returned. 'That was fun,' she said, cramming a handful of the remaining kale chips into her mouth. 'I like Serena. But did you see how Julia came down on her? I don't know what that was about.'

'Oh, it's probably insecurity of some kind.' Katherine sighed with exasperation. 'Julia has come to London and got to know everyone and she doesn't really want another new kid on the block. It's just like school.'

'That old territorial imperative. A basic instinct. Like sex. Although I don't know how basic the sex bit is.' Flo fiddled with her hair, winding it up into a doughnut. 'I certainly haven't been experiencing much of an instinct in that area for a while.'

Katherine considered her next words. She couldn't remember ever having kept a secret from Flo, and she completely trusted her, which was made easier – and she knew this wasn't entirely fair – since Flo was single. When Flo confided in Katherine she could never be absolutely sure Katherine wouldn't share the information with Rick. The flip side was that Flo was proud of her role as gatekeeper and experienced real hurt if she was for some reason shut out.

'But do you really care about sex, really yearn for it, unless there is someone you want to do it with?' Katherine asked, pushing the sleeve of her jumper up to her elbow then pulling it back down and fiddling with the alignment of the cuff. 'I'm not sure I experience free-floating desire. That's what is so amazing when you meet somebody new.'

It came out in a rush, Katherine stumbling as she spoke, but once she had begun she had to get to the end. 'The thing is . . . Look. I know this is insane, but I'm having an . . . well, I don't know quite what . . . with Teo. This doesn't mean anything about my life with Rick. It's just something completely else, and it's going to finish and I'm going to look back on it and think it was lovely and mad. I know it will have to end. But not quite yet. When I'm with him . . . it's hard to explain, but I feel the best of me.'

Flo heard Katherine and saw her face with its silly yet unaffectedly delighted smile and almost immediately heard the words from Olga's conversation in the empty rooms of Drayton. 'Have you missed me? . . . Oh Ricky! . . . I have a little present for you.' Katherine obviously knew nothing about it. During university they had sat on her bedroom floor, the smell of the chip shop coming up from below, while a boy whose parents had just broken up told them that it was better now they all knew what was going on. It was the lying, he claimed, that had been the worst thing, the continual suspicion of their father's deception. He and his sister were never sure their father was telling the truth about where he was or who he was with, but the more likely it became that he was cheating, the more it appeared that their mother wanted to convince them otherwise. It had been sickening to watch.

Flo took a large mouthful of wine and lit a cigarette. She thought briefly of sharing what she had overheard at Drayton, now that her friend had revealed her own entanglement. But she didn't. Maybe it was the thought of Olga's fury if she discovered it was her who told. Maybe it was not wanting to muddy Katherine's excitement. Or maybe it was simply to keep herself out of the firing line from any of them. Don't kill the messenger. There was always an argument for waiting and seeing what would happen. After all, she could have got it wrong.

'He obviously makes you feel somewhere between Madonna and Jennifer Lawrence! But it must be strange. Do you talk about it with each other?'

'Kind of you not to bring up Demi and Ashton,' Katherine continued, smiling. 'You're asking why he wants to shag an old hag like me?' Flo couldn't judge whether that was a genuine question or said for effect. 'Funnily enough, no, we don't discuss it. I couldn't tell you why. But he's gorgeous. What can I say? He's made me feel so much more confident about my body. It's an unexpected gift to be handed when you're our age.' Katherine walked to the far end of the room, closing the shutters against the dark. 'Sometimes I think about how these men get together with young girls and, although we think it's a bit pathetic, we accept it. We tell ourselves they want a piece of that young flesh but we also know the babe's a talisman, warding off mortality. I can tell you it's not like that with me and Teo. He's not staving off old age. If anything, he's made me more able to accept what I am. I guess if he likes my body, then I should. And it's not only the sex. It's just being with him. I can't pretend we have a great deal in common – pretty much nothing – but it doesn't seem to matter.'

'What about Antonella? Does she know?'

'I'm not sure.' Katherine walked over to the fireplace, where the gas flames licked the expensive tableau of fake logs and ashes, and turned to her friend with a smile. 'I know this is bad . . . but Rick's away and it's one of my only opportunities to spend the night with him . . .'

'Sure. I'll be off.' Flo gathered her things together.

'No – I don't mean you have to rush out immediately.' Katherine walked over to her to give her a hug. And both of them knew that wasn't the truth. 'Do you think I'm awful?'

'No,' Flo said, 'but I think you're heading for a right car crash, and nothing I say is going to change that.' She hugged Katherine back before leaving.

The street was silent, but as she left the front garden a cat rushed out from under the hedge and nearly tripped her up. She followed it towards the main road, where the multiplex was tipping out the evening viewers, and joined them in the queue for her bus home. The couple behind her were disagreeing noisily about the film they'd just seen. 'That's the last time I'm letting you choose. I don't need to pay to spend two hours wanting to slit my throat,' a burly man announced to the faded woman in a red anorak next to him. 'Well, you'd seen the trailer,' she defended herself. 'I thought you knew what it was about.'

The room looked completely different from the vantage point of the bed where she and Teo now lay. It had been the nanny's room – well, au pair, really. Sometimes, Katherine felt guilty because she was there in the house paying another person to fry up breaded chicken breasts for tea and listen to Josh's initial daily download, but Rick had thought it was a ludicrous idea not to have help.

Katherine had never before lain on the small double where Kristina, and then Pola, had slept, on the same floor as Josh. It was like being in somebody else's home, hearing the faint noise of traffic drifting from the main road rather than the sounds from the garden side, where their own room was.

The next day she had a deadline. Some friends were hosting an anniversary weekend in Majorca in a month and were giving all the guests a candle with their names and the couple's and the date of the anniversary etched into the thick wax in Katherine's swirl of copperplate. 'We might as well burn through the years in style,' the hostess had said, ordering twenty-four. It was a simple job, but she still had half of them to complete.

Taking up the invitation had seemed like a treat when they had received it just before Christmas, but as she lay with Teo's arm around her shoulder and falling across her breasts, its shape so different to Rick's familiar heft, the prospect had lost much of its original appeal. A night such as this, when they had had sex for so long she was in a trancey state, not clear about the beginning or the end, was utterly addictive. It was never enough. Now her heart sank at the thought of three days of shared reminiscences, hearty laughter and relentless anecdotes as she and Teo lay, speaking little, the smoke of Teo's cigarette in a delicate coil above.

It was true that Rick wasn't at his best on morning-afters. Ideally, he liked a quick blast of sex, a shower, a hit of coffee and then to get on with the day. The long-lingering lie-in with affectionate pillow chat was not his thing at all. But this morning was different, after the considerable effort he had made to entice Olga to Paris, to this room with a view over the Tuileries and the fairground wheel on the rue de Rivoli.

He hadn't yet discovered who had sent the ridiculous but, all the same, disturbing pictures, which he still had on his phone. It would be simple just to delete them but he realized that he would need them at some point to confront the sender. It had certainly taken time but, eventually, he had persuaded Olga that he was close to cracking the mystery and, in the meantime, had managed to lure her to Paris with a rare tour of one of the best private collections. After that evening in the club, where it had become clear that Olga was terrified of Alexander discovering their affair, he knew the end-game was approaching.

They had met outside the pale stone *hôtel particulier* that housed the collection, the presence of Pascal, the sallow-skinned curator in his pale-grey suit, allowing them only an appropriate client-to-gallerist air kiss. It had been the first time Rick had seen Olga since the Weitzmans' dinner and now almost four months since he'd been able to touch her, so just her presence by his side filled him with anticipation of the hours ahead.

Pascal had been eager to demonstrate the depth of his knowledge and spoke in a fast French which Olga understood perfectly, while Rick – decidedly less fluent – missed some of the finer points as they made their way through the series of perfectly proportioned rooms. Once their tour was finished Pascal walked them out to the courtyard, where Olga's driver was parked. He got out of the car and retrieved her small bag from the boot before driving away through the giant gates bordering the narrow street.

'Why did you get rid of the car?' Rick asked, taking her arm and rubbing his hand along it.

'It seemed more discreet. I imagine we are now going to a hotel?' Olga said, with neither excitement nor disapproval.

'That's what I had in mind . . . if it's okay with you.' Rick spoke with schoolboy eagerness, suddenly filled with a surge of general appreciation – for the towering elegance of the Hausmann boule-vards, for the brighter light of a spring afternoon, for the certainty of the sex to come as he walked through Paris with this beautiful woman. He had been about to share some of this with her when he felt her pull away, her attention caught by a man walking towards them while talking into a mouthpiece dangling on his shirt. He waved at them just as he finished his call and Olga introduced Rick to Leonid, mentioning their visit to the collection – spectacular, unquestionably – but leaving it at that. They parted quickly and only a couple of minutes later she and Rick reached the hotel. Rick had the key in his pocket, having checked into their room earlier that day.

Now, he poured himself another cup of coffee and waited for Olga to finish showering. He liked to see her with her hair dripping and combed back into a sleek hood. They were going to leave Paris separately, as they had arrived, him grabbing a cab on the street and catching the train back to London, while she wanted to do some shopping and would get the helicopter to pick her up.

'What time is your train?' Olga asked when she emerged, looking exactly as he had imagined.

'I'll just jump on one when I arrive at Gare du Nord. I've got a lunch, so I'm good as long as I get on before eleven, I suppose.'

He watched Olga dress: a turquoise bra and knickers, a pair of trousers with a jazzy print and a white shirt. It only took a minute all in, then she wound her hair into a small bun and packed her clothes efficiently into a leather bag.

'So, that's it,' she said.

'Hang on, darling. Don't you want a coffee or something?' Rick might have wanted to get on with his day, but that didn't mean he wouldn't have liked Olga to be a little less keen on rushing out.

'No. No coffee for me.' Olga pulled on a navy jacket, considering herself in the wardrobe mirror as she spoke, Rick reflected behind her. 'Rick' – she spoke to the reflection – 'what I mean is that this is it, for us. It has been great – our time together. But we must stop now.'

Rick was watching her expression in the mirror, resisting the urge to shout at her to turn around. 'Why? Is it those pictures?'

'It's not only them, although they are certainly a problem. I consider them a warning shot. Clumsy perhaps, but still effective.' She shrugged, adjusting the collar of her shirt then turning to face him. 'But, more than that, it's just the time. It's important to know when something should end. For me, at least. A good ending is just as important as a good beginning and Ricky, please. Let us have a good ending.'

'So why did you come here with me to Paris? What are we doing here?' Rick asked, gesturing at the large hotel room, the bed a chaos of linen and towels. 'If you were going to dump me, why not do it in Mayfair? I don't understand.'

'I thought it was better this way.' Olga moved a little towards him. 'Perhaps that was wrong. But I have been very fond of you. I liked the idea that we would have a great last night. And we did.' Her voice softened briefly before reasserting its flat purpose. 'Surely you can see that we have to end. It couldn't last for ever.'

'I see. And perhaps you could tell me now – is this also about the child you are trying to have?' Rick heard himself say it, sullen, unattractive, angry; the last person she would wish to be with, and behaving in the way women had on the many occasions when it had been him telling them it was over. He knew just how much he wanted them to disappear at that point. How much easier it was to breathe when they had left.

'You mean, about Alexander wanting a child?' Olga shrugged. 'Perhaps. You heard that?'

'He told Katherine. At the Weitzmans'. He said you were trying. I was shocked by how much I minded when I heard but, obviously, I couldn't show that to my wife. I really hadn't expected it. And, of course, then I didn't know how you were going to manage it . . . you know, sleeping with both of us. It was something I was going to ask you about when I got round to it,' he finished, hopelessly.

'So your wife told you? Aha. Yes. Alexander likes to picture our children at Drayton. It's part of the purpose of the house. When I met you last year, in Venice, I knew a child was next for my marriage, and I guess I took the opportunity of you. Like a last fling, you might say. My life has made it hard for me to believe that anything will be for ever and a way I have survived is to grasp chances

191

when they come. But a child? I do know that is for ever. That will be the real change,' Olga explained, leaving no doubt of the seriousness of her intention. 'I probably surprise you with this way of thinking.'

'I'm not sure it's a surprise, or whether I understand you. But I don't suppose it really matters. If you want to go, you go. I will say this, though: we've had good times together but I never intended you to compete with Katherine or our marriage. I trust in that to the last, and so does Katherine. She heard you on the speaker in the car the other day and said something about you, but I think – and I truly hope – that she has no idea about this. About us. She thinks the best of me, does Katherine.'

'That is as it should be, and it's why we must end it here. We can be the best of ourselves, still.' Accepting Rick's wounded tirade for what it was, Olga collected her bag and walked over to where he sat by the window, his hexagon-patterned tie on the table in front of him. As she bent to kiss his head he saw the same smooth expanse of tanned skin under her shirt he had seen at that first dinner in Venice. When she left the room he noticed that she had left behind the bra she had worn last night, thrown at the foot of the bed. He picked it up and crumpled it into a ball before tossing it with a deliberate aim into the bin across the room.

# Chapter Fifteen

Some days the airport at Palma was littered with private jets perched on the tarmac, alighting like dragonflies before hopping off to the next destination. The Fosters' weekend party walked from one that had been chartered for the occasion into the special arrivals hall past a family waiting to depart. 'Bruno, if you don't behave, you're gonna have to fly *commercial*,' an exasperated young mother shouted across the room to her small son, who was taunting his younger sister.

Only Philip and Mimi Jones (flying in that night on their own Gulfstream) hadn't boarded the plane from London, and the guests were now piling into the minibus, in which the soft leather seats failed to negate the smell of sickly peach air freshener. Despite the age of the group there was the same chaotic indecision about seating as on any school trip; the same hovering anxiety about being stuck for the journey, no matter how brief, next to the class bore or someone you had never liked. Finally, the driver had to call his privileged cargo to order and announce that they were about to leave. The automatic doors slid to a close.

Katherine was seated next to their host, Tim Foster, whom she had known since they were at university, and well before he had made his substantial fortune in Hong Kong. He was an example of life's roll of the dice. Always amiable, and often drunk, Tim had snuck in a 2:1 in Theology and had never given anybody the slightest reason to believe that, thirty years later, he would be wealthy enough to own a Leopard 34 berthed in Bermuda and a house on one of Chelsea's most expensive streets. He'd slowed down at fifty to a well-managed and massively lucrative portfolio life. It was a joke among his friends that he had recently been appointed a trustee of the V&A, given that he had never shown the slightest interest in any form of culture. He put it down to the fact that, although the board would have preferred a woman or, better still, a woman from an ethnic minority, he at least wasn't Oxbridge. And he came with the distinct advantages of his own healthy bank balance and a contact list stuffed with others who had the same. Arty stuff was his wife Lucy's area, he explained with the appealing bonhomie he had carried around since childhood. 'I don't know my Monet from my Manet, but Lu's terribly good on all that stuff. She could do *Mastermind* on that blood-head bloke.'

When they arrived, steel gates slid apart to let the coach continue along a smooth drive.

'We came to a party here a couple of years back, and I said to Lu then, "Problem solved. This is the place for our twentieth,"' Tim remarked, as a large stone house came into view, set into a terrace of olive groves and cypress trees. To the right was a spectacular view of the sparkling Mediterranean below, and ahead a dramatic rocky range of mountains. 'We've been pretty blessed, all things considered, and I wanted to share it with you guys.'

Katherine and Rick had been allocated one of several cottages in the finca's property. Stone paths meandered through orange and lemon trees and oleander bushes. As soon as they were left alone at the cottage with their luggage, Katherine opened the glass door and walked out on to the private terrace, slipping off an espadrille to dip a toe into a personal plunge pool. Above, the sky was a dense blue, broken only by a flock of black buzzards that swept over the house, sharing the space with the glint of a plane many thousand feet higher.

The tone of the party had been established from the first moments they gathered at Northolt, the men set on a course of jovial banter and playful competition, the women sharing faux despair with their menfolk and unimportant confidences. Lucy had revealed that yesterday's Brazilian wax had 'left me, literally, scarred for life. Tim screamed when he saw me last night,' while Tim loudly teased Johnny Beaumont about the big money he had come into now his agency had been bought up by an American conglomerate.

'You're just like one of those mystery oligarchs springing up out of nowhere. You know you never ask those Russians where they got that first million.' Tim grinned, baring his newly whitened teeth, as he mobbed his friend's new riches.

'What do you think for lunch? Should I wear these?' Rick waved a pair of cheerful trunks with a flamingo pattern in Katherine's direction. 'Or are we dressing down?' In his other hand were the regulation khaki combat shorts worn by all in his peer group.

'Live wild. I would,' Katherine replied, gesturing at the tropical trunks, which, with their expensive, noisy print, signified a whole lifestyle. How many men at the party would this very moment be unpacking the same brand, worn around the same pools, from Mauritius and St Barths to Saint Tropez and Mykonos? As she pulled her own swimwear out of the case, she briefly imagined how Teo would look on holiday, his honey-toned legs with their long thighs, straight calves and the sharp bone of his ankles. She shook the image of him away. She had promised herself that she wouldn't think of him this weekend and would enjoy Rick in all his Rickness – possibly, in a certain way, more than she might have done before.

'It's beautiful here, isn't it? I guess the villa is a permanent rental. It certainly isn't a home, judging by this room,' Katherine said. The room was impersonal: a glass-topped coffee table, a plantation lounger in the corner, a ceiling fan that whirred decoratively above the king-size bed as a supplement to the air conditioning. 'I can't believe it's twenty years since Lucy and Tim were married. But of course it must be, because I was just pregnant with Josh.'

Rick was flicking through a leaflet he had picked up from the small desk. It had lain beside the candle with Katherine's writing on it: 'Rick and Katherine' in the middle and, around the base, 'Tim and Lucy Foster', and the month and year.

'They've given us the itinerary for the weekend. I can't decide whether I want to read it or let it all just happen.'

'I think let's just leave it for now,' Katherine suggested. 'I'm keen to look around the place.'

Rick put the leaflet back down. 'It used to be the Germans that owned the island, but I gather the Russians have bought in big time.'

'Like everywhere. Did Olga tell you that?' Katherine asked, pinching the flesh on her upper arm to check how quickly it bounced back in a mildly interested manner, and unaware of the effect of those words on her husband.

'Maybe. I don't remember. Actually, I don't think so. It was somebody recently. Anyway . . .' Rick moved towards the door in an effort to disguise the discomfort the mention of Olga's name had produced in him. 'Come on. Let's go for lunch. I'm starving.' Katherine followed his flamingo-clad behind, the waistband of his trunks falling slightly below its designated level, emphasizing the paunch that had grown a little more evident since they had last been worn.

Whoever had organized the weekend – and Katherine had correctly guessed that Lucy had used one of London's concierge services – had worked on the assumption that there should be no chink where boredom might sneak in. A tennis ladder was set up from the first afternoon and scheduled to end before lunch on the Sunday. Chess and backgammon boards could be found on small tables throughout the house. The cinema housed in the old olive press in the centre of the garden was primed with a selection of old and new favourites – *Usual Suspects*, *American Hustle*, *Rear Window* – while the televisions in each room offered airline-style entertainment from comedy episodes to video games. There were excursions planned on land and sea.

By the second day, the more relaxed were able to read, chat purposelessly, rise late and pad gently around the grounds, while others clutched their laptops like blankies or paced in a corner muttering into mobiles. For the first night's dinner they had travelled a short distance to a restaurant overlooking the sea, returning late to lethal nightcaps and a determination to show each other that they were young enough still to go for it. Leaving several guests dancing to the previous summer's Daft Punk, Katherine and Rick had returned to their room and made love in a committed manner, making the effort to arouse each other slowly and show they were not doing it by numbers. Neither wanted the other to get any sense of their lack of desire. Helped by the unfamiliar room, the brandy, the scent from the jasmine that climbed around the door and a shared desperation to prove to themselves that they were still the couple they once had been, they succeeded well enough and eventually fell asleep in each other's arms.

The next morning Katherine took a walk alone. The air was clear and warm as she negotiated one of the tracks along the mountain. The terraces gave way to wilder territory of gorse, rosemary and broom, which snapped underfoot. Catching a scent, she stopped. She couldn't work out which plant it came from and bent down to pull off a selection of leaves and rub them between her fingers to try and identify the smell that transplanted her back to the days when she, her father and Cindy would hike – as Cindy called it – in the surrounding canyons. She remembered how her father had looked at Cindy with such delight as she strode along in sturdy walking boots, her long brown legs in wide khaki shorts, her hair bobbing in its ponytail. He'd noticed his daughter's expression. 'Such a wonderful thing to be given a second chance,' he had explained, rubbing his daughter's bare shoulder fondly. 'She's like a transfusion.' His joy in Cindy's energy and prettiness made sense. Cindy knew how to make them all feel good.

Early that evening a posse broke off the schedule to visit the local bar, famous in its long-gone heyday as the place that *everyone* would hang out. 'Everyone' was the glorious mix of locals and likeable crims, knowing travellers and sussed ex-pats, Leonard Cohen and Joni, Ginsberg and Corso, which anecdote relates as frequenters of such bars throughout the world. And that same 'everyone', who appeared at the time to be intense and questioning, filled with a passion for discussing ideas and debating all night long and well into sunrise, were never going to be trapped into mortgages, serviceable marriages and the whole money thing. Certainly they were never going to be people like Rick and Katherine Tennison, or Tim and Lucy Foster, or Johnny Beaumont, slung around with materialistic concerns and having to pay lip service to people they didn't give a shit about.

And it was indeed the case that some of the clientele had kept the faith and were still sat there in the bar that evening. Zapata moustaches were now a tobacco-stained white, flip flops had been exchanged for padded, soled sandals, but women still wore their hair in the same rock-chick layers, the same hennaed tint, as when they had first sat at those same tables five decades back. Johnny Beaumont had bossily commandeered a corner under a string of coloured bulbs, and the group was buzzing with a chatty excitement over their departure from the itinerary, as if they had escaped prep.

Katherine touched the potted plant on the table, to discover that the glossy dark leaves were sticky plastic, and saw Rick looking at the posters and notices stuck on the wall at the other side of the terrace. She crossed over, swatting a wasp away, and placed a hand on his shoulder.

'Christ. Some of these look like they've also been here since the sixties,' she said. 'Incredible.'

'Look at the dates, though. They just have that *charming* patina of age.'

'Just like us, you mean.' Katherine leant against him.

'Hi.' A man in loose trousers and a white polo shirt was approaching. Katherine recognized Rick's expression as one that meant he had no idea who the guy was but was going to give him the benefit of the doubt. The newcomer pushed his sunglasses up on to his head and held out a hand.

'Leonid,' the man continued, smiling amiably at the pair. 'We met in Paris. With Olga Oblomovik,' he clarified. 'I think you had just been viewing that wonderful private collection. I must call her and find out how you managed to get inside. Or perhaps it was your arrangement?'

Later, when Katherine looked back, it was a poster of a flamenco festival in Palma featuring black-and-white head shots of the performers and the clattering of several silver bracelets on the man's wrist as he held out his hand to her that she remembered as keenly as his words.

She felt a little buzzy, disorientated, and she didn't want to look at Rick or hear what he was saying. Shreds of information that had floated around the periphery of her understanding – the card on the floor of the gallery; the familiar 'Ricky' on the speakerphone in the car; the distanced tone Rick used when he mentioned Olga – all joined together, making her feel, above all, stupid. Leonid remained chatting for a few minutes, but she moved away, although not immediately back to their table, where Johnny's loud laugh was bouncing off the wall, but to a spot where she could lean over the railing and look across at the houses climbing up the small hill opposite. The bell of the church on the corner tolled the hour.

It took only seconds for her to acknowledge that the shock of the discovery of Rick's infidelity was far less dominant than the feeling of relief. It was okay. She was absolved. Rick had no doubt been in Paris with Olga (not in Vienna for work) at exactly the same time she and Teo had been in the au pair's room having the long, slow sex that had left her molten.

On the road below a group of kids, probably about Josh's age, were returning from the beach below, towels slung over their sticky shoulders. So Rick was having an affair as well. Clearly, none of this was okay. They had totally lost the map. And any minute now she was going to have to go back to the house party, to another two days in their room in the orange grove, with this knowledge. Was Rick better in bed with Olga? He must be doing something he didn't do with her. And Rick would obviously be freaking about what he was going to say to her. But maybe she could act as if she hadn't taken it in for now, not until she knew what to do and they weren't stuck together in Majorca, where it would be hell if they went into the whole thing. And what was the whole thing, anyway? Where did you start?

'Would you like a glass?' Rick offered. There was a bottle of wine sticking out of a Perspex ice bucket on the coffee table when they returned to their room after the bar.

'Would you?' Katherine replied, shivering from the blast of air conditioning that had chilled the room.

'Well, we could.' Rick examined the label.

'Yes, we could, I suppose. Sure.'

'Why don't we, then?' The exchange was at least staving off the inevitable, Rick thought, pulling the cork out slowly, turning around in the expectation of seeing Katherine, her face set and sad, but she had left the room and he could hear water running. He considered taking her glass into the bathroom but decided against it and instead shouted, 'It's here when you're ready.'

He sat on one of the loungers by the small pool. On the terraces below there were ranks of olive trees and a sheep's bell tinkled.

The wine went down easily, and he quickly refilled his glass, cold drips of iced water landing on his bare knees. That meeting with the Russian guy had been unbelievably crap timing. Of all the bars in all the world. He'd been having a great time with Katherine on this trip. A lot of laughs. Watching her earlier that day, he had thought how good she looked. She hadn't fallen victim to remodelling her face like some of the other women there – they had mouths like guppy fish and the eyes of a Pixar child. And she wasn't, and never had been, bored or whining or needy.

Until now, he had prided himself on managing his infidelities, if that was the word. He had never allowed either himself or any of the girls he was involved with to be under any illusion that the relationship was anything more than it was. Of course, they were *something*, but they weren't even the slightest threat to Katherine. When he considered Olga, with that beauty that surprised him every time, and her deep flat voice, which made you want to provoke some expression in it, the way her eyes would slide off centre during sex and the smile that, sometimes, she would make you fight for, he had to admit he had fallen in deep – but, even then, he had been waving not drowning.

Paris had been a shock, and it was still hurting. He wasn't so thick that he didn't understand that part of the pain was because it was she who had ended it, conclusively, with no maybes or taking-a-breaks, no question of a reunion. She had just fucked off. It was unreal that Katherine should have to have learnt about it now, when it was so over.

Some guy had driven them back to the finca, taking the corners with a terrifying lack of concern about the drop down the cliff on one side. Johnny and Tim had kept up a running commentary, and he'd never been more grateful for their gabby camaraderie as Katherine sat silently by his side staring out of the window. Now she was in the shower, where no doubt she was figuring out what to say. As was he.

By the time Katherine joined Rick on the terrace the sun had shifted to daub the view of the hillside opposite with a mellow light. He braced himself for the expected onslaught but instead Katherine bent over her feet, checking her toenails, which were painted a peachy pink.

'Do you think Tim and Lucy are enjoying themselves?' she asked, without looking up.

Rick was so thrown by the lack of accusation or interrogation, the deliberate non-sequitur and lack of engagement in her discovery of his betrayal, that he was silent.

'Are you kidding?' he finally managed. 'There is nothing – *nothing* – that Tim enjoys more than hanging out with his friends and showing us how much better than us he's done.'

'We've all got so much, though, haven't we? It's all ours to lose, right?' Katherine pointed at the moon, a pale smudge in the sky. 'The moon and sun out at the same time. That always seems so strange. I always feel they're competing, even though you know which one's going to win.'

Through the thin green fabric of her kaftan Rick could see the outline of her legs, every inch of them so familiar to him but, even so, the woman standing there with her feet apart, looking at the sky, was distant and formidable. He would have liked to tell her that none of this mattered and that the affair with Olga was over. He would reassure her that he loved her, which was nothing but the truth, and Katherine, in the interests of everything that their life was and could be, would allow him to convince her. But he didn't know how to raise the subject safely. He knew Katherine preferred to avoid confrontation, but he doubted she would have steered completely clear of any mention of what had happened unless she had a reason. Despite the chilled wine, his mouth was dry as he went to dress for dinner.

Under the bridge a man paddled a white surfboard along the canal, past the geese lined up like horses at the starting gate, past a moored barge with a bicycle and a sack of cat food on the roof. Flo attempted a brisk pace so that the walk from her flat to the market could be categorized as exercise. How often had she read that the heart rate needed to be raised for at least thirty minutes every day but that gentle exercise could achieve it? Gentle sounded good – no pounding in the smelly gym. So that was what she was aiming for. A racing heart by the time she got to the market and then she could have a cheese croissant and milky coffee, which would undo all she'd achieved.

For years she had visited a small shop just around the corner from the main market stalls where second-hand books were piled on to shelves that threatened to collapse with a single addition. But one day it had disappeared, replaced by a shop where expensive jumpers and leather backpacks hung in the windows and scented soaps and decorative notebooks were piled on the tables inside, and she had shifted her interest to a collection of trestle tables deeper into the market.

For the past four months, ever since she'd sent over her finished work on Drayton and received an email acknowledgement from Olga's assistant, Flo had returned to working on her own book. She'd redrafted the chapter outline and realized that she was missing a section on the concept of relaxation, but was saved from having to confront the possibility of writing it by being given a research commission for a well-known and prolific historian.

She didn't like to admit how hurt she was by Olga's rejection. It made her feel foolish to think that she had imagined she might ever have been anything more than another hired gun. The splendidly wrapped Saint Laurent handbag delivered by the driver just before Christmas, the sports masseur Olga had sent round when some daft yoga stretch had put her back out, even the discussion they had in the New Year about whether Flo should experiment with highlights, all had convinced her that she had a more intimate relationship with this exotic creature than simply that of employee.

Of course, she could never prove that the change in Olga's behaviour had occurred the instant she sensed that Flo had overheard her conversation with 'Ricky', but that only confirmed what Flo might otherwise have merely suspected. In some ways, Olga cutting her off was easier. She didn't want to be around the woman if she was having a scene with Rick and, though this was perhaps faintly mitigated by Katherine's confession, Flo had had it up to here, really, with all of them. Whenever Katherine spoke of Teo, Flo was tempted to tell her of her suspicions about Rick, but at the last moment she bottled. Rick's marriage to her best friend was a constant in her life. She had a proprietorial interest in its survival, and being the wise monkey at the centre of these events was not the best way to ensure it.

By the Moroccan fish stall she stopped to dig in her bag for a pair of sunglasses. Like her skin, her eyes had not, apparently, been designed with sun in mind. She was about to continue when she saw Antonella and Teo seated outside the café just ahead of her. It wasn't particularly surprising. Over time, she had learnt that London's huge spread was divided into villages, socially and geographically, and after twenty-odd years living there she had made her own map of places, routes and memories, where, more often than not, she would find others she knew. This distillation of the vast capital was surely why it was possible to exist alongside so many strangers, so many people leading their own lives on different tracks.

The pair were, as usual, wearing black, Teo stretching his legs well beyond the territory of their small table, Antonella leaning back on the striped café chair and smoking. She waved at Flo, who was about to cross the road to avoid them, shouting, 'Flo! Come!' When she did, Antonella jumped up, wrapping her arms around Flo's neck in a bony embrace.

There was a glass pot of mint tea on the table. Antonella grabbed a waiter as he passed. 'We would like another of these, and a glass,' she said, while Teo produced a third chair.

'So have you bought anything? We love this market. When we were children we once came to it – the other end, with our parents – and they bought us gifts. Teo, you remember? I had a doll, all in lace with her knickers and chemises, and Teo, what did you get?' Before he answered, Antonella remembered. 'It was an old camera. I think it was a Rolleiflex. You looked into it from the top and you saw out in front. We were fascinated by that.'

Teo added, 'Yes. You wanted the camera, too. You wanted the doll *and* a camera like mine. Nothing has changed, yes?'

Flo pointed across the way. 'You can get the strangest stuff here, can't you? I come to look for books, but often I end up with something I neither want nor need. Really, like you, I just love the place, especially on a day like today.' She sipped the tea, which wasn't sweet enough for her taste. 'So, you've been spending time with Josh? He's my godson.'

'We love Josh. He is so sweet – like a little mouse that runs around.' Antonella ran her fingers along the metal table, enjoying the sound and repeating it, her nails so bitten that they made a padding noise eerily similar to that of a trapped mouse. 'You can play with him. He's super-fun.'

'I don't think he'd like you to think of him as a mouse. I get the feeling he has something else in mind. Nothing mousey,' Flo replied.

'But he is an adorable mouse.' She peered at Flo. 'The lipstick you wear? What is the colour? Can I try?'

'Sure. But you don't wear lipstick.'

'No. But maybe I change. Let me see.' Antonella held out her hand to Flo, who, mildly amused, handed over the fluted gold case. Antonella picked up a knife to use as a mirror, tracing the outside of her lips in the deep cherry colour before filling them in and smudging them together as a finish. She turned to the others for comment.

'You look grotesque,' Teo said factually. 'Like something out of the Commedia dell'Morte.'

And it was true that the dark colour on Antonella looked more macabre than attractive. Finding nothing at hand to clean off the lipstick, Antonella headed to the bathroom, her baggy black dungarees emphasizing her skinniness, as did the heavy Doc Martens on her feet.

That meeting was when Flo really understood what might have attracted Katherine to Teo. As she sat there with the pair, she was behind the glass rather than pressing her nose against the window of their edgy intensity. They could still be anyone, do anything; they weren't set hard, like so many of her contemporaries. Even Antonella's childish playfulness was appealing this afternoon. They could make you want a part of that. Not just to be included, but to be. Was that what Katherine found in Teo?

For a moment she thought of the darker planes of the young man shifting above Katherine's long, pale body. Did he know, and would he care, that she knew?

On her return from the bathroom, her lips still stained with the dark colour, Antonella insisted that they accompany Flo deeper into the market. As they walked she chattered relentlessly, even asking Flo the occasional question: Where did she live? Had she read *The Goldfinch* – incredible, no? Did she have a man? Teo was more silent beside her, checking his mobile constantly and occasionally breaking into a laugh, but allowing his sister to rattle on with no need to compete with or add to her conversation.

When they reached Flo's favourite stall, the owner, wearing his usual wool beanie despite the warmth of the afternoon, nodded in greeting. Although she was a regular visitor they only exchanged minimal conversation. She preferred to browse without someone hanging over her and he left her alone, occasionally attempting harder sells on other passers-by. There were several of the same hardbacks on display as when she had last been there – a first edition of Margaret Drabble's *The Millstone*, a book-club edition of *Lucky Jim*, thick plastic wrapping preserving their decorative jackets. She was interested in looking through a pile of floppy, green-covered vintage Penguins, and was about to tell the others to go on ahead without her, when she noticed what was happening.

The road was crowded with stalls and visitors but the pavements on either side were emptier. Teo was pinned against the angry graffiti on a brick wall by a screaming Antonella, her face inches from his. All the affectionate amiability between them had vanished, replaced by her wailing frenzy. Although Teo could easily have pushed her away, he first made an effort to escape without hurting her, but she knocked him back against the wall, scraping his head against the brick. Until that point it had looked as if he was just going to ride it out and wait for the tantrum to pass, but then he grabbed one of her arms, holding it up in the air as she tried to wriggle free. 'It's enough, Antonella!' he yelled, prolonging each word. 'I *have enough* of this!'

'Oh yeah? For sure you have enough. So do I. I have enough of this relationship with a woman who could be your mother. Even when we are out now you are . . .' And with her loose arm she mimed him jabbing on the phone with a moronic stare. 'When did it become that you had to be stuck to her like this? All the time?'

Teo let her go and she fell to the pavement. He marched away without looking back, quickly lost in the human river. The argument had been watched by the bookseller and a woman seated in the side door of his van, who kept up an amused commentary throughout, as if they were on *Gogglebox*.

Flo ran up to Antonella and crouched beside her. She could see the flickers of fury giving way to hurt. She didn't like the girl – not this spoilt, crazed, self-obsessed side of her, at any rate – but she could scarcely just walk away and leave her like this. She pulled her up, feeling how insubstantial she was. Once upright, Antonella leant against the wall and lit a cigarette, calm returning as quickly as the earlier storm had gathered, her anger exchanged for dull contemplation.

'You know, I love Teo. He is my centre. When he shifts I am thrown – what is the word – off the, in Italian it is . . .'

'Axis, probably,' Flo suggested.

'Did you know about this affair?'

Flo pulled her own packet of cigarettes out, lighting one and taking a couple of short drags as she considered whether to admit that she did would further incriminate Katherine in some way. Given Antonella's warped mind, it was almost certainly better neither to admit nor deny. She attempted a quick, casual shrug, about to move on to another topic and get away.

But Antonella wanted to talk. 'Everybody is the same. They are all fucking around. To start with, I thought she was just dull and maybe bored with the marriage and so Teo fucks her and it's some kind of therapy. No problem. She has that husband who is obsessed with Olga – good luck to him.' She swiped a piece of dirt off a strap of her dungarees. 'I was amused by it all. It was fine. But now Teo. He has changed. I feel I am losing him.'

'Don't be so stupid. Of course you're not losing Teo. I've never known a pair so close. The Velcro kids.' Flo could see a couple at the next stall deciding whether to buy a maimed Ercol table. 'But you should look at why you behave like this, Antonella. You just went mental. I suppose Teo's used to you turning like that, but I think you have a problem. Anyway' – she hitched her canvas bag up to a more secure slot on her shoulder – 'I have to be getting on.' Flo hoped that if she made her escape quick enough it would prevent Antonella from talking more about Katherine. This was a scene too many. She was leaving them all to it to work it out for themselves. It was time to get her head back down. At least Josh had been kept out of the mess her friends were making of their lives. Who was acting the teenager in all this?

# Chapter Sixteen

*June*

It was one of those rare London evenings when the heat that had accumulated through the day gave the city's occupants an opportunity to pretend that they didn't live on some island in the North Sea protected only from the climate of Iceland by the fortunate currents of the Gulf Stream. The summer was still young enough for warmth to be a much-appreciated favour bestowed by a benevolent weather system rather than a rightful due. In a month's time, if the days were grey and damp, all conversation would inevitably return to the question of whether summer was going to be as epically bad as last year and, if it was hot, the very same people would complain of poor sleep and how their gardens had become the Kalahari. But tonight the temperature was delightful, and Rick and Josh were fortunate enough to grab the last table on the pavement outside their local pizza place.

Rick ordered his usual Quattro Stagione with extra pepperoni and Josh his usual American and a side of garlic bread, although ritual dictated that they read the menu thoroughly before finally revealing their choice.

'If you want some, why don't you order your own?' Josh asked his father, as Rick leant over to tear off a piece from the bread on his plate.

'We can always have another one. What's the big deal? I don't get why it annoys you so much.' Rick gestured at one of the waiters a few tables away for another portion of garlic bread. 'I blame Katherine. She's always indulged you.' He hoped that this comment would be taken in the affectionate way he intended, but he couldn't always call it with Josh. Sometimes those freckled, hazel eyes and

that long, pale face would be full of light and humour, and sometimes it would assume a sullen cast that was hard to ignore.
Katherine always pandered to it, always had done, ever since Josh
was born, turning her whole attention on him when he was playing
up in that way rather than just ignoring it.

Tonight, as had been the case for weeks now, Josh seemed distant. Usually, Rick could spend time with his son in an easy intimacy
that didn't necessarily rely on conversation. But this evening Rick
found himself hunting through possible topics he thought might
provoke chatter, then realizing, not by any means for the first time,
how little he and his son had in common. Sport was always Rick's
default subject with other men. A discussion of England's tragic
performance in the Test against Sri Lanka would have taken up a
considerable portion of the meal if he had been eating with anyone
else, but he knew full well that cricket gained no traction with his
son.

'Are you okay? You seem a bit down,' Rick said, having exhausted
the plot twists of the latest box set he'd watched, a series Josh had
already seen online, talked about a sale he hoped to finalize and
made a few enquiries about those of Josh's friends whose faces he
could match with names.

'I'm fine.'

'Well, perhaps you could talk to me? I'm kind of rabbiting on to
myself and not getting much back. It's not a particularly rewarding
way of spending a dinner.'

Josh didn't answer, instead focusing on the table behind Rick,
where a group sat talking in the same speedy mix of English and
Italian as Antonella, their noisy conversation punctuated with
shouts. He envied them. The girls had coloured tips to their long
hair and short tops that revealed flat bellies tanned from weekends
in the sun – Portofino, Saint Tropez, Ibiza – that were as much a
part of their existence as a journey to Exeter on First Great
Western.

He was annoyed with himself for being caught up in this pizza
outing. When term had ended two weeks back, he had considered

staying on in the city but almost everybody he knew at uni had abandoned the place already for summer travels or their families. He didn't want to be at home, where he would have to be close to his parents. No matter how much he tried not to think about it, the unwelcome knowledge of his mother and Teo's affair was insistent. A kaleidoscope of images would come into focus then break up and multiply immediately when he woke, and more often than not the images were still there when he went to sleep at night.

At the same time, he couldn't really believe it was happening. There had been no point when he'd spotted his mum coming on to Teo, or the other way round. He knew what his mother was like when she was flirting. She put on an intense look, her laugh ratcheted up several degrees and she sounded like she was super-interested in whatever she was being told while laughing at the same time. And he hadn't seen anything like that when she'd been with Teo, not for a second. As for Teo, he had hung out with him enough times to see him in action. The guy would enter places like he owned them, checking out the room from the door as he decided whether he was going to grace it with entry. And once he was in, well, he was a poon magnet for sure. But then, in a weird way, he never seemed that interested. Josh assumed he took girls home, but he never heard Teo mention them.

The whole thing was crap. He didn't want to go near Antonella after that last evening. He'd been avoiding her for weeks and she was sucking him dry with her endless texts and messages. If it went on like this he'd have to get a new number, which would be a real pain. When he thought about the photos he felt nauseous, and the moment when the idea might have seemed in any way funny or clever was so far off he couldn't connect with it. Okay, so his dad might have fancied Olga – it wasn't impossible – but that wasn't in itself a crime and, in the light of what he knew now about his mum, it was fine. Totally fine. It didn't justify him and Antonella messing with Rick's head in that way. Sitting across from his dad, now chomping on his favourite pizza, he just wanted to run away. He couldn't deal with it.

'It's bad luck on your mum to have one of her headaches on an evening like this,' Rick said. 'She thinks they might be caused by some kind of pressure to do with the weather.'

Josh remained silent.

'Not that she likes pizza, anyway, does she? You know how she always looks at the menu here with surprise that there aren't more pizza-free choices.' Rick imitated Katherine, furrowing his brow in concentration and then pushing aside the imaginary menu with a frustrated wave. 'And then she's disappointed.' Usually, they would have shared a laugh about the predictability of Katherine's response, but tonight Josh just looked away at the street.

'When are you starting that work experience? Is it next week?' Rick had called Johnny Beaumont to ask if he could take Josh on for a couple of weeks of the long holiday. He imagined it wouldn't be a problem, since he'd found a place for Johnny's daughter, Sophie, just before Christmas. 'I'm not meant to start till later in the month,' Josh answered. 'I might go away before that.'

'Oh. Where?' Rick latched on hopefully to this potential topic for discussion. 'That sounds good.'

Josh shrugged. 'Stay with a friend. I'm not sure.' He took his phone out, speedily tapping a message. 'Are we finished?'

There was no point in prolonging the unsuccessful occasion any further. 'Sure. You go. I'll settle up.' Rick watched Josh lope away, his white T-shirt hanging over his chest and his saggy jeans. Once his son had disappeared from view he ordered another beer. The Italian kids at the next table were having a load of laughs, and he liked hearing them, and it delayed his return to the company of Katherine and her migraine.

Nowadays, if she spoke to him, it was clipped; she briskly avoided any kind of discussion and only raised a point if it was completely necessary. Wherever possible she organized her days independently of him and, most tellingly of all, she showed none of the tenderness which, now that it had evaporated, he realized he hadn't properly appreciated when it was there. A kiss when he got home, a touch on his arm, understanding in her voice, allowing him the benefit of doubt, unlike so many wives he knew. And then, in bed, she simply said it was too hot whenever he approached her, turning away and banging cool into her pillows to make the point. He had been hopeful that Josh's return would change this state of affairs and there might be some life in the house, but it hadn't worked out that way.

Rick checked his emails, scanning the ones that had arrived in the last couple of hours and opening a link he'd been sent with some information about a major new Chinese collector. He was a man who had started in one of those cities that nobody had heard of but which had a population larger than the whole of Greece and had made an unimaginable fortune selling chickens. Just chickens. Now he lived in Shanghai, and in the past year or so he'd become obsessed with buying art. Everything and everyone from the past fifty years. The collection was massive and, although it seemed like he didn't really care about the art itself, what he wanted, he was determined to have. There were artists everywhere banging out stuff for people like him, just as if they were on the factory floor.

Having paid the bill, Rick strolled the short distance back to the house. The terrace was empty, apart from Mrs Vlychnos, who was clipping her yew hedge, the only woman who took care of her front garden herself. Everyone else hired a team of matching T-shirted gardeners to make sure the geraniums and petunias in the large pots were free from brown leaves, the topiary outlines immaculate on the paving slabs where, originally, there had been beds and lawns. Should any plant demonstrate disobedient tendencies – blackspot, wilt, aphids, the lacy legacy of snails – it would simply be whipped out and replaced.

Mrs Vlychnos had lived in the house for fifty years. Her husband had bought it for what at the time had been a considerable sum but, with their canned-food import business, they could afford it. Ten years ago he had woken one morning to sling a pyjama'd leg out of bed but had toppled over with a heart attack that left no time for an ambulance. His wife had said to Rick in their first conversation, as the Tennisons' packing cases were being lifted into number 30, that everybody had told her she should sell the house and move some-where smaller when he died.

'"Why?" I ask. "Why should I move? This is my home and I want to stay here."' Now she took in lodgers, filling the children's old bedrooms with foreign-exchange students from the local language school and renting out the basement, currently to a young couple who tubed it to the City every morning and earned over 100k between them but couldn't afford their own home anywhere they wanted to live. The house was now worth over three hundred times Mr Vlychnos's original investment, and there was nobody left in the street from the old days. The new people were all working in finance. When they had been discussing some recent arrivals a year ago, Rick said that he wouldn't have been able to afford to buy if he was buying today. The prices had gone insane.

'Evening, Mrs Vlychnos,' Rick said.

'A lovely evening,' she replied, in the throaty accent she'd retained despite leaving Cyprus as a teenager, struggling on with the long hedge clippers.

'Can I help you with that?' Rick offered. He had never volun-teered before, but he was keen to avoid his own house, where there was no sign of life, despite Katherine being at home. Its dispiriting appearance reminded him of the unasked and unanswered ques-tions that hovered in a permanent cloud he knew would dissipate only if they had the conversation they had always managed to avoid. Discussing his affair with Olga would inevitably lead to Katherine's discovery of his other affairs. If she thought Olga was the only one, then his liaison with her would seem to have more importance than it had. 'Why now? Why her?' she would want to know. What did it mean about *them*? About *him*?

'That's very kind of you. I am finding it a little difficult. It is my age, you know. At my age everything is working less well. And the heat. I don't manage so well in this heat.'

'Let's see what I can do.' Rick took the clippers from her. 'I can't imagine my own mother, who is at least ten years younger than you, looking after her garden as you do – hauling bags of compost around, or anything like that. I have to admit we use a gardener, like everyone else round here, to do all the big stuff. I just stick to a bit of deadheading now and again.' Considerably taller than the elderly woman, Rick was able to reach the highest spikes of the hedge with ease. There was something extremely satisfying about snipping the individual branches and watching an even surface emerge as they fell on to the pavement.

'I like to take care of things myself. Round here now, I don't recognize the people. Where do they all come from? All parts. Sometimes I don't know where I live any longer.' She tugged at her thick, much-worn gloves, finger by finger, to remove them. 'At least we don't have the Roma round here yet. They are all sleeping on Park Lane. Manny, my eldest, he says it's all Turks now, up where they are. His wife is waiting for me to die so they can move,' she concluded, not sounding unduly concerned.

'But we've always gained so much as a city from people like yourself arriving from elsewhere.' Rick walked to the furthest end of the hedge, where a branch was still sticking out. 'Of course, it's all about balance.'

The house was quiet when Rick went in. He glanced into the living room, despite knowing there would be nobody in there, before getting a glass of water from the fridge. The door to his and Katherine's bedroom was shut which, tonight, he felt further represented Katherine's chilly attitude towards him.

He had a look into Josh's room on the next floor, knowing he was unlikely to find his son there. What a tip. The striped duvet was in a tangle and the pillows were on the floor. Strands of tobacco covered the side table next to a few rollie stubs and an empty water bottle.

The desk on one side of the room was piled with stuff he'd brought back from university and dumped there without bothering to sort through it. Rick flicked through some of the books and photocopied articles – 'Health and Place', 'Environment and Sustainability in Cities'. God knows what was up with him, but it would pass. That was the great thing about being older. You knew things passed. Most of the time.

It was rubbish being young in many ways, he could still remember that. Sometimes, it was easy to think back to youth as an Elysian field of possibility and irresponsibility. But a lot of the time it hadn't been like that. The range of options, the question of what life was going to be as it stretched endlessly ahead brought its own anxieties. It wasn't all sunny pastures. Of course, at the time, he'd dealt with it by self-medicating – not that he'd considered it as that then. If he'd considered his actions much at all, he'd have thought he was just having a good time, but looking back, the drugs had definitely helped him avoid any self-examination. Thank God, Josh didn't appear to have an issue with drugs. Rick was pretty sure he'd recognize it if he did.

He pulled open the top drawer of the desk: Rizlas, pens, postcards, a compact camera, a bottle of Tabasco. There was an old iPhone at the back, under a used Jiffy bag. Compared to the new ones, it looked so clumsy. Rick supposed that it must belong to one of Josh's mates, since he knew Josh had just got an upgrade for his.

He pressed a switch in the expectation of there being no charge but the screen sprang into life immediately. There were just a few basics apps: Instagram, WhatsApp, Facebook, Twitter. Pressing Photo, dense rows of small pictures appeared. He opened one. There was Teo, seated on a metal chair in a garden, a dark ball of box and the curve of terracotta behind him. He scrolled through a few more from what appeared to be the same day – young people he didn't recognize, arms around each other. The next batch was taken at night, and he saw his son, bundled up in a puffa jacket on the street, his grin reaching the apples of his cheeks, as it always had. There were several of Fred, too, standing in the doorway of the gallery, his face either bleached ghoulishly by the flash or too dark to read from backlighting. Rick was pretty sure they had been taken the night of the Christmas party. Whoever had their hand on the trigger was no Mario Testino, that was for sure.

The next was a picture he had seen before. There it was, that first picture of Olga, the one he'd been texted when he was meeting CeeCee for lunch. Even though he had looked at it time and again – on his camera, on his computer, on his iPad – trying to work out what it was, where it had come from, to discover it on this anonymous device in Josh's bedroom was nasty. What on earth was it doing here? Olga's clichéd pose, the skin he knew the feel and the taste of, cheapened by clumsy retouching so that a plastic girl stared out, available to any viewer of the phone. He scrolled on to the next picture, not sure whether he wanted to discover it was another of Olga. Josh again, this time standing beside a desk chair, but the focus was poor. And the next, another of the Olga pictures, and the next and the next. All those he had been sent, and one that he hadn't. It was taken from the side as she lay on her front, bum raised in the air and her arms tied behind her. She was looking sideways at the screen, her mouth slightly open and those clear blue eyes too wide for the pose not to be ridiculous. There was nothing about it that was anything other than laughable – or would have been if the woman hadn't been Olga and it wasn't on a smartphone next to his son's first-year reading.

Taking the phone, he walked down to his study. It didn't make sense that it had been Josh sending those pictures to him. He couldn't be that fucked up. Anyway, it hadn't been Josh's number. He switched on the desk light and started to investigate what else there was, but it only held the pictures – no contacts or emails – and the only texts were the ones to his number. It was a loaded gun and, apparently, he was the target. Just along the corridor, Rick's wife was lying in bed, pickled in silent fury, and now it was looking highly likely that, over the past months, his son had been aiming psycho messages at him. For the first time, Rick considered the possibility that, when all this had passed, he might be left somewhere very different.

Since it was only shortly after eleven, Rick knew that Josh was unlikely to return from wherever he was anytime soon. He called him from his mobile, listening only to the first two words of Josh's message before ringing off and texting: 'Call me now. It's urgent.'

He knew there was no guarantee that Josh would reply. He poured himself a whisky at the small bar he had had installed as a treat to himself when they first moved in. When people came round, he enjoyed standing behind the marble counter to pour his guests champagne or mix Martinis. Bar equipment had quickly become the obvious gift and, down in the basement, in the neatly organized storage spaces, Mariella had several shelves of cocktail shakers, ice buckets and shot glasses that had been given to him over the years.

Josh phoned moments later.

'What's the problem?' His voice was only just audible over music but, even so, it managed to convey an utter lack of interest and complete resentment at having been called by his father.

'Well, Josh, where to begin? But it's a big one, and you're going to explain it to me.'

'What do you mean?'

'I want you back here now. Immediately. No fucking around. This is serious.'

'I'm out, Dad – miles away. What's so important? Can't it wait till tomorrow?'

'No. Just get back home.'

'I haven't got any cash. I was going to crash here.'

'Get a cab. I'll pay. Just do it, Josh, for fuck's sake. Just do it. Where are you?' Rick shouted, as much to make himself heard over the music as out of anger.

'Brixton. Okay,' Josh muttered. 'I don't believe this.'

Rick looked out of the window, where shapes which Katherine and her lighting designer had selected as worthy of illumination were picked out. The small spots set into the curving garden path had always reminded him of the emergency lighting on a plane, but by the time they were installed he couldn't be bothered to object. The moon hung right outside the window, and for a moment Rick wondered whether, if he concentrated hard enough on it as a calming, meditative exercise, he might see it move. Katherine would know the exact term for the stage of that moon. She liked that kind of information. On one of their first nights together they had lain on a smooth, damp lawn. She had pointed out the seas and craters she could name on the moon's patterned surface and he, not wanting to be thought lacking in interest in the Sea of Rains or the Ocean of Storms, kept his eyes focused on the sky, when all he had wanted was to turn them to her naked body.

It was almost an hour before he heard Josh return.

'I'm in my study!' Rick yelled.

'So what's the problem? It had better be something important.' Josh stood in the doorway in an effort not to commit entirely to the meeting, positioning himself in a way that showed he had no intention of getting sucked in to whatever it was his dad was on about. He still had the sound system crashing around in his head, and he wasn't entirely straight – he'd done a bit of stuff earlier and had a few beers, not much, but enough to know he wasn't as quick as he might have been. He pulled himself up in an attempt to feel more together.

'This.' Rick waved the phone at him. 'I want you to explain what's going on.'

'What do you want to know?' Josh asked, walking over to the bookshelves and pulling several spines out just enough to see their front covers, then pushing them back again. Shit. He'd found the pictures. Briefly, the room whirled around him, but when it stopped he was still in the same place.

'Stop doing that!' Rick snapped as he closed the door. 'Look at these. I want to know what they are and I want to know why they were sent to me. I'm assuming you know about this' – he waved the phone again – 'since it was in your desk.'

Josh continued to look at the bookshelves and paused before saying, with a forced hopeful smile, 'It was meant to be a joke. I mean . . . we didn't mean anything serious.'

'We?'

'Oh Dad.' Josh's long arms flapped. 'Me and Antonella. She found the pictures and she kind of thought it would be a laugh to send them to you. Well. For me to send them to you. Obviously, it was an absurd thing to do. I know that now.'

Hearing Antonella's name, Rick wasn't the slightest bit surprised to learn that that scuzzy headcase had been responsible. He had known she was bad news, both her and that brother of hers, from the first time they had come for dinner. He had thought they were affected and spoilt but, for Katherine's sake, he had been prepared to tolerate them. But this was different. Now he wasn't sure that they – or at least she – wasn't mentally disturbed. He was about to share this thought with Josh but stopped, as it dawned on him that, first, he needed to know why Antonella had wanted to send them. What did she know, and what had she told his son? The blame game had suddenly become a lot more complicated. It was one thing Katherine finding out about Olga, but it was a whole other thing if Josh knew. In the case of Katherine, he was having to deal with her hurt, but when it came to Josh he was embarrassed. Nobody wants to hear stuff like that about their dad.

'Where did the pictures come from?' he asked, picking his way to the answers.

'I've got no idea. Antonella just said she'd found them on the net. I thought they were so old you'd get that it was a joke.' Josh sensed that, although his father was furious, he wasn't really letting rip in the way he had expected. The pair of them were testing the ground to see when it was going to completely give way.

'I obviously don't share your sense of humour.' Rick stood up abruptly from his chair and pulled one of the pictures up. 'I mean, these aren't exactly charming pictures of Olga Oblomovik, are they? It's not like you were just posting a few holiday snaps. And I suppose part of the joke was that I wasn't to know where they came from.' He had started his interrogation with a measure of control, but now he couldn't work out how much Josh knew, and a sense of his own culpability combined with his fury at what Josh had done made him lose it.

'You are a complete idiot. You are, frankly, a total waste of space. There's a missing link somewhere. Don't get me wrong. I can see what you thought was funny. And it's obvious that girl has your balls in her claws. What I don't get is you.'

'Yeah!' Josh shouted back. 'Well, there's a lot you don't get, Dad. Take it from me, I'm not the only thing in this place you're not getting. Or if you are, then it's all even more ridiculous.' Josh headed for the door, but Rick got there first, preventing him from leaving. 'Let's face it. They're just pictures of some woman you fancy. Just pictures.' Josh's face showed its usual guilty flush. The pair of them stopped as they heard Katherine outside, banging on the door and shouting as she opened it.

'What's going on? Why are you screaming at each other?' she asked. Rick stood aside to let her in, immediately joining forces with his antagonist, each of them as unkeen as the other for her to see the phone and its tacky contents.

'It's fine. We're just sorting something out. Get back to bed. You look wiped,' Rick said, attempting to put his arm around Katherine, partly to reassure her, but more to reassure himself that such an action was possible. His wife, standing there in her pale-blue dressing gown, an interloper in the messy confrontation taking place, might yet be the thing that could hold it all together. But she turned around. 'I'm not up to this, whatever it's about. For heaven's sake, just keep it quiet. My migraine's still murder.' She left Rick and Josh together in the room, neither sure what the next step was, or where it would lead.

# Chapter Seventeen

## July

Katherine had parked the car just down the road from a school gates, as the adults waiting at the gates were caught out by a thunderstorm, their thin, colourful clothing suddenly insufficient. The rain stopped as quickly as it had arrived, and Katherine opened the car door just as the first children emerged, clutching their term's paintings and lumpy pottery, rucksacks humped on their small backs, yelling with excitement. She walked quickly to Teo's flat, picking her way through the puddles.

'Sure. Come over. I'm alone all day,' Teo had answered when she had called earlier and suggested their meeting 'for a coffee or something'. Ever since the other night, when she had walked in on Rick and Josh, and discovered Rick, overbearing and furious, confronting Josh, equally angry and, she could tell, close to tears, and had been told by both of them that they were 'fine' (a word that she was finding increasingly pointless), she had badly wanted to see Teo. Although Teo was central to the co-dependent bubble of suspicion and blame that surrounded her and Rick, and although it was in her control to prick it and see what would change, she didn't feel capable of doing so until she had been with him again.

And now she was slowly running her lips along the smooth saltiness of his body, feeling the muscles that always surprised her with their strength and burrowing her face where they dipped in a concave 'V'. As they moved together, what had once felt shocking and compelling was now a panacea, a rush of smelling salts brought out to revive her senses and dull her doubts. The windows of Teo's bedroom opened on to the same ironwork balcony as the sitting room, and from the bed the large trees lining the street reflected a green light, their canopy of leaves still dripping.

'Did you hear last night's storm?' Katherine asked, watching the shadows from the trees dancing on the wall. Teo reached across her to the floor, groping for his cigarettes.

'No. We were with friends. There were a lot of us. A lot of noise.' He took a deep drag and held the cigarette up above his face as if it were a candle. 'It was light when we left. Maybe it was raining?' This was a reasonable answer, but the reply left Katherine wishing she hadn't heard it.

His evening would have been so different from hers: crowded, careless, noisy. There would have been girls with glossy hair, coloured for fun rather than necessity, bright eyes framed by huge sweeps of mascara, their lids smooth and wide below their brows. She conjured up an Impressionist background of bare limbs, bodies and laughing chatter in which only Teo was clearly defined, enjoying himself without her. In contrast, she had been alone, watching two episodes of a series she had recorded, while Rick had gone out.

Summer had begun to drain the city and the usual dinners and parties that made up so much of her and Rick's life were thinning. The caravanserai of collectors, socialites, gallerists and curators were leaving town and wouldn't return to London until September. Usually, she enjoyed these few quieter weeks with Rick, but in their current toxic space she wanted to keep apart from him as much as possible, avoiding meals alone with him and confining talk to the cul-de-sac of logistics and daily formalities. It was hard to imagine the future for them, or if there was one. Rick was sleeping with one of his clients, and she was sleeping with a boy only a few years older than her son. Did that mean they were even?

Katherine slid off the bed and put on Teo's black T-shirt before walking out on to the narrow balcony. She leant against the damp railing, feeling the pressure of the metal against her ribs. Teo joined her, cupping her breasts from behind, his nakedness shielded by her body from the street below as they stood there for a moment, him pressed against her back, before returning to the room. Now that they had made love, Katherine was nervous about Antonella coming back. She was tense, listening out for the bang of the front door to the building or, worse, the key in the door of the flat.

'Let's go for a walk before I leave. We could go to the café up the road,' she suggested, reaching down for her jeans and the patterned smock, lying on top of her phone, which had begun to ring.

The pavements were still sodden from the flash storm when Rick left his meeting with John Steele. John was one of the good guys in Rick's book. He'd started his business in the late sixties as a middle man for artist friends, and they had all been beneficiaries of that zeitgeist in which the canniest operators were able to monetize in the most traditional of ways. His Pimlico Road gallery was a cooler and younger scene than Michael Tennison's, but the two men liked each other and shared a teasing honour-among-thieves camaraderie.

John had closed the gallery itself years back, but he still did business from his flat, where the work of artists he had launched hung on the walls, along with a valuable collection of Indonesian textiles. Rick always felt better for an hour or two in John's company; the older man's passion was invigorating and he always came away having learnt something.

It would take him about an hour to walk home. He wanted and needed the exercise and was enjoying the humid wind blowing in after the rain. They were meant to be going on holiday in a couple of weeks – him and Katherine and Josh – ten days on the island of Patmos sharing a house with another family, then a week in Puglia with some other friends, before ending up on the opposite Italian coast in Portofino. The three 'P's had worked well for them last year and they had thought it was worth a repeat.

But, last year, things were different. He had only just met Olga, and all summer was cruising the high, the one that got him again and again. It wasn't about conquest or escape. It was, he had always thought, an almost innocent joy. Once, he'd gone to see someone about it. Josh was thirteen, maybe fourteen, and Katherine was fretting about his growing up and needing her less. He knew he should do something to restore her confidence, but the plain truth was that nothing he did made her feel better. Despite breaking off a brief liaison with a pretty girl he'd met at Frieze (an action he privately regarded as a gesture of support), he remembered desperately wanting to find somebody else. It was the first time he'd moved from one to another so quickly, and that need had worried him. So he'd tried a few therapy sessions with some woman, in a room where prints of the Grand Canal hung on the wall and a dusty spider plant sat on the table, and she had told him that he had self-esteem issues and that she could detect a sadness at his core.

No, last year he and Katherine had been in a great place, or so it looked from where he was now. At a crossroads there was a flower stall that had been there as long as he could remember, selling lush, expensive bouquets. If he bought some for Katherine, though, he suspected she would just ignore the gesture. As he continued through the residential streets a white van sped past, spewing out the water from a pool in the gutter and spraying his trousers. He looked back after it in irritation. A taxi rank separated the unusually wide road and way across, several houses back, behind one of the thickly leaved trees, he could just see a blonde woman standing on the iron balcony that ran across the front of the houses. She was wearing a black T-shirt, or possibly a short dress, and her legs were bare. He'd go to the grave noticing great legs. From this distance, he could just make out that she was a version of Katherine – tall, blonde, pale – but Katherine would never hang out there in such a louche way. He watched her turn to someone behind her before going back inside.

It reminded him that he had been going to suggest to her that he booked somewhere for dinner and he stopped to make the call, leaning against a low wall. He had a plan. He didn't want another evening like last night, when he'd had to go and have a drink on his own to avoid spending time in the house, swamped by Katherine's passive aggression. Obviously, the answer was to come clean and sort it out with her. He had to stop being a child and hoping it would just go away. Clearly, it was going nowhere.

It took a few rings before she answered.

'Hi. I thought I'd book somewhere for dinner. Let's get out of the house tonight.'

'Where are you?'

'Just walking back from John Steele's. And you?' The woman across the road had returned to the balcony door and was leaning against it as she spoke on the phone. The thick leaves of the tree in front moved to and fro in the wind, frustratingly blocking her for seconds and then exposing her to his view. He listened to his wife on the phone as he watched the woman. He was intrigued by her. Wondered what she was like, who else was there with her.

'I'm just doing some stuff, round and about,' Katherine replied.

As she talked, the woman on the balcony bent to rub her calf. How often had he seen Katherine massage her calf after one of her runs, always bending straight from her long waist, just as the woman he was watching did, her hair falling forward. He watched her stand back up and raise an arm to her hair. *Was* it her? It was like people said, as if time had gone slo-mo. He was shocked but fascinated, wanting to pull the strings as if he were a puppeteer, say something that would make her move in a way that would identify her indisputably. He couldn't think quickly enough; in his head he heard her in the car home from the Weitzmans' when he'd asked about where the Fullardis lived.

'See you at home later. I'll be an hour or so.' Katherine ended the call and he watched the woman – his wife – move the phone away from her head and step back into the house while he remained fixed to the spot.

Teo bypassed the tables outside and headed for a booth in the corner of the local café. Unlike the pavements, the room was almost empty, the only other customer a man alone doing a newspaper crossword. As they came in from the brightness, the room was dark and cool. They sat, and a waitress, her hair in cornrows and a tattoo up the inside of her arm, handed them menus.

'*Ciao*,' he greeted her, without looking at the menu. 'An espresso, double.' He looked at Katherine, waiting for her order.

'Do you have fresh mint tea?' she asked.

'Yes, we do. Do you want anything to eat?' The waitress spoke with a French accent. 'We have an amazing raspberry cheesecake today.'

'Not for me.' Katherine was pretty sure Teo wouldn't eat either, but he ordered a bowl of ice cream. When it came, after the first taste, he offered her his spoon and she sucked off the mound of icy bitter chocolate, wiping her lips with a finger.

'You know, I have meant to tell you,' Teo said as she looked for something to clean it. 'We are leaving soon.'

Katherine watched as he dug into the ice cream but without lifting the spoon so it began to melt in the small metal bowl.

'For the holidays?'

'Yes – Pantelleria. There are lots of people out there. We go for a time most summers. Antonella likes the scene and I like the sea. There is incredible diving.'

'When will you be back?' Katherine asked, wondering if she would be home from her own holiday before him.

Outside on the pavement, Katherine could see a group of young mothers chatting in long, patterned dresses, their children bribed into sitting at the table by dishes of ice cream like the one Teo was toying with.

'It's probably a good time for us – for this – to finish.' It was unclear from Teo's gentle smile whether he was simply unaware of the effect this news had on Katherine or if it was a deliberate attempt to deflect any reaction.

'Why do you say that? Why now?'

'Things. You know, sometimes, things, they pile up and – hey, it is the time. I guess it started when there was an argument a while ago. Me and Tonne. You know how she is. She was in one of her crazy moods – nothing was right. She was angry with me and she wanted to hurt me, and Josh was there, in the firing range, so she told him about you and me. Maybe a part of her thought it would balance things.'

'*Balance* things? You've lost me. What did you just say? I *can't* have heard you right, can I?' As Katherine took in the fact that Josh knew about her relationship with Teo, her shame, building up by the second, at first emerged as a series of questions. 'What on earth would be the point of her telling on us? What could possibly justify that? I mean, I know she's crazy but surely she's not certifiable. He's my son. He's barely nineteen. What's he done to her? What, if it comes to it, have any of us done?'

'Everything all right? Can I get you anything else?' The waitress appeared at Katherine's elbow with magnificent ill-timing.

Teo nodded her away and Katherine turned to look at a child who was crying after tripping over. The mother picked up her daughter and gave her a kiss on the knee, then placed her on her lap and stroked her hair. That was what mothers did. They made every-thing all right, didn't they, rather than making it all wrong as she had done? She couldn't separate out the emotions that were tumbling in on her one after another.

When she had called Teo that morning she had known that the relationship must be coming to its end, but that didn't mean she had wanted it to happen. Now, though, as panic took hold, as she con-sidered how revolted Josh must have been when he found out, and how vindictive Antonella must feel towards her and Teo, her feel-ings for him only moments earlier became unrecognizable.

Tears threatened, humiliatingly. 'This is unbearable. He must have been so upset. What did he say?'

'I don't remember much about what he said,' Teo answered, with a lack of concern that added to Katherine's dismay. 'He left, I think. We were meant to be going to a party and Antonella was angry that I was late. She was probably playing around with him. Her little mouse, she calls him.' And he swiped an imaginary paw on the table. 'Sometimes, I wondered. Should I warn him not to bother with her, because I know how difficult she can be, how complicated. But then' – Teo shrugged – 'if someone ever told me to stay away from someone it would make me want to be closer to them. He was entranced. She has that power. In London I have learnt, finally, that we must separate. I thought she couldn't manage without me. But now I know she can survive. All the hurt I thought she might turn on herself, well, she turns it on to others. It's how she manages. She doesn't need me.'

'And what did you mean when you said she thought it might "balance things"?'

'So Rick hasn't told you?'

'About what?'

Teo waited to answer, finally pushing the ice-cream bowl aside. 'I guess that now we are talking about everything . . .' He paused, before relaying the information with a lack of emotion bordering on boredom. 'Antonella and Josh have been texting him these pictures of Olga. Stuff my sister found that came from some old Russian porn magazine, I guess. I'm not sure. She told Josh to text them to your husband – she thinks he has a thing for her. I suppose she was, like, Olga and Rick equals Teo and Katherine. Neat. She really hates that I have been involved with you.' He added, simply and unexpectedly, 'She knew I cared, in my way, and Antonella has never wanted me to care about anyone other than her. And you have changed things. You have been a good person for me. You have made me realize that it is time to move on alone. Go to New York. Break the patterns that we do again and again and again.'

Listening, Katherine grew more and more furious. The childish self-absorption of Teo's explanation, the way he appeared to view the mess she and Rick had made as a kind of self-help exercise for him and Antonella, and the way he described his feelings for her – 'I cared, in my way' – so much less than her own obsessive lust. The risks she had taken to be with him, the fizzing anticipation she had carried around for months like perfume on her skin . . . all this was now simply pathetic.

So much had changed since Katherine had parked her car that she wouldn't have been surprised if it was no longer where she'd left it.

The wind and rain had littered the windscreen with sticky buds and flaccid petals that needed the wipers on as she turned on the ignition. The music playing when she had arrived, a favourite Oasis track, blasted out with inappropriate good-time fervour. She switched it off, preferring to drive home in silence. There seemed no way to find the beginning of it all, and she couldn't be sure that she was at the end. Yes, her relationship with Teo was at an end but the fall-out – that had only just begun.

It was nearly seven by the time she walked into her home. She couldn't bear the idea of confronting Josh immediately. She hadn't seen him since he and Rick were screaming at each other in the study, then silenced but also embarrassed by her arrival. Now she understood why.

Rick was in the kitchen sorting through the mail stacked on the table. There was already a pile of torn, empty envelopes and cellophane and beside them a delivery company's 'while you were out' card. He had thrown his jacket on one of the dining chairs and his checked shirt was hanging over his trousers. The doors to the garden were open and a wash of early-evening sun covered most of the garden, from the stone terrace down to the pleached limes at the far end; it was one of the reasons they'd chosen this house. In the cherry tree, now empty of the fruit that had dangled there only a few weeks earlier, perched two parrots – one a vivid pale green and one a bright yellow. The beady dark eyes of the green one appeared to watch the proceedings inside the house; the other turned its back and stretched to peck at the higher branch.

'Where did you decide to book for tonight?' Katherine asked, dropping her bag on a chair next to his jacket and pulling at the thin fabric of her smock to cool herself down.

'I didn't,' Rick replied.

'Oh. Why? Did you change your mind? I mean, that's totally fine by me. But I thought you wanted to go out.'

'I did.' Rick's staccato delivery was unusual. She had frequently sounded like that during the past few weeks, she knew, but Rick had constantly chatted, meaningless stuff much of the time, trying to compensate for her unwillingness to engage in anything but the most necessary and brief exchanges. She was about to leave the room when he continued.

'I was going to book a restaurant but then I thought it would be better to have the conversation here. In private. In what, until recently, I had thought of as our happy family home,' he said, with blunt irony.

A conversation with Rick about his affair with Olga was the last thing Katherine wanted at this point but, after the last hour, she had reached the point of 'just bring it all on'. Even so, she was surprised how angry he sounded.

'Is Josh here?' she asked, walking towards the garden. The sight of the neat lawn, the climbing roses and honeysuckle, the teak Adirondack chairs on the terrace and the trickle of the fountain on the southern wall failed to offer her the reassurance it usually did. Another parrot swooped in briefly as she stepped outside, dipping low and then climbing to a tree in the distance with an echoing shriek that rallied the original pair, who followed in a noisy rush.

'I haven't heard him. I don't think so. He's probably avoiding me, the same way you are. It's been just great for me here recently,' he sneered, and she realized that, whatever it was that was going to follow, it wouldn't be an apology.

'Okay. What is this *conversation* you want to have? You're right. It *is* time we talked.' Katherine moved in his direction, to sit at the table.

She could hear that Rick was attempting to exercise a control over what was happening that he didn't feel. 'It's obvious that I should apologize,' he began. 'I know that you learnt about Olga in Majorca, and I should have said something then. I should have explained, or tried to.'

'What were you going to explain?'

'Well, that's the point. I would have explained that what had happened had no effect on what I felt for you – it was over by then, anyway. That yes, I had been having an affair with her – we saw each other occasionally, not that often – but that it was as if it happened in another world from you, from Josh, from this. I would have told you how I always knew that you were my lodestar. That I would never have wanted to hurt you and it was possibly foolish on my part to think I could behave in that way, which, obviously, did run the risk of doing just that. And that I realized that, of course, the opposite had happened. I *had* hurt you. Betrayed your belief in me. But this afternoon, that changed. I have to hand it to you, Katherine, you had me fooled.'

He flung the ball of blame neatly over to Katherine, taking her completely by surprise. She had thought the confrontation would be about his guilt and his apologies, and that her own burden would be dealing with her deception.

She tried to work out what he had discovered. 'Perhaps we've both uncovered more than we wanted to about each other.' Even to her it sounded priggish and hollow.

'Don't be ridiculous, Katherine. What have you been doing with that boy? I saw you there. Standing on his balcony in – let me guess – his T-shirt. How sweet: boyfriend's T-shirt,' Rick mocked. 'The funny thing was, I saw that woman and thought, I bet she's got no knickers on under that. It was kind of a turn-on. Just taking a break after a good fuck, were you? Yes? Am I correct? A boy nearly your son's age?' He shook his head, ramping up his indignation. 'You really have got me there. I would never have expected it of you.'

'I wouldn't have expected it of myself, but I don't suppose that makes much difference. And it's finished as well, whatever was going on between us. It ended this afternoon. When Teo told me about Josh and the photos.' Not for a moment did Katherine think of trying to deny Rick's accusation.

Rick shrugged but remained silent.

'Nothing I say can make this okay. I'm not even sure what the definition of okay would be,' Katherine continued. 'So we've both been unfaithful – it happens, doesn't it? I suppose the question is why, and what now. But, to be honest, I can't work that out at the moment. All I care about is Josh. How he's dealing with it all. Because I also discovered this afternoon that he knows about me

231

and Teo. Before that, I thought he had no idea. Imagine what he must be thinking. Actually, I can't bear to.'

'It's a fraction late for that now,' said Rick. 'But why that kid, Katherine? Of everyone. Why him?'

'Oh, come on. You, of all people, know guys who have affairs with girls twenty, thirty years younger than them. It's scarcely groundbreaking. I loved the person I felt I was when I was with him. I was someone new. He made me feel – not young, but . . .' Rick could see she was trying to hold herself together, just as he was. 'It doesn't matter, really. It doesn't. He's leaving. He and Antonella – they'll both be gone in a few days. And here we are, dealing with the consequences.'

Rick wished that he could hold his wife and gain comfort from her. But he couldn't. When he looked at her he saw the woman on the balcony, with her long bare legs below a boy's T-shirt, and, although it was entirely his imagination, he couldn't get rid of the smell of long, damp sex carried on that warm afternoon wind.

# Chapter Eighteen

As a small child Josh had been told that counting elephants would help him sleep. He should use their stately procession, lumbering across the landscape, tail to trunk, trunk to tail, to lull him at night, and it had often worked for him. It hadn't worked last night, though, and he'd drifted in and out of semi-sleep, getting up for a glass of water, then peeing, then finding it hard to get comfortable in bed, flinging a leg out for cool and then curling up. His bedroom was stuffy and hot, but if he kept the windows open he could hear the noise from the street below. Most of the time the road was quiet, with only the occasional sound of a car but sometimes it was the quiet that spooked him. When he was stressed, like now, he would lie constantly on alert to hear a sound that meant something was wrong – a scream, or voices shouting.

By around eight o'clock in the morning he gave up and reached down for his phone to check Facebook. The way life was at the moment, his bedroom was the best place in the house to be, given that it contained neither Rick nor Katherine.

The phone vibrated with a message – Antonella, again. Would she never give up? 'We're in the park. It's a sunny day. Everything is going to be fine now. Come.' The text was followed with a line of stupid emoticons. He threw the phone to the end of the bed and instead picked up his laptop to look at Buzzfeed, where, for a few minutes, he was absorbed in '21 ways to turn beer into cash'. But he knew he was really thinking about Antonella. It had been weeks now, and though he pretended to himself he was ignoring her texts and crazy messages, in the end, she was still filling up his head. He just wanted to erase her, and Teo, and pretty well everything that had been going on for the past few months. It would be great if he could just restore his life to factory settings.

If she was hanging out in the park this early, she must be pretty out of it. No way did he want to go. He heard another buzz from the phone. This time the message was from Teo. 'Hey, man. We need to talk. Call me.'

The bedroom was filled with a soft light seeping through the striped blue-and-white blinds. He raised one and the sight of the curtains still drawn in the house opposite and the brightness reminded him that he was knackered. He called Teo back. Even though he didn't want to hear his voice or see him, he was curious to know why they needed to talk.

'Hi. It's cool here. You know we are leaving in a couple of days? It would be good to meet.' Teo sounded fine, and spoke as if it was normal to suggest them meeting so early. 'Come, and we'll have a coffee. We're near the fountain.'

Josh knew where they were. A few months ago they had walked through the park late one evening and, when they reached the stone terrace where the fountains played, Antonella had wanted to sit and smoke a couple of joints. They'd been there for ages in the end, until they'd been moved on by some security guy.

'What's the point?' Josh replied.

'Hey, man. Just to say goodbye. You know. It would be good. We have had some great times together. And we need to make it good. We don't want to leave with this bad feeling.' Teo spoke in his usual slow way, teasing out the syllables.

Josh imagined the scene downstairs. Katherine would probably be dressed for a run, and his dad would be kind of reading the paper but not really, as he'd be looking at his BlackBerry, and there would be the *atmosphere*, which he was properly fed up with. It did his head in, being the only person in the place who knew everything that was going on. The pictures he had sent his dad, the thing with Olga, and now Mum and Teo. It was like some crappy TV series. Nothing inspired, like *True Detective* or *Breaking Bad*, which would have been major, and they'd probably all be dead by now. No. It was more like an afternoon soap. But this wasn't a soap, it was real life – his life – and it was ridiculous.

234

At least Teo had said they were leaving. That was the best news he'd heard for ages. He gave his eyes a rub and tugged at his hair, which felt sticky and needed a wash. Staying here in the house with his parents, or a quick goodbye in the park?

'Okay,' he said. 'Give me half an hour.'

By the time Josh reached the park entrance the jangling of his night's poor sleep had eased. On a Saturday morning, the streets looked different: people moved around like they had a choice. During the week, everyone seemed to be going places they didn't want to be, shut into their own world, rushing and pushing their way into the day.

Even though it seemed so early to him, the park was already busy. The paths were heaving with joggers on their own or in groups, some of them looking as if they weren't going to make it, the sweat pouring off them. He knew that his mum liked to run in this park. She was pretty fit compared to some of her friends – Flo, for instance, who wouldn't make it once round the pond, let alone manage the circuit that Katherine did. Once again, the idea of his mother having sex with Teo whammed back, splayed and noisy.

Meeting Teo and Antonella wasn't going to make him feel better, that he was sure of, but there was this sense of unfinished business. Perhaps in the bright sunshine it would be easier to avoid the shadowy areas where he found himself whenever they were around. Nothing much ever happened in the morning. Josh considered it dead time and usually dull, but dull was a good thing where Antonella was concerned. He could do with a bit of dull.

As he walked down the path towards the fountains he could see the pair sitting some distance to the left, on the grass below the playground, where there were a load of dads pushing swings. The music in his headphones failed to override the thumping in his chest as he drew nearer. There was a moment, just as he reached the terrace, when he was tempted to turn around, but he made himself walk on, through the crowd of pigeons that were flapping and strutting about, encouraged by a lady muttering to them and scattering the contents of a bag of crusts.

Antonella was wearing a mini dress streaked with a colour that glittered in the sun. She waved wildly at him, while Teo lay beside her, stretched out on the grass. He was wearing a black suit and looked like some surrealist freak.

'How long have you been here?' Josh asked, standing above the prone Teo.

'A couple of hours. Maybe,' Teo answered, his eyes hidden behind dark glasses, his arms out in a 'T'. He didn't move; it was as if it hadn't been him that had called and asked Josh to come and meet them.

'We wanted to . . . to be loose and float around. Didn't we, Teo?' Antonella was slurred and speedy at once, and stumbled as she came up to him. He could smell whisky on her breath, but it didn't dim the familiar scent he associated with her and, briefly, he felt the same pull as he had when he first smelt it. It was part of the spell she wove. There was a story about the edelweiss he'd been told in Germany; it lured you to the edge of the cliff where it grew, tempting you to lean too far over in an attempt to reach it. But he knew now, didn't he? What lay below. Just a load of mind games and trouble. Nothing he couldn't live without.

'So when are you leaving?'

'We were just talking about it,' Teo said, now sitting up.

'Where are you going?' Josh dumped himself beside them as he asked.

'Pantelleria – probably. But after, in the autumn, I am planning to go to New York,' answered Teo.

'He knows I want to come with him.' Antonella giggled first, then exchanged the humourless giggle for a shout. 'He knows I need him! That it is not the same if we are not together.'

'I said you could come on later. But it would be good for you to look after yourself. And for me also. Antonella – *you* will survive. The issue is collateral damage.' Teo laughed drily.

'Teo has changed here. He's left me, like a doll he doesn't want any more, a broken doll.' Antonella had now turned to self-mockery, loosely hanging her neck and arms like a string puppet but then straightening herself and grinning.

'A broken record, yes; doll, no. Don't be so tragic. This is not why we asked Josh to join us. This is not what he wants to hear.'

'No, I don't. It's just the same old crap. And I don't much appreciate being collateral damage either.' Josh wasn't prepared to let Teo get away with acting like he was the good guy. 'Not from either of you.' He stood up as if to go but Antonella grabbed him and, with surprising strength, pulled him down again, ignoring his crossness. 'You come with us to Pantelleria! You would love it there. It has the wonderful sea and rocks. It's super-cool.'

Teo had stood up and was strolling towards a large horse chestnut tree. The gnarled trunk was bare of low branches but, by jumping, he could just reach a few stragglers. It took him several leaps until he was able to tear a couple off and return. Antonella started to massage Josh's shoulders under his T-shirt. She was good at it. Able to find the sweet spot and get her fingers right in and under his skin. She whispered to him to kneel so she could do it properly. But the moment passed as images of men kneeling before having their brains blown out came into his mind. He stood up quickly, blood rushing to his head with the sudden movement, so much he thought he was going to faint.

Teo dangled a branch from his hand as he walked back to them. He took off his jacket, laid it out on the grass and sat on the black fabric before reaching into the inside pocket for the penknife Katherine had given him. Josh wondered whether it meant anything to Teo that it had been hers, or if he remembered it was that knife that had given the game away.

Antonella put her arms around Josh. 'Okay. So let's dance.' She was doing that thing she did when she was out of it, bouncing from one subject to another. The discussion of who was going to Pantelleria or New York had vanished. Her thought process had no trail that you could follow. Not that he wanted to any more. He reckoned that if he just played along with the pretence of dancing for a minute or so it would be easier to leave, but Antonella held him tightly against her, shuffling him around like he was the partner in an exhausted couple in a dance marathon. He felt her bones through the dress, her ribs, her hips. The dizziness from standing hadn't passed, and the way she was moving him was making it worse.

Teo ignored them, slowly skinning strips of bark from the branches and filleting the leaves silently. Every now and again he held a leaf skeleton up to his face or raised the naked branch nearer his eye to carve something. The noise of the playground drifted across to them, more loudly than the rumble of the nearby traffic, as Antonella unhooked one arm from Josh and bent down in an attempt to pull her brother up to join them.

'Teo, Teo! Come and dance with us. It's good to dance.' The edge of hysteria had returned to Antonella's voice, increased by Teo's rejection of her hyper mood. She was going to try and make him react, Josh thought. He wanted to seize the opportunity to move away as she loosened her arm, but instead they tripped and fell, both of them crashing on to Teo so that he toppled beneath the pair of them. Antonella was laughing as she collapsed on her brother but then she was quiet. For a second Josh thought she had passed out. Her dress was hoicked up to her knickers, her bare legs twisted as she slumped over her brother's white shirt. A dark stain spread down his collar.

'Antonella. Get off him. Something's happened. Look. He's bleeding!' Josh shouted, grabbing hold of her dress. It slid through his fingers so he had to bend lower to lift her off. A sound – not a groan, more a gurgle and a faint hiss – came from Teo, and it was only then that Josh saw the engraved handle of the knife. Antonella saw it at the same time and, kneeling back down beside her brother, unhesitatingly pulled the knife out from the smooth tanned flesh of his neck. The blood ran faster.

'Teo,' she whispered. 'Teo. Look at me. Can you speak? I'm sorry. We were dancing. Remember. We were dancing.' Teo turned his eyes to her face, which was inches from his. She pressed her fingers over the wound, and the blood, a bright red, trickled in between.

'We need to stop it. Not like that. Wrap something around it!' Josh shouted, pulling his phone from his pocket to dial the emergency number. '. . . Hyde Park. By the fountains. You know, near the playground!' Josh shouted into the phone as Antonella ripped off her dress then tried to tear it into strips. 'I don't know. He's bleeding massively. No. He's not speaking.' As he spoke, Josh was pulling his T-shirt off to throw at Antonella. 'Use this!' he yelled before returning to the operator. 'How long? I don't know. I don't know. How tight? Won't it make it harder for him to breathe?' He was desperate for the voice on the other end to keep talking. Although the calm, disembodied instructions seemed useless, as the blood continued to seep through the new cloth, it was better than being left with silence on this patch of grass in the huge park. Antonella was stroking Teo's forehead, her hair falling across his face as she wept and whispered into his ear, words that Josh couldn't hear. He didn't know what else he could do. He called his mother – it was better than doing nothing. He was put through to voicemail – 'You have reached Katherine's phone. Please leave a message' – and rang off.

The red air ambulance arrived within minutes, circling the playground, the trees and the grass where Teo lay. Waving his arms above his bare chest, Josh pointlessly yelled, 'It's us! We're here!' as if the pilot could hear. He watched them land a short distance away, where the dry, scrubby grass was flat, the noise of the engines momentarily blotting out his thoughts but not the fear. A group of people was moving towards them from the playground, lured by the helicopter, a child running excitedly in the lead.

Before the blades had stopped, the door opened and the paramedics jumped out, crouching with hefty backpacks and small bags of equipment. It was no longer up to him to save Teo. Josh watched as one checked Teo's pulse and put a mask on his face with a valve attached to a bag, packing the flow of the blood with thick gauze, while another brought a stretcher. He tried to call his mother again without really knowing why, but hoping she would answer, calm him down, tell him what to do. This time he shouted into the voicemail.

'Mum, we're in the park. It's gone properly wrong.'

# Chapter Nineteen

Rick walked on to the terrace at Charlwood followed by Katherine and, just behind, like a sleepwalker, Josh. The stripes of the newly mown lawn spread out towards the brick loggia, scented and serene. This visit had been planned weeks back, before the trauma of the previous day, as a last lunch before the holidays. After returning from the hospital Katherine had wanted to cancel, but Rick had said, 'We've got to do something, be somewhere. Charlwood's probably as good as anywhere to get through the day.' And, in the end, she had thought he was probably right.

As Katherine sat in one of the wicker chairs on the terrace she could feel the warmth of the sun on her arms and smell the lavender and box planted beside her. It seemed inconceivable that this was the same world as yesterday's – the one where she had met Josh and Antonella at the entrance hall of the hospital where Teo had been taken. They had travelled up the building in a cavernous, shuddering lift and walked – it felt, for miles – along corridors of pasty linoleum to reach their destination. While they waited at the reception desk of the ward they saw nurses, visitors, doctors passing them on their own urgent business as if the shattered trio were invisible, until a young Asian doctor arrived. Antonella, no longer crying, was wearing her bloodstained dress, ripped around the armholes by her attempts to turn it into bandages.

'Where is he? I want to see him!' she said, her voice cracking and hoarse. 'You must take me to him!'

The doctor had ushered them into a small, windowless room. 'I'm afraid it's not good news,' he said gently, but firmly, to all three. 'The emergency team tried everything they could on the journey, but your brother' – he looked at Antonella – 'was in a very bad state when he arrived here. We couldn't resuscitate him. I'm very sorry.'

The doctor's eyes were smudged with tiredness as he revealed this most tragic and intimate information to a group of complete strangers. 'The loss of blood wasn't the chief problem, but the haematoma from the wound had blocked the airway. It's a common issue when there's a penetrating trauma of the neck area.'

Katherine would never forget Antonella's expression. There was no incomprehension or confusion as she heard the doctor's words, but a recognition of total loss. For a moment, she stood there as the doctor began to explain the process of what would happen next, then she turned without a word and walked down the corridor to the swing doors at the far end, a stick figure under the insensitive hospital lighting.

'Go with her. I'll see what I can do here. Try, if you can, to keep her nearby. They will need a family member,' Katherine said to Josh. 'I'll call Ann.'

When the doctor had left and she was alone, Katherine felt the sadness break. Until then, the need for her to take control had propelled her through the period where hope that he might survive dangled before them, but as hope had turned to bleak fact she was left with the knowledge that Teo had gone for ever – his beauty, his youth, his touch, his desire for her; he was now nothing more than a cadaver ready for a mortuary slab.

She needed a moment before she could bear to make the call to Ann, no longer as an old schoolfriend, certainly not as a bereaved lover, but in the ghastly role of a fellow mother sharing the news of a child's death. The waxy sterility of the hospital corridor was unbearable and she left to find a place to make the call that was full of a normal life, hoping it might make the task a little easier.

The rest of that day was spent in the juxtaposition of practicality and agony that accompanies death. By the time Katherine arrived home in the early evening, her previous day's misery and loneliness was wiped out by what had happened. When Rick approached and put his arms around her, massaging her back in a wide, circular movement, as he had done so often, she was simply immensely grateful.

On the terrace Josh was stroking Roland when CeeCee appeared on the lawn from the direction of the small walled garden. She was carrying a large trug filled with sweetpeas from the cutting beds and, as she walked, one occasionally toppled on to the grass, causing her to bend slowly to collect it.

Approaching Katherine first, she put down the trug and laid her hands on her shoulders. 'I was very sorry to hear about that young man. Such a waste,' she sighed. 'Robert, could you fetch me a vase so I can put the flowers straight in?' When Robert had greeted the group at the front door, he had also murmured his condolences. Katherine had wondered then whether the staff in the house had been chattering around the kitchen table when they learnt the news, just yards away from where she and Teo had first made love.

A rectangular cream umbrella sheltered the table laid for lunch. CeeCee slowly unpicked the tangle of fine pale stems, positioning each individually after taking time to consider the height and colour of each – lilac, scarlet, pink, magenta.

'It's Josh who had the worst of it,' Rick explained. 'He was with them, you know, when the accident happened.'

'I gather it was a penknife?' CeeCee asked. 'When the children were young I was always worried when Michael gave them those knives, but I must confess it never occurred to me they could be dangerous for an adult.'

Katherine saw Josh glance at her as CeeCee mentioned the knife. When they had been travelling to the hospital and he was telling her exactly what had happened in the park he had included the detail that the knife was hers. 'You know, the one you used to have on your desk with the carved handle. He had a couple of the blades pulled out.' He didn't need to tell her any more for her to understand he was admitting that he knew of her and Teo's relationship. She had looked out of the cab window, at a young couple who were drinking from takeaway cups as they walked down the street.

'And the girl? Is she with her mother now?' CeeCee gave an appreciative look at her flower arrangement before taking it over to place it in the centre of the table. She stepped back and slightly adjusted a few of the stems.

'Yes. Ann is dealing with all the nightmarish bureaucracy. She flew in immediately. There's so much stuff they have to go through before they can take Teo . . .' Katherine broke off for a second before continuing '. . . Teo's body back to Italy. As it's Sunday today, they can't get much done, but I'm going to help her tomorrow.'

'I thought, Josh, you might like to swim after lunch,' suggested CeeCee. 'The pool was a wonderful temperature this morning.' She led them to the table where the meal had now been laid out on large dishes – slices of rare fillet of beef, new potatoes dappled with butter and mint, a salad of soft lettuce and peas. In their own way, each was grateful to the older woman carrying them along in her imperturbable wake that day.

Katherine didn't feel like eating anything, but helped herself to a small slice of the meat and some salad, pleased to see that Josh's appetite remained unaffected and that his jumpy panic of the previous day had calmed a little. He wasn't speaking much, but CeeCee's bright chatter never flagged and she could tell that Rick was keen to keep the conversation light. His frequent irritation with his mother was, on this occasion, superseded by an eager acceptance of her ability to negotiate the emotionally fraught atmosphere and her overriding conviction that the status quo should be maintained. CeeCee would never pretend that something unpleasant had not occurred, but she would alight on it only long enough to acknowledge its existence before swooping off in a less troubling direction. It had served her well.

'Talking of happier things, when do you leave for your holiday?' she asked now. 'You're going to be with a crowd, aren't you? I've always found the company of others on holiday is a great help in many ways. It's excellent timing to have a change of scene.'

'We're meant to leave in a couple of weeks. But I'm not sure. Apart from anything else, there's the funeral. We don't know when that will be,' Katherine said. Before yesterday, she had been dreading the holiday, but now, with Teo dead and her floundering in a pool of guilt and regret, life-saving driftwood came in the shape of Rick and Josh. If they were careful. If they tried to be gentle with each other. If they could resist the recriminations that would now be so pointless, perhaps they would survive. That was what she asked. It couldn't be the same as before. They would never be the same.

'Oh, you must stick to your plans. Death always has a tendency towards the inconvenient,' CeeCee replied.

'Honestly, CeeCee. Even for you, that's pushing it,' Rick said, wiping his mouth before reaching out for the carafe of wine in front of him.

'Not at all. I simply meant that you have to try not to let death veer you off course any more than necessary. Anyway' – CeeCee changed tack – 'on a happier note, I gather Olga Oblomovik is pregnant. Drayton will be a family house – I'm pleased for them. I've rather come round to Alexander. And children, as we all know, are so grounding.'

The long shadow cast by the umbrella had moved over the lawn in front of them. When the meal ended CeeCee left the table in search of a picture that she wanted to show Rick, leaving the three alone. From the gardens and fields all around a chorus of birdsong, varied and blithe, from the larks and swallows, blackbirds and wagtails, lapwings and bullfinches of the English countryside, filled their silence.

# Acknowledgements

I would like to acknowledge the help some people have given me during the writing of this book. Simona Baroni, Melanie Clore, Lu Guthrie and Offer Waterman all took time to give advice on areas I was unsure about.

*Behind Closed Doors, At Home in Georgian England* by Amanda Vickery (Yale University Press); *The Making of Home* by Judith Flanders (Atlantic); *Contemporary Calligraphy* by Gillian Hazeldine (Robert Hale); *The Fish that Ate the Whale: The Life and Times of America's Banana King* by Rich Cohen (Jonathan Cape) provided useful information.

My special thanks to my agent, Eugenie Furniss, for keeping me at it when I was discouraged and to David Jenkins who, apart from being generally lovely, has been patient and helpful when I got lost in the plot.